Santa did not want to go away again.

He could not imagine anything more wonderful than being here among people, seeing how they lived, how they felt. Cold fear made a knot in his belly. He did not recall what it was like before he had appeared on that street corner. The thought of not existing again worried him.

It was the nature of life to want to remain alive. What did he have to do to stay that way?

And it was all around him. Twinkling lights that were not made of fire, encased in light bubbles of glass. Everywhere he walked, he saw fascinating new inventions, wonders in themselves. Human beings defied the darkness, pushed back ignorance, spread knowledge in new ways. They had chained the lightning. Small wonder that it had pushed from them that little comfort of someone giving them simple gifts out of love. Was he no longer relevant?

Peddlers pulling carts glanced up and saw him. Women doing their day's shopping noticed him. Men in waistcoats, collars and ties peered his way . Most smiled, and then looked away hastily. A few stared openly. He greeted them with a cheerful wave. They saw, they hoped to believe, and they doubted.

As he walked through the bustling city, he saw no place where he belonged. He touched upon the lives of people only once a year. Here and now he was misplaced in time. *I'm not satisfied to exist only one day*, he thought.

—from "The Very Next Day" by Jody Lynn Nye.

Also Available from DAW Books:

Boondocks Fantasy, edited by Jean Rabe and Martin H. Greenberg

Urban fantasy is popular, but what if you took that modern fantasy and moved it to the "sticks," with no big city in sight? Trailer parks, fishing shacks, sleepy little towns, or specks on the map so small that if you blink while driving through you'll miss them. Vampires, wizards, aliens, and elves might be tired of all that urban sprawl and prefer a spot in the country—someplace where they can truly be themselves without worrying about what the neighbors think! With stories by tale-spinners such as Gene Wolfe, Timothy Zahn, Mickey Zucker Reichert, Anton Strout, Linda P. Baker and others.

Zombiesque, edited by Stephen L. Antczak, James C. Bassett, and Martin H. Greenberg

Zombies have long stalked and staggered through the darkest depths of human imagination, pandering to our fears about death and what lies beyond. But must zombies always be just shambling, brain-obsessed ghouls? If zombies actually maintained some level of personality and intelligence, what would they want more than anything? Could zombies integrate themselves into society? Could society accept zombies? What if a zombie fell in love? These are just some of the questions explored in original stories by Seanan Mc-Guire, Nancy A. Collins, Tim Waggoner, Richard Lee Byers, Jim C. Hines, Jean Rabe, and Del Stone Jr. with others. Here's your chance to take a walk on the undead side in these unforgettable tales told from a zombie's point of view.

After Hours: Tales from the Ur-Bar, edited by Joshua Palmatier and Patricia Bray

The first bar, created by the Sumerians after they were given the gift of beer by the gods, was known as the Ur-Bar. Although it has since been destroyed, its spirit lives on. In each age there is one bar that captures the essence of the original Ur-Bar, where drinks are mixed with magic and served with a side of destiny and intrigue. Now some of today's most inventive scriveners, such as Benjamin Tate, Kari Sperring, Anton Strout, and Avery Shade, among others, have decided to belly up to the Ur-Bar and tell their own tall tales—from an alewife's attempt to transfer the gods' curse to Gilgamesh, to Odin's decision to introduce Vikings to the Ur-Bar...from the Holy Roman Emperor's barroom bargain, to a demon hunter who may just have met his match in the ultimate magic bar, to a bouncer who discovers you should never let anyone in after hours in a world terrorized by zombies. . . .

HUMAN FOR A DAY

Edited by Martin H. Greenberg and Jennifer Brozek

DAW BOOKS, INC.

DONALD A. WOLLHEIM, FOUNDER

375 Hudson Street, New York, NY 10014

ELIZABETH R. WOLLHEIM

SHEILA E. GILBERT

PUBLISHERS

http://www.dawbooks.com

First Printing, December 2011
1 2 3 4 5 6 7 8 9

DAW TRADEMARK REGISTERED
U.S. PAT. AND TM. OFF. AND FOREIGN COUNTRIES
—MARCA REGISTRADA
HECHO EN U.S.A.

PRINTED IN THE U.S.A.

ACKNOWLEDGMENTS

TABLE OF CONTENTS

THE MAINSPRING OF HIS HEART, THE SHACKLES OF HIS SOUL

Ian Tregillis

As the *Christiaan Huygens* made its final approach to New Amsterdam harbor, carrying a princely gift of 100,000 tulip bulbs for the colonial governor, the chief engineer and his mates fired up the wireless. The Breuckelen Dodgers were playing a double-header.

Jax wondered if they played baseball in Quebec. Maybe, after they escaped, he and Willem could attend a game.

But he couldn't join the others where they sat with their heads clustered around the tinny speaker, straining to hear box scores over the rumble of turbines and the clacking of Jax's metal body. The chief had commanded him to ignore the game and work the boilers. So Jax had no choice but to shovel coal: he had no Key, and thus no free will.

War's end meant a cessation of open hostilities between the Brasswork Throne and Montreal. But to French Canadian privateers and fifth columnists, the Treaty of Dublin was just a piece of paper—suitable for the privy and nothing more. Hence the order from the commodore of the queen's naval entourage: be ready to move at the drop of a kerchief. The Frenchies wouldn't catch the world's only superpower asleep in port. The fleet would whisk the queen back to the Netherlands at the first sign of trouble.

Not that Her Majesty was likely to tarry in the war-ravaged colonial backwaters. She'd deliver the tulips, thank the governor for his service to the crown, and return to civilized Europe. Even a million tulips couldn't dispel the infamous stench of New Amsterdam, fodder for jokes long before three decades of warfare had scoured the colonies.

Jax didn't mind. Surely even the most noisome human sewage couldn't taint the thrilling promise of freedom, of unlocking his soul, of drawing breath and speaking as a human man. Each revolution of the turbines brought him closer to the fabled secret locksmiths of Montreal.

Meanwhile, he shoveled.

Coal crunched beneath the blade of his shovel. Reticulated gearing rattled along his spine, brass clattering against brass as he heaved another load into the cherry-red maw of the boiler.

"Quiet down!" said the chief. He spat. "Worthless goddamned Clakker."

Jax adjusted his posture. It made shoveling more difficult, but marginally quieter.

Firelight gleamed on the humans' bare chests, sweat-slick in the close heat of the engine room. Jax tried not to notice how the flickering light played across their smooth brows. Humans didn't have keyholes. They owned their souls from birth.

Jax slumped in imitation of a sigh. *His* keyhole sat in the center of his forehead, at the spot some considered an outward extension of the third eye, and where currently (and more prosaically) soot caked the alchemical sigils etched into his metal plating.

The ship shuddered. A minute tremor ran along the keel from stern to bow: the captain had called the order to reverse engines. Jax's feet clanged like a pair of cymbals against the deck. He creaked to his toes, forced there by the geas laid upon him by the chief's casual outburst. Shoveling became extremely difficult, but it lessened the noise almost imperceptibly. Jax heaved a dozen loads of coal while contorted like a circus performer before the captain called a halt to the engines and the decking fell silent. The *Huygens* coasted the last few hundred yards to its berth. Down here among the boilers, the queen's historic arrival in the new world was announced by nothing more grand than a faint *bump* as the flagship snugged into its mooring lines.

Queen Margarethe, Blessed Sovereign of Europe, Light of Civilization and Benevolent Ruler of the Dutch Colonial Empire, had arrived in New Amsterdam.

And Jax, the very least of her clockwork servants, had arrived at the home of the Underground Railroad.

A strong wind followed the East River. It ruffled miles of blue and tangerine bunting, snapped the queen's standard like a lion tamer's whip, and blew across the

deck of the *Huygens*, where it evoked a strangled cough
from Willem. The lieutenant fished a handkerchief
from his pocket and pinched his nose. The cloth, Jax
knew, had been soaked in chypre.

Jax wiggled his fingers. *Is it as bad as they say? The
stench?*

"It smells like a herd of elephants drowned in an
open sewer," said Willem.

*That doesn't sound so bad. You squishy humans. So deli-
cate.* Jax signed this along with a trill of gearing from
deep in his torso: the Clakker equivalent of a chuckle,
though most took it for a growl.

"They drowned a month ago," said Willem. "And
they're getting ripe."

In the centuries since Jax's primary mainspring had
been wound and sealed into his torso, only Willem had
ever taken the time to know him. Only Willem recognized that being mute didn't make Jax a halfwit. Willem alone had ever wondered about the thoughts
imprisoned within the brass jail of Jax's skull, and only
he had seen fit to set them free with sign language. Willem was his only friend and the best human he had
ever known.

Soon Jax would have a Key and a voice. His
chromium-plated exoskeleton would undergo the
alchemical transformation that would render it soft
flesh. He'd be able to hug Willem, and thank him,
without cutting or crushing him. His love would not
be deadly.

The wind sculpted snowdrifts of confetti against an
empty grandstand. The Mayors of New Amsterdam
had been in attendance when the queen presented the

lord governor with his medal, his title, and, most extravagant of all, the tulips. He'd gained her favor by pushing the French back across the border, and lavish were her rewards. But now the celebration was over and the sterile glow of electric street lights bleached color from the rainbow-hued streamers. Wind-strewn crepe flittered through the legs of the motionless clockwork servitors lining the approach to the *Huygens*. The rest of the queen's guard had accompanied her to the ball at the governor's palace.

The buzz of saws and the percussion of hammers echoed across the harbor. Carpenters were already hard at work dismantling the stands. Wood was in rare supply these days.

The wind died. The queen's standard fell limp against the flagpole. But Willem kept the handkerchief pressed to his nose. Jax pretended not to hear him blowing his nose; politely turned a blind eye to the way he dabbed at his eyes. He felt the same way, but envied Willem his tears. Jax couldn't cry. That was the province of humans.

But that didn't mean he couldn't worry. Willem would pay dearly if his role in Jax's escape were uncovered.

Are you having second thoughts?

Willem gave his nose a final blow, tucked the handkerchief back in his pocket. A rueful smile touched the corners of his eyes. "Miss my chance to see you finally free? Don't be silly. But now that I'm here, I find I'll miss being a sailor."

Jax shook his head. A passerby at that moment might have thought a steam engine had slipped its bearings. *You should stay*, he signed. *Let me go alone.* A Dutch naval officer caught sneaking into French Quebec is likely to be shot on sight. Worse, it could reignite the war.

Willem said, "Let's make an effort not to get caught, then." This time the smile missed his eyes. Instead it speared Jax in the hollow where a human's heart would have been. It hurt worse than a grain of sand pinched in the coils of a mainspring, or a cracked tooth on a cog.

"Are you ready?"

Jax nodded.

"Very well, then." Willem stood straighter and looked Jax in the eyes. The regal bearing couldn't completely erase the wetness in his eyes. The tears, Jax knew, signified both joy and sorrow. He'd observed humans for a long time before he understood this.

"Jackivantus, heed my words, for as a human being I claim my right to lay this geas upon you: I demand that you forsake your duties aboard the Christiaan Huygens. I demand that you venture into New Amsterdam with the sole and unwavering purpose of seeking freedom in Quebec. I demand you seek the maker of counterfeit Keys, who is said to live above a machinist's shop on Vermeers Street, and that you make every effort to do so, including doing violence to those of your own kind if such is necessary. And I demand that you take every precaution to avoid receiving any further geas that would supersede this compulsion." The seriousness around his thin lips gave way to the smirk. "And, as your friend, I demand that you let me help you."

Willem meant well. He didn't know how much the compulsion hurt. No human did.

The words were a lightning bolt to the helpless dry tinder of Jax's soul; an unstoppable brush fire that would burn him to ash, over and over, until he satisfied the geas. He could not but obey. He had no Key. No free will.

Willem's bootsteps evoked a quiet rattle from the gangplank. Jax crouched beside the taffrail, his knees hinging backwards in the manner some found grotesque. They ratcheted closed with the tick-tick-tick of an outsized pocket watch. He rocked onto his toes, pressing his ankle joints tighter against the springs of his haunches. Willem set foot on the pier. He ignored the guards and went straight to the carpenters, clever and bold and oh-so-handsome in his lieutenant's grays. Only a man with nothing to hide would be so brazen.

Jax's anxiety grew with every pulse of hydraulic fluid into the pistons that drove his legs. He quivered like an overheated boiler. The compulsion had stiffened the springs in his legs, made them stronger, almost too strong to withstand. Light glinted between Willem's fingers when he pulled the silvered flask from his pocket. The carpenters gathered around: the price of good liquor had increased a hundredfold during their adulthoods.

Jax waited until after Willem had taken his own sip and passed the flask around. And when the lieutenant had captured their attention, he jumped.

A quiet puff belied the explosive release of potential energy that launched him from the deck. He arced over the pier, over the Clakkers tirelessly protecting the *Huygens* from French perfidy, over the flagpoles and the queen's standard. Jax soared beyond the ring of electric lights toward the shipping offices and warehouses. The carpenters might have seen a glint of light streaking across the sky and thought it a shooting star.

On the way down, Jax unfolded his arms to their fullest extent. As the shadows of the wharf enveloped him, he tightened the springs in his arms and torso.

Like a steel javelin, Jax's outstretched body speared a warehouse roof. His arms buckled to their fullest compression with a spine-rattling clank. The impact pulverized roofing tiles. The handstand persisted for a fraction of a second, and then he somersaulted through the air, flipping along the roofline like a Chinese acrobat. Each landing absorbed more energy and slowed him further.

Until he crashed through a skylight. Jax flailed at nothing on the way down and came to rest atop a flattened pile of wooden crates. His landing launched billowing clouds of dust and debris through dark aisles.

He stood. Glass tinkled and wood creaked. Nails jutted from the demolished crates, scritching across his armatures. Something soft and round bounced away when he brushed himself off. Jax stepped out of the wreckage and crushed another soft something underfoot.

A tulip bulb.

The queen's gift, he realized. He untangled himself from a length of tangerine bunting.

Electric arc lights flared to blinding life. A shout echoed through the warehouse. It was followed by the rumble of a loading-dock door and the unmistakable clatter of brass on concrete as a squad of the queen's guards poured inside.

The tulip shipment was the most valuable thing to enter the harbor in a very long time. A king's ransom, or a city's, or an entire winter without hunger for those desperate and bold enough to risk tulip soup. Of course it was guarded. Metal troopers, machines like Jax, weren't the worst problem. The real danger was their human commander, once he realized a rogue Clakker was loose in the warehouse.

Willem's compulsion rose within Jax: a searing ember that couldn't be extinguished, hot enough to consume him if he resisted.

Jax shredded the bunting and then shoved the rags into the holes in his skull with enough force to bend the rims of his ears. No matter. They could always be hammered back into shape. But now he couldn't hear an order to desist.

Nor could he hear the guards. But he'd served in more than one army in the centuries before he was sold to the navy, and knew the tactics of the human minds who commanded the clockworks. They sought human offenders: impoverished thieves weak from hunger, or French saboteurs.

Jax leapt upon one of the iron pillars spread throughout the cavernous warehouse. Stiffened fingers and toes punched rivet-sized holes through the beam as he scrambled into the shadows above the lights. A rain of iron doughnut holes pattered upon the concrete slab, oddly silent to Jax's close-packed ears. A waxy half moon shone through the empty skylight frame.

Bullets ricocheted through the iron scrollwork of the ceiling beams. They struck sparks that flickered in the darkness like fireflies in high summer.

Jax swung himself up through the broken window and back to the roof. One round creased his foot and another dented the plating where the small of a human's back would have been. He sprinted to the edge of the roof and flung himself over the alley to an adjacent warehouse. He crossed the gap between buildings folded into a sphere, while the queen's guards on the streets below mustered into squads with clockwork precision.

He rolled to his feet, sprinted to the edge, and repeated the process. He couldn't stop to watch the search. Even now, the Clakkers from the warehouse would be climbing after him. Any delay threatened failure to comply with the geas Willem had laid upon him, and that was impossible for a Clakker without a Key.

Jax crossed one rooftop, and another, always following the tug of the compass rose in his chest. According to the map he'd studied with Willem, Vermeers Street was a narrow slash northwest of the city center.

The pounding of his heavy feet dislodged a roofing tile. It cracked free, bounced along the eaves, and tumbled three stories to shatter on the street like a flowerpot. It drew his hunters as sharks to blood, warlords to weakness. He bounded over the next alley faster than the humans could bring their weapons to bear, but not faster than the Clakkers could respond. Three more bullets pinged from Jax's balled-up body.

The mechanical men carried rifles, which they

wielded and aimed far better than any mortal could achieve. Their human controllers carried tar guns and sand sprayers.

Any Clakker found in possession of a counterfeit Key—any slave with the gall to pick the lock on its own soul—was subject to summary execution in the dreaded forges of The Hague. So said the Highest Law since the time of Huygens, when his publication of the Horologium Oscillatorium begat three centuries of Dutch ascendancy. Even the British, with their insistence that Huygens had stolen the alchemical researches of an obscure natural philosopher named Newton, had fallen silent when elite legions of clockwork fusiliers marched through Westminster. Only the French had stood firm in their enlightenment: first Paris, then Montreal had been the seat of a government that espoused the ideal of universal human rights for mechanical men; a dangerous and irresponsible policy to the Dutch point of view. And thus the holy crusade.

The compulsion flared anew, like a white-hot fishhook snagged in Jax's mind. He stumbled. He would fail Willem and violate the geas if he led his pursuers to the machinist. He turned west, and made a show of it.

It brought him closer to the guards from the warehouse. They brought their clockwork perfection, and their rifles, to bear on the bunting wrapped about Jax's ears. He ducked, spun, and flipped over another alley. Their shots drew more sparks where they dimpled his body, flares of pain that lit the night like flashes from a semaphore lamp. One round snapped his head back; another shattered the crystal in his left eye socket. The world went flat.

Jax kicked up a tile. He hefted it while he ran, got a sense of its weight and aerodynamic properties, while turning to again cross over the human pursuers. The loss of binocular vision made it difficult to aim. And the geas raged like a conflagration against the hard boundaries of the mechano-alchemy that had imbued Jax with life. No Clakker could harm a human being unless specifically bidden to do so with elaborate bindings and special geas; a simple compulsion like Willem's could never overcome that.

He could, however, knock the tar gun from unsuspecting fingers and use it against his pursuers. Jax let the tile fly and dove into the alley.

Several hours later, when he finally limped to Vermeers Street alone and unpursued, his chassis had more dimples than a golf ball. His knees groaned with metal fatigue. The piston rods in his right arm were warped and immobile. Sand scoured his cervical bearings when he turned his head. Smears of tar covered his face and dripped from his ears.

It hurt to move. But not moving, ignoring the geas, hurt more.

He knocked at the machinist's. The door opened almost at once. Willem gasped. Jax couldn't hear what he said. The AWOL lieutenant pulled him inside.

They stood in the shadows of presses and lathes, saws and drills and welding equipment. Their feet kicked up eddies of sawdust. A mundane and law-abiding workplace: not a pentangle or pendulum to be found; no sign of grimoires or gears. Clockmaking, and the associated arcane arts, were the sole province of the queen's forges.

The man who emerged from the shadows had the large callused hands of any laborer, but the peculiar haunted eyes of one whose study of alchemy hadn't deadened his conscience. He appraised Jax with a long look, and betrayed no reaction when doing it. The machinist snapped at Willem. The lieutenant looked abashed.

The machinist retrieved a metal can from a cabinet. Jax saw it was turpentine. It didn't take long with the two men working together—one on the left ear and one on the right—before Jax could hear again.

Willem said, "Jackivantus, heed my words, for as a human being I claim my right to release you from your geas."

This snuffed the blistering heat of compulsion more completely than an avalanche could extinguish a candle. Moving still hurt, but not moving was no longer agony.

"I'm so sorry," said Willem. The machinist kept working to clean the smears of tar from Jax's head. "I didn't know. They never told us it hurts you." He looked ready to cry. "I thought I was helping."

The machinist glared at him, and spat. He dipped his wire brush in the turpentine, splattering all three of them in the process, and set to work scrubbing Jax's forehead.

I wouldn't be here now if not for your geas.

Jax slumped as the sense of urgency left him. He'd found the Underground Railroad. Soon he'd have a Key to unlock his soul, and not long after that he and Willem would be in Quebec. He closed his eye and thought about baseball.

The machinist stopped scrubbing. He muttered to himself. Jax watched him produce a pair of spectacles and squint through them. Then he tossed the brush aside and said, "I can't pick this lock."

"What?" *What?*

The machinist poked Jax in the forehead with his little finger. "A bullet sheared part of this sigil." Poke, poke. "Changed its meaning. That could be fixed, given enough time and somebody who knew the work. But this"—his thumbnail made a tinny *clink* against the keyhole—"is the killer. Lock's damaged. It won't rotate the sigils."

The spiral of symbols on every Clakker's forehead formed a unique alchemical anagram that, when properly reconfigured with a Key, would unlock the soul, transmute brass to flesh, and imbue free will. His finger traced a dent along the hairline seam outlining the tumblers deep within Jax's skull. Jax knew this for truth, because he felt no tingle when the machinist touched the keyhole. It was dead, the soul-freeing magic shattered.

I, I, I don't need a Key. Jax's fingers clicked against one another, stuttering like stuck typewriter keys in his haste to respond. *Tell him, Willem. We jus–s–st ne–e–ed to get–t t–to Queb–b–b–ec.*

Willem did. And he added, "We'll find somebody who can fix the damage once we're safely north."

The machinist knelt beside Jax on the cold, hard concrete floor. His hard eyes had softened, and his voice came out quiet and flat, crushed beneath the onus of destroying one dream and two lives. He spoke to Jax.

"It's not a matter of skill. Fixing the lock requires

forging a new anagram." He touched Jax on the temple with a gesture both firm and compassionate. "It would mean taking you apart. Melting your skull and the lock and recasting them anew. Your soul would burn like a moth on the sun. It wouldn't survive. You wouldn't be you any longer."

"The fix needn't be permanent," said Willem. "Just until we reach Quebec."

"The railroad won't take you, son. Not while he's incapable of disobeying an order. They won't tolerate the risk. You run into trouble, the men hunting you can make him to turn on you and anybody helping you. That's why I'm the first stop on the railroad. But they won't take you if I haven't picked the lock."

I'll plu–u–g my ears again.

"I know these men. They won't risk it. I'm sorry."

When Willem spoke again, his voice came out cracked and brittle, like a ceramic roofing tile. "Please."

The machinist sighed. He removed his spectacles, bowed his head, pinched the bridge of his nose. Without looking up, he said, "Given the choice, would you live forever as you are now, or die like a mayfly with a soul?"

I have wanted nothing more these past two centuries, Jax signed, *than to become human.* His fingers didn't stutter. Willem relayed his answer.

The machinist strode into the shadowed recesses of his shop. He returned with a diamond-tipped chisel, hammer, steel vise, book, block of maple, and an electric drill.

"This is mending tattered cobwebs with hemp twine and a railroad spike," he said. "It won't last. If it works."

"How long?"

"Impossible to know." The machinist shrugged. "A few hours. A day, perhaps."

One day seems nothing to you, whose soul is his birth-right. To my kind, it is an eternity.

The men helped Jax lie on a workbench. The vise bit into his temples. Pulling a jeweler's loupe over his spectacles, the machinist said, "This will hurt. Far more than any damned geas."

Willem stroked Jax's hand. But the machinist pulled them apart. "Don't do that if you ever want to use your fingers again," he said, then placed the maple in Jax's empty palm. "Now be quiet."

He spent many minutes studying the damaged sigils. Then he pressed the tip of the chisel to Jax's brow and—

Jax convulsed. Wetness ran down his arm and dripped to the concrete. And he did something he'd never done before: he screamed. His birth cries cracked the foundation of the machine shop.

Jax stood on the roof, facing east, catching the first rays of dawn on his face. Sunlight had become something warm and silky, no longer sliding across his body with a sterile, slick disdain for metal. It lingered and caressed.

This skin, this strange moist elastic covering, it fairly burst with sensation. He'd never imagined. Even the simple play of a borrowed shirt across his chest—he was *breathing!*—made his toes curl with delight. (He had toes, and they *curled with delight!*) Unimaginable treasures to a creature that all its long life had only known yearning for freedom and the torment of compulsion.

"I could stand here all day," he said to himself. He said what he thought just for the twin pleasures of feeling the words bubble up in his throat and hearing his voice. It was raspy and inconstant, unlike Willem's. The machinist judged this a result of the screaming. It would heal, eventually, if Jax lived long enough.

He wouldn't. Already there was a flutter in his chest where his heart beat. (*Where. His. Heart. Beat.*) Faint, but growing.

"If you wish," said Willem. "It's your day." Tears thickened his voice, but he hid it well. "But we should leave soon if we're going to meet our guide."

"As you say," said Jax, bracing for a lightning bolt that never came.

He turned his back on the rising sun. It was more difficult than it might have been a few hours earlier; the steep angles of the dormer challenged his frail human ankles, threatening to snap them like green timber. Capricious things, these human bodies.

But then he realized what he'd done, and laughed. (Laughter felt like sunlight in his belly.) Two hundred years of ingrained behavior made for difficult habits to break. It came with a twinge of sorrow that he wouldn't have longer to relish breaking them. (Sorrow and laughter together? Miraculous and contradictory, too, human bodies.)

And then Jax said the words of which every Clakker dreamed: "No. I don't want to do that." He looked at Willem. "I don't want to run for Quebec. It doesn't matter any longer."

Willem wept openly now. But he nodded. "Any-thing you want, Jax. Anything."

"I want to eat an apple." (The gurgling in his stom-ach, was that the thing called hunger?) "I want to be tickled. I want to sing in the bathtub. I want to lie in green grass. I want to see the Breuckelen Dodgers play baseball. And when I die, I want to be in your arms.

"That," said Jax, "would be my perfect day."

THE BLADE OF HIS PLOW

Jay Lake

They tell stories about me. A lot of those are wrong. I was never called Ahasver. I wouldn't know how to make a shoe if you paid me. No one cursed or blessed me. Really, I just am.

When you realize you are deathless, you gravitate to certain lines of work. Not a lot of call for immortal bricklayers. Doesn't take much luck or skill to follow a plow, beyond knowing the business of your own fields. Standing behind the sharp end of the sword is what I do.

Used to be I kept count of how many men I'd killed. Then I just counted the battles I'd been in. After a while, I lost track of that and started counting the wars. Now, well, they count the wars for me. Finally, you people are finishing the job that Yeshua Ben Yosef started all those years ago on top of a dusty hill too far from his home or mine.

Thank you. Thank you. Thank you. Blessings upon

you, all that are in my power to give. I know God has an eye on me; lets me direct His gaze to your heart.

Well, maybe not that last.

Longinus had already walked the earth six times longer than the life of a mortal man. He had fought in Syria, in Scythia, among the Parthians. He'd changed his name a dozen times. No matter how far he ranged, he eventually found his way back into the legions.

He'd settled on the rank of *tesserarius*, always being vague about his exact history while showing enough of his experience with weapons and maneuver and the business of wrangling men to be convincing to a *signifer* or *centurion* desperate enough for skilled bodies to ignore the irregularities. The older the empire grew, the easier this became. There were always men discharged for drunkenness or brutality who drifted back into the ranks.

And by the gods, Longinus knew one end of a spear from the other.

This time, though, he could see the end coming. Not his own end. Not anymore. He'd taken enough blows, caught enough arrows point first to know what would happen to him. It hurt like crazy, but the wounds always closed up. So far no one had tried to cut off his head. He wasn't looking forward to finding out how that went.

This time it was not his body absorbing the blow. It was the Eternal City herself. Alaric's armies were at the gates for the third time in two years. The Emperor Honorious was long since decamped. Everyone of consequence in the senate and the army had gone with him.

Only the broken legions, and those whose masters could not arrange their timely withdrawal, remained.

Longinus watched the smoke rise from the fires near the Salarian Gate. Rumor among the centurions and their troops was that slaves had let the attackers in. Not that it had done the poor bastards much good. The Visigoths seemed pleased to kill anyone unlucky enough to be in their path.

Now, atop a house part way up the Aventine Hill, he no longer wondered how long it would take them to reach him. A band of the Celtic warriors had ridden into the Vicus Frumentarius perhaps half a glass earlier and set to the serious business of smashing their way through the homes here.

He had four men with him—two of them drunkards, one barely old enough to shave, and another veteran like himself. Longinus had only bothered to learn the old soldier's name—Rattus—as the others wouldn't live long enough for him to need to remember them.

"We could just bugger off." Rattus was slumped against the rooftop parapet sucking down the last of a broken amphora of wine from the house stores. The kid had been useful at least in handling the petty thievery on behalf of the older veterans. It wasn't very good wine, though. The vinegar stink rose up like pickling time in the kitchens.

"Bugger off where?" asked Longinus distantly. He wondered how many of the Visigoths would make it to this house. They were visibly drunk, and not moving with their reputed efficiency.

"Skin out of our kit, flee with the rest of the meat."

Longinus understood from Rattus' tone that the old soldier wasn't serious. "Die here, die there," he said. "They kill everything."

Rattus burped. "What's so special about dying here? If we die there, might have a little longer to live first. Something could happen along the way. A man can be lucky."

"Here is where we were sent to die." Longinus remembered a hot, dusty hilltop in Judaea. He'd learned a lot about being sent to die at that place.

"Fair enough." Another belch.

One of the drunkards poked his head up from the narrow ladderway. "You coming down?" he asked. "We got duck in brine."

"Eat, drink, and be merry," Longinus replied. He heard the raucous laughter of the Visigoths spilling back into the street, two houses down. Smoke was already rising—they'd finally set a real fire here, too. "For all too soon we shall die."

There was no purpose defending this place. Their handful of legionaries had been set here to guard against looting, should the Visigoths be turned back or otherwise overlook the house. Now, well, it was a worthless fight. Nothing more.

Longinus regarded his *gladius*. As swords went, his was not a bad one. He'd claimed eleven lives thus far with the blade. Perhaps a few more today.

When they came, the Visigoths killed the drunkards out of hand. Rattus died swiftly as well, to his mild surprise. When they got bored with Longinus holding off three of them on the roof, they shot him with arrows until he could not stand. The kid they used like a girl until he begged them to permit him to die.

He watched it all through the filmy eyes of an apparent corpse. If speech had yet been granted to him, Longinus would have begged them to take his head as well.

I tell stories about them, too. Or would if I had anyone to listen to me. Another grumbling old man in a world with no patience or place for grumbling old men. Veterans have war stories that no one cares about but the men they fought beside.

Charles Martel is as a dead as Abdur al-Rachman. Nobody but me remembers them, or what happened in that rainy autumn deep in the forested country of the Franks. Anybody I might tell wouldn't believe me anyway.

Sometimes I've thought to write it all down. My memory used to be real good. A man isn't made to remember everything, not even last week's breakfast. But he should remember taking a life, a night with a woman, helping birth a baby.

I've done all those things, a thousand times over. Most of the details are gone. Sometimes it's like I've never lived at all.

Longinus had never felt much sympathy for the English. Once a Roman, always a Roman, he supposed. The English were edge-of-the-Empire rubes grown too proud of their mucky little island. But here in France, Charles VI, *le roi*, was a fool. The men who commanded his armies were little better.

One thing Longinus had never done, not as legionary, mercenary, or soldier, was turn his coat. Desert, yes—there was small point in remaining with a defeated army. He had never fought for his own flag, or whatever surge of patriotism drove the sons of farmers and butchers and priests to seek blood. But he did not leave in the moment of battle, and not to the harm of the army he fought for in that season.

What he never could forget was that the men at his side were just like him. The only difference was that none of them had ever been on a Roman execution detail one hot morning in Judaea. Other than that, they were all the same: soldiers in uniform who would kill or die for the sake of their next hot meal and the pay to come. Whichever came first.

These names he knew, the pikemen in his line. Longinus was a *caporal* just lately. A dozen men to wrangle, and a sergeant to avoid.

The French had not paid sufficient attention to longbows. Longinus had. He'd served at Crécy. He knew what the English could do. Even a generation later, the idea that a peasant could slay a sworn knight still seemed too difficult for the French nobility to comprehend. Longinus understood. He'd taken a clothyard shaft in the breastbone and been left for dead. One of the worst injuries he could recall, in fact, a deeply blossoming field of pain that had almost overwhelmed even his strange, accursed gift.

Finding new and interesting ways to die was an occupational hazard of going for a soldier, but that didn't mean he had to search them out. The frightened squad around him deserved better than their commanders would give them. Longinus was recalled to that by the smell of urine—Petit Robert had wet himself again. Mist and birdsong might have raised the dawn sun from the fields, but it was the smell of piss and blood that really reminded a man that he was at war.

"When you see the knights fall as if struck down by God, we will fall back into the woods," he said, wondering how many different languages he'd given orders in. After a while, they all faded with disuse, except the Koine and Aramaic of his youth. Those were languages of his dreams. "Sieur d'Albret has promised us a great victory and revenge for the defeats of our fathers."

The squaddies muttered, elbowing one another, a few grinning.

"I have a different promise," Longinus continued. "I promise to keep you alive, if I possibly can."

"Our names will all live on in victory," shouted Henri le Doyeux, surely the most ardent partisan of their little unit.

Longinus met the glance the *caporal* of the next squad in their line—a hard-bitten Basque who reminded him of Rattus, except for an unpronounceable name. *Idiot*, their eyes said to one another.

"I think you'd rather your body lived on," Longinus replied. "Carrying your name with it."

A bit more elbowing and grinning met that remark, then they settled down to the serious business of breaking their fast and tending their pikes.

When the arrows came, they chittered through the

air like blackbirds on the wing and fell through the skin like knives. Longinus never did get his men to the woods, but he found out once again how badly a long-bow could hurt a man.

A woman once told me that only in dreams are we truly free. I think she had it backwards. Only in dreams are we truly ensnared. A waking mind knows better than to hope for certain things. Wishes can be avoided for the sake of sidestepping the pain of life. But the dreaming mind, like the heart itself, wants what it wants.

I've spent centuries cultivating the art of not wanting. Married a few times, along the way. Even once staying around long enough to see your children grow to doddering age, then burying them, will put a stop to that.

Cultivating the art of not getting killed took more of my time. Like I said, I don't die, but otherwise fatal injuries still hurt like blazes. Even so, I've walked off more battlefields than anyone in human history. Of this I am certain.

I've kept a few kids alive. I've sent a few fathers home. I've slain a lot more, of course, my own side's and others. Loyalty is where you find it. Kind of like those dreams.

Even as bad as the English archers were, it was gun-powder that made things impossible. When you could be killed without even knowing you had been fighting, that changed everything.

*   *   *

He hated trenches. Worst invention in the history of warfare. Worse even than guns and bullets. With trenches came mustard gas and bombing runs and tanks and all the things that could befall a man pinned down by position.

Longinus wasn't too happy about his Lee Enfield 0.303, either. With bayonet fixed, it was an incredibly inefficient spear. Mostly, though, it was a finger of death. One that didn't even require the training and sweat of an honest bowman.

The newest lieutenant came down the line, yammering about orders and an attack. Longinus figured he'd last three days at most. Given that the man's first act on arriving was to root out all the booze and cigarettes, then lead a prayer service to stiffen everyone's souls, no one was going to ask too many questions about who fired the bullet that would soon kill him.

After almost two thousand years of warfare, he'd long since realized that every army ever constituted had precisely the same process for producing foolish twits recklessly in love with the power of their commissions. Most of those armies also had an informal process for weeding out the foolish twits on the ground.

It would be pleasant to at least consider that natural selection, except the quality of the officers never seemed to improve.

"Corporal Longo!" shouted the twit.

"Sir?" Longinus gave the man his best tired old sergeant's stare. He knew the noncoms and the company commander had him pegged as a disgraced sergeant-major serving under another name. You just couldn't hide the kind of experience he carried in every step, every glance, every word. The new lieutenant saw corporal's stripes and assumed malingering, as that's what the lower classes by definition did with themselves in the absence of proper leadership. Or so Longinus had been told.

A red face sweated at him despite the chilly, fogged-in morning. "Do not eyeball me, Longo. You may be my father's age, but you will respect my authority."

"Sir." Longinus didn't bother to conceal his contempt.

The Lieutenant leaned close. "I'll be sorting out the order for our next assault. Would you like to be first out of the trench?"

"If you'll be leading the way, sir, I'd be pleased to follow your example."

The resulting stare down ended poorly for the officer, who finally stomped off muttering.

When the order to go over the top came down the next morning, Longinus shot the Lieutenant himself, saluted the captain, then took his squad through a barbed wire forest into a hail of Boche bullets.

Did you ever figure how much of it all was connected? Just what you can remember now, at the end of the Imperial age, should be enough. Andersonville, Isandlwana, Katyn Forest, My Lai.

A curse, Christ's Harrowing of Hell.

I have been the blade of His plow down the centuries of history. Only now, the numbers catch up to me.

And so they have. A man came to me last night. He wore a suit and snakeskin boots and he ate an apple as he spoke. "Longinus," he said in my own native Koine. He was the first person to call me by my right name since the fall of Rome. "Your days have numbered beyond counting."

I was drinking coffee from a wretched paper cup on a sidewalk in a city of Africa. No one here should know me or speak my tongue, this I well knew. There was only one answer I could give. "I have waited for you a very long time." *Whichever one you are,* I thought but did not say.

His eyes were violet, and spread wings were reflected in them as if an angel stood just behind me. "Are you finished?"

"Ever have I been finished. Good for evil's sake, evil for the sake of good." I added, "I am tired."

He touched me, just once, saying, "You are free to go."

Where his fingertip had brushed the back of my hand, blood welled up. Two hours later, the scratch had not healed. The lingering pain was a marvel I had not seen since Judaea.

To test his word, I cut off the least finger of my left hand with a hunting knife. *It did not grow back.*

Then I knew I was free. The only question was what to do with my freedom? I could only go where I had ever been, the battlefield, but that was no longer so easy.

In these days, the recruiters can number the lines on a man's thumb. They can number the flecks in his eye.

They can number the patterns woven into the seed of his loins. I have never bothered to learn the crafty skills of forging paperwork and changing records. Always I could walk away and take another name.

Now, though, even the least of African tyrants wants a resume and a cell phone number for the mercenaries who might bear weapons in his name. Tramp freighters of no fixed flag won't hire gunmen on their deck unless references are provided. There is no place left for me.

Sunrise greets me now with a sky of fire, as it has done down the long centuries. I have made my preparations. Just in case this last promise is another deceit, I will strike my last blow so well they will not find me after.

I used to wonder what it was to die. Eventually I stopped, but on this last morning, another wretched paper cup of coffee in my hand, it occurs to me once more that my reward and my punishment are likely just the same.

A soldier's death, and a silent, restful peace with no grave at all. If God wants me, He will have to take some trouble to find me.

So I am walking up that dusty hill for the last time—my still wounded left hand throbbing in time with my heart. Going over the top of the trench. Claiming the fire for my own. No one will miss this truck until it is too late. The fertilizer and fuel oil in the back will serve. If I have been lied to, not even my God-given invulnerability can survive being vaporized.

I hope.

I am tired, I am old, and I am sick of being the plow

blade. The dust like stars shall be my tomb. All those who went before me have borne my name to Heaven or Hell. It does not matter which.

Really, I just wish I still had my old spear. That would bring a proper end to all stories.

CINDERELLA CITY

Seanan McGuire

San Francisco, California, 1901

I awoke covered head to toe in a slate-gray cloak of pigeons. This was not, in and of itself, unusual; I spend most of my time covered in pigeons. What was unusual was the fact that I was waking up at all.

"Miss?"

The pigeons took off at the sound of a human voice, leaving me lying naked on the cold cobblestones of the alley floor. I sat up, trying to figure out the appropriate reaction in this situation. Screaming was popular, in my admittedly limited experience, and so was covering oneself with one's hands. I settled for looking warily toward the speaker and asking, "Yes?"

Not the most memorable, as first words go. The man didn't seem to mind. He held a coat out to me, an earnest expression on his broad, serviceable face, and said, "Miss, ma'am asked me to see if you were the source of the pan-e-ther-ic dis-turb-ance." He looked extremely proud of himself for managing all those syllables. I didn't have the heart to tell him they'd been managed completely wrong. "Would you like to come with me? Ma'am says I'm to tell you there's rum."

"I suppose that yes, I *am* the pan-etheric disturbance." I took the coat, slipping it on before reaching for his hand and letting him pull me to my feet. "Rum would be lovely. Thank you."

"Yes, miss," said the man. He smiled blandly as he led me out of the alley and onto the street—a place I'd never been before, and had been constantly since the day I first came into being. I stumbled slightly. I couldn't help it.

The man gave me an anxious look. "Miss?"

"Rum would be *very* lovely." I said, stunned, and followed him.

The man led me down several blocks, seeming not to notice or care that I was barefoot and being pursued by an ever-growing number of pigeons. A few people waved as we passed, and one man called, "Nice catch, Andy. You find her down at the docks?" His companions laughed. My companion—Andy—didn't.

He also didn't scowl or walk any faster. I squinted at him. "I believe those men were implying that I was a woman of negotiable virtue."

"Yes, miss."

"And that you paid me for my company."

"Yes, miss."

"Doesn't that bother you?"

"No, miss."

"Why not?"

"Because it isn't so, miss." Andy stopped in front of a storefront that seemed to consist primarily of a grimy plate glass window with the name NORTON'S painted across it in gold leaf. I couldn't remember ever seeing it before. That, too, was worrisome, since there shouldn't have been anything in the city that I'd never seen. Not unless it had been constructed since I woke up, and this building was too old for that.

Andy didn't appear to notice my dismay. "In here, miss," he said, opening the door and stepping inside. There was nothing to do but follow him.

The sound of the door closing behind us was accompanied by a series of dull thumps as my attendant pigeons tried to fly through the dirty window. I winced in sympathy before turning my attention to the room that we had entered.

It was clearly a public house of some sort—surprisingly clean for such an establishment—with a vast bar of polished ash dominating one wall. The shelves behind it were loaded with an assortment of liquors, only some of which were immediately familiar to me. Of equally questionable familiarity was the only other person in the room, a redheaded woman with her hair braided in a tight crown around her head and a barmaid's apron tied around her waist. She was regarding me with an unblinking stare that was almost as unnerving as my current condition.

"I brought her, ma'am," said Andy.

"Very good, Andy," the woman replied. She stepped around the bar, untying her apron as she approached us. Stopping a few feet in front of me, she looked me critically up and down before saying, "You're rather shorter than I assumed you would be."

I bristled. "And you are?"

"I'm Mina Norton, and this is my establishment." Her expression was grave as she added, "I may be your only hope for survival."

"Ah," I said, faintly. "Well, isn't that lovely. The pan-etheric disturbance would like some rum now, if you please."

"Certainly," said Mina. "While we drink, we can attempt to figure out what the incarnate city of San Francisco is doing in my bar."

"And won't that be a lovely change?" I muttered.

Mina left Andy in charge of the bar after presenting him with a long list of instructions, including things like, "Don't serve gin to gargoyles; it makes them rowdy," "Tell Tom he has to settle his tab before he gets another drink," and "Don't let anyone into the back unless you hear screaming." Then, armed with a bottle of rum, she led me through a door behind the bar and into the well-kept storeroom beyond.

"Why have I never seen this place?" I asked her. "It's not new."

"Far from it. My father built it during the Gold Rush, before your attentions were fully formed. He thought it best that we be protected from certain forms of spiritual observation, and I've maintained those protections." Mina tapped a wind chime that hung incongruously from the edge of a stocking shelf. A low tone rang through the room. "It's not that I dislike you, really. It's simply that I dislike being watched when I didn't invite the observation."

"But you're in my . . ." I hesitated, trying to find the appropriate word. There didn't seem to be one. I followed her through the door at the back of the storeroom and down the stairway on the other side, finally saying, "You're *in* me. Don't you think that means you've invited the observation?"

"To be quite honest, no." Mina stopped at the bottom of the stairs to light a match and touch it to a length of wick protruding from a copper pipe. The flame flared briefly, and gas lamps came on all around the room, illuminating a space I would have sworn I didn't contain.

Catching my expression, Mina shook out her match and said, "The walls are reinforced. Just let me know if you feel an earthquake coming on, and we should be fine."

"Yes, of course," I said. A variety of arcane seals were chiseled into the floor and ceiling. I pointed to one of them. "Are those why I can't normally see you?"

"Yes, they are." She walked calmly across the room to the twin of the bar upstairs, where she put down the rum and bent forward, leaning over the wood to extract a pair of glasses. "As for why I don't believe we've invited observation, the spirits of cities are born when a sufficient number of thinking beings have moved into the area. Those thinking beings don't get a vote in the matter. My father had no objection to you, and neither do I, but that doesn't mean I want you looking over my shoulder all the time."

I frowned as I followed her. "You could move."

"We were here first." She poured two fingers of amber rum into a glass and pushed it toward me. "Here. This should make you feel better."

"Thank you." The rum didn't have a taste so much as it had a sensation, like fire running down my throat. I choked a little, coughing into my hand before putting the glass aside. "Much better," I managed to wheeze. "Now, can you tell me what I'm doing here?"

"I haven't a clue," said Mina, pouring herself a much larger glass of rum and downing it in a single impressive swallow. "I didn't know anything was going on until my orrery of the Bay Area started spinning out of control. It was as if one of the largest gravitational forces—that being you—had vanished from the model. *Something* was disturbing the natural order of things. My books indicated that it might be a matter of incarnation, so I sent Andy looking for a naked, confused person who wasn't meant to be a person at all. He has an eye for that sort of thing."

"Why's that?" I asked, reaching for the bottle of rum. Getting drunk was sounding more appealing by the moment.

"Because he's a person who wasn't meant to be a person at all. What's the last thing you remember?"

I stopped, blinking at her for a few seconds, before I poured myself another glass of rum and said, "I was . . . it's hard to explain where I am, when I'm in my natural state. I'm everywhere. I'm the sidewalks and the rooftops and the houses. I'm the shops and the theaters and the stands the food vendors set up along the beach.

I see things, but they aren't immediate. Not the way they are right now."

"Small gods," Mina said, turning to begin rummaging through the shelves of liquor behind the bar. "Lares and Penates. That's where all this began. You would have been a household spirit, once, when everyone carried their own gods with them. Now, you're the soul of a city, and you're sitting here wearing my golem's coat, drinking rum, leaving San Francisco just this side of completely unprotected."

"What?" I looked at her with alarm. "I can't be unprotected. I have police, firemen, pigeons—"

"None of whom will be able to defend you if whatever—or whoever—caused you to incarnate shows up with a shotgun," Mina said, sounding entirely too reasonable. She turned back to me, holding a bottle of something green. "Did anything unusual happen before you took on flesh? Anything at all?"

"I . . . I don't remember."

"Try." It wasn't a suggestion. She poured a glass of the green liquid and pushed it across the bar to me. "A great deal depends on it."

Lacking any better options, I picked up the glass and drank.

This time, when I awoke, I was lying flat on my back on the basement floor, and there were no pigeons. Mina was standing over me, a quizzical look on her face. "Well?"

"There was a man." I pushed myself into a sitting position. My throat felt raw and tender from whatever it was she'd given me to drink. "He was . . . he was the summer! The whole summer, walking around like a man!"

"That's James Holly," said Mina, dismissively. "He's the Summer King. Did he do this?"

"No. He . . . he was running away from something. Some*one*. The man who did this to me. This one wasn't the summer."

"Most men aren't," agreed Mina, helping me to my feet. "What was he?"

"He was like you. The same sort of construction."

Mina's eyebrows lifted. "He was an alchemist?"

"Is that what you are?"

"Since I doubt you can use your magical city powers to detect bartenders, yes." She sighed. "His name is Stuart. He's a little unbalanced. And apparently, he's learned how to incarnate the souls of cities. Oh, won't this be fun?" She started for the stairs.

"Wait!" I cried, alarmed. "Where are you going?"

"To telephone the Summer King and let him know that we're all about to die. You can come, if you'd like. Or you can drink more aconite absinthe. I understand that even geographic fixtures can become drunk, if they consume enough. Feel free to try."

Then she was gone, walking back up the stairs to the storeroom. I stayed where I was, wobbling slightly on my unfamiliar legs, and tried to figure out what, precisely, was going on. When I realized that I wasn't going to succeed, I followed her.

I took the absinthe with me.

It took approximately thirty minutes for James Holly to cross me and arrive at the bar. That was sufficient time for Mina to find me a dress—too big at the bust, too long in the skirt, but still an improvement over Andy's borrowed coat—and a pair of shoes. James burst into the room, ignoring the CLOSED sign on the door, and demanded, "Where is she?"

Mina looked up from polishing a beer stein and replied, mildly, "James Holly, Summer King, meet the City of San Francisco. San Francisco, meet James Holly, the source of all our troubles." Andy didn't even grant this much of an acknowledgement, but simply continued sweeping the floor.

"That's unfair," objected James, before bowing in my direction. I remembered that gesture, even though I'd never seen it before, and smiled at him in answer. "My lady. I am very sorry for your current inconvenience."

"I have absolutely no idea what's going on right now," I said, still smiling. It seemed like the best thing to do. "Are you really the *entire* summer?"

"To my occasional chagrin, yes." He straightened. "Miss Norton, are you sure this is my brother-in-law's work?"

"She saw an alchemist chasing you shortly before she was given human form, James. What do you think?"

James scowled. "Blast and damn."

"Precisely."

I held up a hand. "Could you please explain what's going on? I don't appreciate being talked around, even if I'm not customarily in a position to join the conversation."

"It's simple, really. He," Mina pointed at James, "is

married to the Winter Queen, and the Winter Queen's younger sister is married to your embodying alchemist."

"Stuart and Jane Hauser," interjected James. "They want to claim our Seasons. Margaret and I would rather they didn't, as this would kill us."

"What does that have to do with *me*?" I demanded. "I'm not really involved in this line of succession. I just want to stay alive."

"I'd assume Stuart was planning to sacrifice you to gain power, if he'd been there when you incarnated," said Mina. "As he wasn't, I have to assume that he wanted you out of the way for a time. He wanted San Francisco stripped of mystical defenses."

"Are you humans always this complicated?" I rubbed my forehead. "I'd like to resume being a city, please."

Mina frowned. "You never stopped," she said. "You just stopped paying attention to yourself. James, grab a bottle of Scotch and follow me. We need to find out what Stuart is up to."

The gas lamps in the basement were still on. Mina stormed down the stairs with the two of us behind her, muttering to herself. "You!" she whirled, pointing at me. "Where is Stuart?"

"In an abandoned warehouse two blocks east of here," I replied, without thinking about it. I froze. "What—what did you do?"

"Nothing. You did it. You can't be completely sundered from yourself, or we'd have fallen into the ocean by now." She moved behind the bar, grabbing a large stein and several bottles. "James, the Scotch. City, tell your pigeons to watch Stuart. If he moves, you need to know."

"I can try," I said, uncertainly.

"Don't try. Do it or we're all going to die."

James frowned as he passed the Scotch. "A bit apocalyptic, don't you think?"

"No." Mina half-filled the stein with Scotch before beginning to add splashes from her other bottles. "Why incarnate the city of San Francisco? Why distract her from her usual occupation?"

"Boredom?" he ventured.

"He's trying to start an earthquake." My voice surprised even me. James turned to stare at me, but I was distracted by the sensations in the bottom of my feet, the itching I hadn't recognized until I started trying to focus on what I was, rather than the body I was wearing. "He's pressing down on one of my faults—he wants to shake the city into the sea. Why would he do that to me?" I looked at them pleadingly. "Why?"

"Because he's mad," said James.

"Because he wants to blackmail us into giving him the summer," said Mina. She picked up the stein and swigged half its contents before pouring the rest into a flask she produced from inside her bodice. Dropping the empty stein to the bar, she tucked the flask away and said, "All right. Let's go save you."

Walking through my own streets was even more disconcerting now that I had a vague idea of what was going on. It didn't exactly help that I acquired an escort of pigeons, stray cats, and wharf rats as soon as we stepped out of the bar. Mina ignored the wildlife, scowling at shadows and taking occasional swigs from her flask. James also ignored the wildlife, perhaps because he was distracted by the way flowers kept sprouting from the cracks in the pavement as he passed.

"Oh, yes, we're *very* unobtrusive," muttered Mina, glaring at a dandelion that had suddenly popped up in front of her shoe.

James looked abashed.

"If we can stop the earthquake, does that mean he'll stop doing whatever he's done to me?" I asked, hurrying to catch up with the pair of them. "This is very distracting. I don't like it."

"The human condition is so rarely welcome," said Mina.

"That isn't an answer."

"It wasn't intended as one." She sighed. "I don't know, all right? So far as I know, no one has ever incarnated a Lare of your scale without their cooperation. This could be permanent."

I stared at her, horrified. "What do you mean, permanent?"

"I mean it could last until you die. Now come on. This will be entirely moot if we all plummet into the Pacific Ocean. If you don't mind?" Mina sped up, forcing us to follow or be left behind.

"I don't think I like her," I muttered.

James just smiled.

The warehouse was old, crumbling, empty, and most importantly, mine. Unlike Mina's bar, it had never been shielded against me, and when I pressed my hand against the wall, it was happy to tell me what it contained. I would have had no trouble interpreting its message in my natural form. As it was, my knees nearly buckled before I gasped, "He's in the back. There's a woman with him. She's . . . on fire?"

James and Mina exchanged a look. "Jane," they said, in unison.

"He's reading something. I don't understand the words. No one in me speaks that language."

"Probably Babylonian, or something dreary like that," sighed Mina. "Well, then. In we go."

I pulled my hand away from the wall. "What? What about a plan?"

"That *is* the plan." She held up her flask, smiling sardonically. "Last call. Place your orders and get out." With that, she shoved the warehouse door open and strode inside. James shook his head and followed.

"I won't do it!" I called after them. "I'm going to stand right here until you come back here and have a better plan!" They didn't come back. The itching in my feet was getting worse. Scowling, I motioned for the pigeons to come along, and ran after them.

James and Mina were striding through the warehouse, making no effort to move stealthily. I caught up to them easily, my pigeons soaring overhead and roosting in the rafters. Neither James nor Mina said anything, and then I heard the sound of chanting, different now that I was hearing it with ears, but also what I'd heard before.

"Stop that rubbish right now, Stuart!" half-shouted James. "You're being silly. Dropping the entire city into the ocean doesn't make you clever, it makes you a bit of a bastard." He paused. "Ah, apologies for my language, Miss the City."

"People are saying worse inside me right now," I reassured him.

That was when the first fireball hit the rafters, and things became too complicated for conversation.

The flaming woman charged out of the back, her hands filled with dirty orange fire. She flung it at us indiscriminately, rapidly filling the warehouse with the smell of singed pigeon feathers. Mina and I dove for cover while James raised his hands, heat like the sun baking off him until the flames were dwarfed by its power. "This, again?" he asked. Sunlight surged, and the flaming woman was blown backward, slamming into the wall with a bone-rattling thud.

"City, come on!" shouted Mina, skirting the burning patches of floor as she made for the back of the warehouse. "I need you!"

With no better idea of what to do—and no real desire to be set aflame—I followed, pausing only to stomp out any embers I passed. I was too aware of how old and dry the wood around us was. My pigeons, rats, and cats came with me, and they, too, stopped to extinguish any flames small enough to be handled by their wings and paws.

Behind us, the woman shouted something spiteful, and James answered with another burst of heat. It was like all of July was trying to happen at once. Then we passed a large stack of boxes, and I lost my concern for anything but the man kneeling in front of me, still chanting in that language I didn't understand. It made my teeth ache, but not as much as the sight of the chalk circle around him. Something about it was *wrong*. I couldn't look directly at it.

"Stop that!" I shouted, involuntarily.

The man looked up and—to my dismay—laughed. At least that meant he wasn't chanting anymore. "Oh, this is cute. You've brought me the city, Miss Norton? How did you even find her?"

"I have my ways, Stuart," snapped Mina. "Listen to your habitation when she tells you to do something, and stop that."

"This is giving me a headache," I complained. "I'm not used to having a head. I don't like this."

"The headache is probably from the rum, but we'll have worse than a headache in a few minutes if Stuart doesn't stop playing silly buggers with the laws of nature." Mina started to uncap her flask.

"I wouldn't do that, Miss Norton." Stuart stood, shouting something in a different language I didn't recognize. This one made my eyes water and caused a gust of wind to sweep Mina off her feet and slam her into the wall. Her flask hit the floor, still capped.

Stuart turned toward me, smiling. I took a step backward.

"Don't come any closer," I said. "Or . . . or else."

"Or else what? You'll shout at me? Behold the City by the Bay, reduced to harsh words and questionable allies." He stepped out of the chalk circle. "You're a brilliant work of transfiguration. Lead into gold, city into girl. Oh, the things I'll be able to do once I've taken you apart—"

Mina wasn't moving. James was shouting something in the warehouse behind us; that, and the waves of heat washing against my back, told me there was no assistance coming from that quarter. Stuart was advancing on me, looking entirely too pleased with himself. I did the only thing I could think of, futile as it was certain to be. I raised one hand, pointing at Stuart, and used the other to gesture my animal attendants forward.

"Pigeons," I said, "kill."

With a raucous din worthy of Chinese New Year, the urban wildlife descended. Stuart screamed. After that, the feathers obscured the worst of it—at least for a little while.

My animals stopped shy of tearing Stuart to pieces, but only because James came around the corner with Jane's unconscious body slung over one shoulder, looked at the scene, and groaned. "Don't kill him if you have a choice, please?" he asked. "My wife will be annoyed if I let him die. It's a family thing."

"He was quite happy to kill *us*," I said. "He was going to use me for parts!"

"And now he's not, so please?"

"Very well." I sighed and clapped my hands, calling, "Everyone come away from the bad man. He's probably terrible for your digestion, anyway." The animals came with only a few complaints, moving to cover the floor all around me. Pigeons settled on my head and shoulders. I didn't shoo them off. "Now what?"

"First, this." James dumped Jane next to Stuart, who

was scratched and bleeding but still breathing. Ignoring them both, James picked up Mina's flask and uncapped it, pouring the contents onto the chalk circle. The lines blurred and ran together, becoming a muddled mess.

"Get the books," rasped Mina. I turned to see her sitting up, one hand pressed to her head. "I'll need them to return the city to its original state, assuming it can be done at all."

"What about them?" I asked, pointing to Jane and Stuart.

"Leave them," said Mina. "This is enough of a setback that they shouldn't be a problem for a while."

I scowled. "I'll be watching them."

"Good," said Mina, and smiled, before wincing. "Now can someone help me up?"

It took us substantially longer to make our way back to the bar. Mina shuffled slowly, with James supporting her, and the sidewalk in front of me was carpeted with living bodies. Their eyes watched every step I took, furred and feathered bodies parting for my footsteps. My companions weren't so lucky.

"I had no idea there were this many rats in the city," muttered James, after the fifth one he managed to accidentally step on. "Can't you send them off?"

"No. They're worried about me. They're afraid I'm going to leave them."

"Of all the conscious worshippers a Lare could have, you chose pigeons and rats," sighed Mina. "Tell them that if they don't let us get back to my establishment, you *will* be leaving them, because I won't be able to send you back to your original state."

The animals seemed to understand her. They scattered, leaving the way clear for the remainder of our walk. The CLOSED sign was still up on the bar door, and Andy was still behind the counter. He didn't appear to have moved while we were away. That might have been because he hadn't.

"Storeroom," commanded Mina. "James, help me."

"What are you going to do?" I asked.

"Drink a great deal. After that?" She flashed me a pained smile. "I'm going to settle your tab."

"Stuart used a poorly advised variation on the Cinderella Cordial," said Mina, looking much better now that she'd consumed most of a bottle of rum and something green that smelled like fermented herbs. "It allows you to transform an ordinary girl into a princess for an evening—or, if used without safeguards by a suicidal idiot, to transform the spirit of a city into an ordinary girl for the same period of time." Her hands moved as she spoke, pouring an ominous assortment of liquids into a tall glass.

"Why was this poorly advised?" asked James.

"Beyond the part where the city didn't grant consent, she has no shoes to leave on the palace step." Mina picked up a spoon, giving the mixture a stir. "It's losing the shoe that undoes things. Without that, we must improvise. It's that or have a permanently human city cluttering up the place."

"No, thank you," I said quickly.

Mina smiled. "I thought you'd feel that way, although I admit my motives are selfish. Stuart may have succeeded in damaging the fault. If he did, I need you to delay the earthquake as long as possible, to give us time to prepare. Can you do that?"

"I can try," I said.

"Good." She added a final shot of liquid to the glass and handed it to me. "It was very nice to meet you. Now drink this and go."

"Thank you." The liquid was sweet and sharp and spicy, all at the same time; it burned my tongue and throat, until it felt like I was drinking the fire Jane had been flinging at us in the warehouse. As I drank, I realized that it was getting harder to feel my fingers wrapped around the glass, and harder to keep my eyes from closing. I kept drinking. The burn intensified, sharpened—

—and it was runoff from last night's rainfall trickling through my gutters, it was puddles on the sidewalk and saltwater foam blowing up against the beachside houses. I couldn't feel my fingers because I didn't have any fingers, and I couldn't open my eyes because I didn't have any eyes. I didn't need them. Every pair of eyes in the city belonged to me. Every hand was mine. I was home.

I never left.

James looked at the spot where the city had been standing. Only her borrowed clothes remained, lying empty on the floor. "How long do you think we have before whatever Stuart's done comes due?" he asked.

"Not long," said Mina, flatly. "I recognized those symbols. He was willing to create another Atlantis, if that was what it took to take the summer. We'll have to deal with him sooner or later."

"I'll tell Margaret, when she wakes up." James rubbed his face with one hand. "Can the city hold back the quake?"

"I think so." Mina smiled, bending to pick up the dress San Francisco had been wearing. "We sent our accidental Cinderella home. She'll try to help us, if she can, but it can't hold forever."

"Well, then," said James. "Let's get to work."

One of my pigeons comes to me, eyes bright with wonder. "Is it true, ma'am?" he asks, in coos and chirps—and I was never "ma'am" to them before this. I was their city, and now I am their mother. "Were you human for a day?"

"Yes. I was."

"Can you tell us about it, ma'am?"

I would smile, if I still had lips. Instead, a rainbow shines through the spray in the fountains of Golden Gate Park, and a hundred dogs bark for joy.

"It began," I say, "with waking up, covered in pigeons . . ."

TUMULUS

Anton Strout

The gnarled roots at the thick tree trunk's base atop the hillside burial mound looked normal enough, Jeanine thought. That was until the clouds finished passing over the harvest moon and she saw that the yellowed finger bones, with their dried cracked skin peeling away from them, were real, not a trick of her nervous eyes. She wished for a moment that the *Samhain* revelers were still there and not already long gone back to the Irish village down the hill in fear of the witching hour. All that remained of their presence were the half dozen straw men standing on makeshift posts around the edge of the very mound itself.

The long green earth that covered the top of the mound gave way as the hands flexed and closed, pulling themselves up out of the ground at a pace nothing like the speed in which movies always showed the dead digging themselves up from their graves. This process was much slower, the near skeletal arms working hard against the press of dirt, grass, and stone to free the figure below.

As Jeanine stood there clutching her overstuffed backpack like some sort of protection or talisman, the smell of death and rot was what caught her attention most. The the smell overpowered the more familiar smells of the surrounding forest and the lush Irish grass that ran along the hillside. Part of her wanted to run screaming off into the night, back down through the village until her legs gave out, but Jeanine stood her ground, watching and waiting. This *had* been what she wished for, hadn't it?

No, she thought. *Not wished.* Worked *for.*

By the time the gnarled, bent figure of an old woman had worked its way out of the burial mound, the moonlight revealed the bones beneath the torn gray rags it wore, the remaining skin a thin coat of flesh that matched the rags themselves. The blackened sockets of its empty eyes hid behind limp strands of tangled white hair clumped with wet earth. The broken flesh of its neck twisted as it craned its head back and forth, struggling to look around, but without eyes, it was a futile gesture.

With every passing second and movement, more and more of the dirt and debris sloughed off the figure. The hair continued growing, darkening to black, and the skull beneath it filled in with a wrinkled skin that formed down over the empty sockets until eyelids ~~sat~~ closed in their place. Seconds passed before ~~the leath~~ery lids fluttered open, revealing eyes bene~~ath~~ halos of bright green around pupils black as itself. Cracked lips parted on the ancient face as if to let out a mighty screech, revealing brown-black teeth, but nothing came. *A hag*. Among the festive straw men that had been erected upon the burial mound, she was the only figure that moved outside of Jeanine herself.

The old woman closed her mouth, her eyes seeming to notice the young woman for the first time, and she pointed crooked fingers in Jeanine's direction. After a moment she opened her mouth again, the tongue inside it forming as Jeanine fought back the urge to vomit rising in the pit of her stomach. Sound came from the hag, a garbled ancient voice that spoke words Jeanine barely recognized despite the books she had studied, yet some connection in her mind filled in the missing parts and words in her mind's eye.

"I have risen," the voice in Jeanine's head boomed, startling her. Goosebumps rose up and down her arms beneath the sleeves of her sweater and heavy fall coat, but she steeled herself.

"Yes, your majesty," she said, laying her heavy backpack down at her feet. *Composure*, she reminded herself, and gave a polite if not awkward curtsey to the woman. The hag's face twisted into a manic smile, her eyes widening.

"I see you know your manners among your betters."

"Yes, ma'am," Jeanine said, pulling her wool coat closer around her, the chill radiating out from the hag almost unbearable.

The old woman shuffled toward her a few steps before stopping, surprise and confusion registering on · face. She looked down at her feet to a thin white line that ran around the top of the burial mound. "Salt," she hissed through clenched teeth.

"Yes, ma'am," Jeanine said, backing away even though she was well on the other side of the line. "Begging your pardon . . . I did not want any trouble with you."

The hag's eyes looked at the line of salt, hoping, no doubt, for a break in it. When she found none, she turned back to Jeanine. "Do you know what they call me, young lady?"

Jeanine nodded, lowering her eyes to her backpack. She reached down into it and pulled out a five foot length of rope. "*Mongfhionn*," she said, tying a knot in it as she said the name, sounding it out slowly. *Monk fin*. She repeated the name seven times, tying a new knot each time until she had seven of them as well. The sound of the nonsensical words only conjured up strange images in Jeanine's head, but given the circumstance, the humor of it was quick to die there on the hillside.

The hag gave a throaty laugh. "*Mongfhionn*? Once, perhaps. But I am her no longer. Your kind calls me a *bean sidhe* now."

"*Bean sidhe*?" Jeanine let the words run though her mind while she fished a red velvet binding bag out of her backpack and slipped the knotted rope into it. The words felt familiar, something she had studied, but recognition refused to come to her in any sort of intelligible thought.

"A *banshee*," the hag reminded her. "A harbinger of impending death. This is my penance for my crimes, to wander, to haunt, although I see by your circle here that you have denied me even that."

"I know enough to protect myself, ma'am," Jeanine said. "That much I know."

"Undo this circle, girl," the hag said, almost growling through clenched teeth. "I have not the time to tarry with you."

"Why not?" Jeanine asked. The hint of a smile took to the corner of her mouth.

The hag shut hers in response, wary. "Suffice it to say that I do not wish to bandy words with you," she said. "You would not understand."

"Understand what? That your time is precious to you, my lady? That perhaps *this* doesn't happen all that often? Only, say, every hundred years or so . . . ?"

The hag stopped and stared at Jeanine, narrowing her eyes until they bore into the young woman, causing the young woman to squirm in discomfort.

"You know my name and my legend too, I see," Mongfhionn said. "What kind of witch *are* you?"

Jeanine shook her head. "I am nothing of the sort," she said, her voice shrinking. "Just a girl concerned with her own future . . ."

"Then you know that my time in the flesh is short, from moon to moon," the hag said. The risen woman's features were still transforming, the hair growing, untangling, and coming in thicker, her body becoming less and less bony as the flesh flowed and stretched out over her form, becoming fuller and fuller. "A time I have, in fact, come to cherish more and more with the passing centuries."

"Do you cherish it more than those people you killed?" Jeanine asked, reaching down into her backpack once more. She pulled out another cloth bag and stepped to the edge of the circle. The hag's face went dark.

"Yes, I know you, 'fair mane,' " Jeanine said, opening it. She pulled out a broken shard of mirror and laid it in front of the hag. "Mongfhionn, wife of the Irish High King *Mugmedón* and . . . mother, yes?"

At the word "mother, " the hag doubled over like a knife had been thrust into her gut, one made of grief. "Aye," she said, lifting her head as her eyes lit up in remembrance. "*Ailill, Brion,* and *Fiachrae* . . . All fine boys; all deserving, loving sons."

"Deserving of what, ma'am?" Jeanine asked. She moved around the outside of the circle, placing one shard after another every few feet as she went. "The crown? So much so that you murdered your own brother?"

A low growl arose from the hag as she turned away from the young woman.

"The King of Munster," Jeanine said from the far side of the thick trunked tree at the top of the mound. She came back into sight on the other side, laying down pieces until she completed the circle. "*Crimthann mac Fidaig.* He would have been the next High King of Ireland, wouldn't he? But *you* thought your own sons more worthy of the position, yes?"

"They were born for greatness," she hissed, pacing along the edge of the circle like a great beast of a cat. "I was trying to ensure their future! Yes, it is true I put the king's second wife *Cairenn* though hard work while she was pregnant hoping her to miscarry. Then I demanded *Eochaid* put all our children through several contests to prove mine worthy of the throne. To that end, he trapped them in a burning forge, ordering them to save what they could, but ruled his own son *Niall* victor for rescuing the heavy anvil while they foolishly chose wood, swords . . . even a bucket of beer. I would not accept his judgment."

"So a hunt was arranged, and a hag as hideous as I am now met them at a well in the woods. Water would be exchanged for a simple kiss, and all refused—"

"Except *Niall*," Jeanine said, cutting her off. "Transforming her into an attractive young maiden, once again ensuring the kingship for himself and several generations after."

The hag's face fell again. "Darkness and death followed me those days. Why else would the pagan Irish choose to worship me at the onset of winter's embrace? I died too, for all the good it did me. My brother insisted that I drink from the same cup as he to prove I had not poisoned him, and . . ." The old woman gave a dark smile, the teeth white now. "Well, here we are now, aren't we? They called me kinslayer."

"Your misguided mother's love murdered your brother, the king," Jeanine said, wonder in her words as she spoke them. "Poisoned him, all in an attempt to let one of your sons assume the throne instead."

The old woman lunged at the edge of the circle, still unable to cross it, but the hag terrified Jeanine nonetheless. "I will not be judged by you," she snarled. "History has judged me already, and there are those among your people who worship me as a sorceress queen to this very day. Why, look at the straw men who cover this very barrow! People pay me homage.

Samhain is my singular time, a time of great power for me. *Féile Moingfhinne.*"

Jeanine shook her head. "I meant no judgment or disrespect, ma'am," she said. "Only this time, this rising, is not a time of great power for you now, is it?"

The woman cocked her head to the side like a bird. "How do you mean?"

"You walk among us, us mortals, *as* one of us," Jeanine said. She reached down into the backpack at her feet and pulled out a thick binder, flipping it open. "I have done my research on the legend, *your* legend. I did not randomly pick this tumulus by chance, hoping to catch a passing spirit during *Samhain*, when the veil between both worlds is thinnest. I came seeking you, Mongfhionn."

The woman eyed her with caution. "To what end?"

Jeanine's face went red and her voice went quiet again. "I come to ask a boon," she said. "My husband Joseph and I . . . aren't able to conceive a child by natural means. Lord knows we have tried, but we have had little hope or luck. We even turned to medicine, but it seems I am unable to bear a child. I do so want to have one of my own so badly . . . please, you must help me, your majesty."

A look of impatience grew on the woman's face, which was no longer that of the hag she had been moments before. A simple, plain woman in her fifties stood there, the same bright green eyes with long black hair with wild Irish curls now. "Is this not a matter for the *Beltaine?*" she said, her voice younger sounding. "Why do you trouble me this time of year, this time of harvest and death? Why not bother a spirit such as the *Morrigan* instead?"

"I thought you of all the *spiorads* might understand my plight, and I thought you might be able to help," Jeanine said, looking down at her feet, "by . . . supernatural means. As you say, you are a revered goddess of sorcery, and a mother on top of that. One who was willing to kill for the success of her children."

She threw her head back and gave a dark, bitter laugh. "But I did not succeed, did I? My drinking of the same poison as my brother condemned me to his ill fate as well. I failed at my task, condemning me to this form for eternity."

Jeanine's eyes filled with desperation. "But surely you have the power to help . . ."

"Why in the name of the gods would I help one such as you?" the woman asked. "Being allowed to be in the flesh is supposed to remind me of the very humanity I so quickly dispatched of in life, the same humanity that worships me now. Yet every 100 years, I am allowed to taste the dark bitter sweetness of that form, and you deny it to me with this circle. You ask my help yet you imprison me, make demands of me . . . ."

The angered woman tensed, her eyes catching Jeanine's, refusing to let them go.

"Would that I were in my usual form right now I would tear your flesh from your frame with my very voice," Mongfhionn said, viciousness filling her. "So you knew of my legend and my demise, but do you truly understand what I am capable of now as a *banshee?* My voice alone can bring humans to their knees in terror."

Jeanine nodded. "I have heard of the *bean chaointe*, the keening washerwoman whose voice can shatter glass from its pane. I have also heard it sounds like two slabs of wood slapped together in the dead of night, piercing one's ears."

The pretty but plain woman spoke through pressed lips and clenched teeth. "Again, why do you chance yourself with me at this fall time of harvest when those springtime spirits of May would no doubt be more willing to provide?"

"Perhaps I am too impatient," Jeanine said. "I am growing older and the idea of waiting until the spring seems like another lifetime spread out before me. I suppose some people would find a desperation in that, but I have little shame in admitting it. I want a child, one of my own, and I found hope in choosing you, a spirit that others might not think to ask such a boon of."

"Hope?" the woman laughed. "How did you ever find hope in my legend?"

Jeanine flipped through the notes in her binder. "Because even the creature you are now holds a hope for me." She slammed her finger down onto the middle of one of the pages. "Here. They say that your voice is not *always* a terror. They say the sound can come as something pleasant, a soft singing . . . almost a lullaby, a child's song. Surely that's a sign that this boon is within your power to grant me. That is why I chose you, and the fact that this location in particular is strong with magic, not only a burial mound but a fairy fort as well. It is a liminal, a place of magic, ma'am. It is even said that leprechauns know of hidden gold in fairy forts such as this, but that is no concern of mine tonight."

"Your concern is of a more *carnal* nature," the woman said.

"You understand the *want* of being a mother," Jeanine continued. "I thought perhaps it would be best to ask your favor while you were in this form. Please, I've tried, researched so very much. My husband Joseph and I know of no human way."

The woman inside the circle of salt stepped to the edge of it. "You waste my time," she said, her body transforming even further, until she stood there a young black-haired beauty with a body that her grey rags barely covered. "I could not help you on this day, even if I wanted to . . . which I do not. I do not hearken to demands made of me."

"I have done my best to show you no ill will," Jeanine said, shamed a bit by the way the risen sorceress queen stood there showing no modesty. "Have you no mercy to show me? Can you not help me?"

"Do you not listen? I said I could not help you on *this* day. You should understand all too well that fact. Today I am only of the flesh, as you well know from your studies."

"I thought—"

The woman gave her a dark smile. "I know you have thought, girl, but I do not think you have considered everything."

"Meaning what exactly?"

"Consider this circle, for instance," Mongfhionn said, tracing the toe of her bare foot along the edge of it. "As you said, you built it to contain me, to hold back the spirit within, and it has. Yet . . ."

The woman paused. A ball tightened in the pit of Jeanine's stomach, causing her to step back.

"You forget," the woman said, and stepped beyond the barrier that encircled her, her toes breaking the circle, scattering little white crystals across the grass. "I am no longer spirit now that I am fully risen this night. As you noted, I am merely human."

"Shite," Jeanine said, fumbling for the backpack at her feet.

There might be nothing preternatural about Mongfhionn now, but still, the woman was fast and closed with Jeanine before she could even move. The woman's now perfect hands rose up in a flash and grabbed Jeanine by a huge chunk of hair.

"I am not afraid of you," Jeanine said, struggling to pull herself free from the woman's grip but it was no use. "You're only human now."

"Then more the fool you," she said. "For I know the damage one human can do to another. I've had centuries, and I will not be denied my day. Not this century."

"I only sought your help!" Jeanine said, no longer able to hold back her tears. "Will you not help me?"

"There *is* no help to be had from me. I have neither pity nor remorse for you. I am Mongfhionn."

"Then you have truly learned no penance," Jeanine said. The woman pulled her hair hard, making her cry out.

"There are reasons that my followers worship me at the time of *Féile Moingfhinne*, *Samhain*. They are celebrating death and tonight; you too will join that celebration, foolish woman."

"I am not foolish," Jeanine said, grabbing her own hair and pulling it as she tore away from her attacker. "I did my research—"

"You *are* foolish," the other woman shouted at her. "In coming here after the festival and staying alone. Your mistake will bring you little comfort in death."

Jeanine backed away, standing up fully. "I never said I came here alone," she said, and looked past the woman back up the hill. "Joseph!"

The woman spun around, hunched down like a wild animal. A brown-haired young man the same age as the girl stepped out from behind the thick trunk of the tree at the top of the burial mound, a book clutched in his hands. The man looked unsure.

"Read!" Jeanine called out. "Now!"

He looked down at the book, his voice wavering, barely audible as the wind began to whip through the surrounding trees.

The woman straightened up. "What is he doing?"

Jeanine gave the woman a sad smile. "Reinforcements," she said.

The woman returned the smile, but hers looked much less sad, triumphant even. "I think not," she said.

"What do you mean?"

"He is a man, after all," she said, looking down her body's now ample curves. "I understand how men work."

Although she still wore the torn gray rags from the grave, they now lay over fair alabaster skin and a body that even Jeanine felt herself drawn to. Before she could respond the woman spun and walked over to

Jeanine's husband, her hips swaying with a rhythm that drew his eyes up from the page he was reading.

"Tell me, *Seosamh*," the woman said, with a soft sultry quality that Jeanine wouldn't have thought possible from so dark a woman. "Wouldn't you rather give yourself over to a woman like me? I can offer you things no other can, sins of the flesh that would split your very soul in two with pleasure."

Jeanine ran to her husband's side. He stood there, not moving. Mongfhionn wore a look of triumph on her face and Jeanine turned to her husband, squeezing his arm.

"Joseph . . . ?" she asked, worry thick in her voice.

He shook his head as if clearing it and turned to give Jeanine a small smile. His eyes met hers, and she could see the momentary fog on his face lifting, then he cast his eyes back to the woman.

"Forgive me, enchantress," he said, turning back to his wife's eyes, "but do you think I'd be standing out here at the midnight hour incanting some crazy spell if it weren't out of love for my Jeanine? I am not so easily swayed by a dead queen." He looked down at the page again, then turned his gaze upon the woman herself. "*Ó gach gairm bheatha!*"

The wind picked up all around them on the hillside as Jeanine fought to piece together the words from the Old Gaelic. She wasn't sure of all of it, but *come to us from all walks of life* filled her head as the weather changed.

The gale blew harder, branches swaying and snapping, even knocking over the straw men that stood upon the burial mound. They fell to the grass as their crude mountings gave way, the hill looking like it was littered with the shadowy figures of the dead. Then four of the fallen strawmen proceeded to stand up of their own volition, clumsy, awkward, rising like new-borns taking their first steps.

"*Máthair . . . ?*" The word floated out into the air from one of them. The faces were nothing more than jumbled twists of twigs and straw with no mouth to even say such a word, and three of them closed in on Mongfhionn as she simply stood there in shock.

"*Ailill . . . ?*" she asked, abject horror on her wide eyed face. "*Brion, Fiachrae . . .* my sons."

The three figures moved to stand all around her, grabbing her, the sticks and poorly articulated arms and hands piercing through the skin of Mongfhionn's arms. She cried out in pain and the fourth figure strode up in front of her.

"*Deirfiúr,*" it said. Sister.

"Forgive me," the risen queen said.

"Forgiveness?" Jeanine said, almost laughing. "You've proved that you have learned nothing from your penance or your time as a human. You are beyond forgiveness."

"Please," the woman said, desperation heavy in the word, the first time her voice had sounded remotely human. "I will give you what you wish."

Jeanine buried her head in Joseph's shoulder, look-ing away from the woman. "I am sorry, but I cannot trust you at your word," she said. "I . . . I have made a mistake coming here tonight."

The woman struggled amid the straw men, but the

blood running from her pinned arms was proof enough that she would not escape.

"As a *banshee* you may have stood a chance against us, but no," Joseph said, hugging his wife to him. "You understand nothing about loyalty. *Léirscrios!*"

Mongfhionn went to speak, but the straw men holding her struck, crushing in on her as the final word of the incantation set them to their final task—to destroy. A flurry of action rose up in front of the young couple, obscuring the risen woman who all but vanished as branch and root and twig tore into her. The pile fell in on itself as the wind calmed, and when the night was quiet once more, the only evidence left of her ever having been there was the hole Mongfhionn had crawled out of, covered in what looked like a bonfire piling.

"Is she dead?" Joseph said, stepping to it and scattering the debris around with the toe of his boot.

"No," Jeanine said, walking over to her backpack on the other side of the tree, "but I suspect she won't be bothering anyone in the flesh for another hundred years." Her mouth tightened and her forehead wrinkled. "Not that we'd have any ancestors for her to take revenge on."

Joseph moved to her as she broke down with a keening cry and she collapsed into his arms. He held her tight until the worst of it passed.

"So what now?" she asked, wiping at her tears, still shaken. "What do we do now, Joseph?"

He shrugged, but gave her a warm smile as he lifted her chin and met her eyes. "We always have the first of May," he said, taking his hands in hers, squeezing them. "Didn't she suggest herself that the *Beltaine* spirits are a bit more receptive to proposals of our kind?"

"Aye," Jeanine said, a glimmer of hope slowly filling her eye as she smiled back at him. "That she did."

The two walked back down the hillside to the lights of the village below, guided by the light of the harvest moon, leaving the burial mound, the pile of broken sticks, and death behind them.

THE SENTRY

Fiona Patton

Physical sensations came on slowly, so slowly that he hardly recognized them for what they were at first. A disturbance and a shifting far away brought feelings near to hand: the scratch of a pigeon's claws against his shoulders and the whisper of the wind against his cheeks. He stood frozen, marveling at them and wondering how they'd come to be.

He'd known the strength of stone and the serenity of silence. He'd known the call of duty and the slumber of the fallen. He'd stood, weapon clutched against his chest, guarding them from any who might disturb their rest. A candle in a distance burned for all of them, but not all of them could reach it; their time on earth had been too terrible and far too brief. For those, he took their memories of pain, loss, and sacrifice. Comforted, they took the path illuminated for them and passed away beyond the trees. A boy in face and form, and a man in duty, he knew death but he did not remember if he'd ever truly known a life that might have once been his.

He heard voices speaking words and strained to hear them, a strange unnatural ripple of anticipation traveling through his limbs.

"I found something."

"A body?"

"Maybe. Bones, anyway. See, those would be fingers, there and there."

"Be careful with them."

Whisper soft, a brushing motion swept across his hands and the voices spoke again, more clearly now.

"It's definitely a body."

"A soldier?"

"Looks to be. There, that's a brass button. See? And here's another."

Hundreds of the fallen had left their memories in his care and they flooded through him now; the screaming of the shelling in the distance and the corkscrew twist of fear as it came closer. He had sudden urge to freeze, to hide, or rise and run, to do anything but carry on slowly forward. A pain so sharp and bright it took his breath away, then falling.

"See here, the vestiges of a uniform tunic."

The scratch of wool against his wrists and throat. The stiffness of it when it had been clean and new, the stiffness of it when it had been old and caked with clay, the heat and then the cold of it as it had filled with blood, but through it all, the hard unmoving armor of it as stone. He held on to that one image as his own as the voices carried on, unrelenting as they dredged up the past and layered it on the present.

"I found some metal."

"A weapon?"

Jamming, shattering, flung away, tossed aside, or held as tightly as a talisman.

"No, it's too fine, more like wire. Yes, see here's a roll of it around what was probably a wooden spool."

Crawling in the darkness and the mud, a line of wire unraveling behind him in the darkness.

"Wait. There's something here tucked up beside the ribs, something leather. A small book, I think, or a piece of it, anyway."

"A journal?"

"Could be."

"Can you open it? Can you make anything out? Words or a name?"

"I think so. Shine your torch here."

"Careful now, careful."

The rush of memories froze in place as he waited for words he'd hadn't known he'd ever hear or ever thought he'd need to.

"Private William Falkner."

A boy in face and form, and a man in duty, lost, and honored to be carved in stone by the ones he'd left behind. Found.

He opened his eyes.

A white-dressed cemetery filled his vision: a jumble of old gravestones and iron markers radiating out to lines of stark, grey trees. He heard birds and far away a single church bell tolling morning. As the dawn sun warmed his face, he stepped off the monument that had been his sentry box and heard the crack of hard-packed snow break beneath his boots. The wind whispered past his face and, as he turned, he saw a single candle flame beckon in the distance.

He followed it.

The gravestones became older, darker, covered in moss and worn smooth by years of rain and snow. At the far end of the cemetery, the land sloped steeply down into a line of trees and he stared at them for a long time, feeling them stare back. They and their kin had been fed by the dead for so long that it was impossible to tell where trees left off and the dead began. But he could see the candle flame flickering behind them. He took a single step forward and suddenly the memories he had carried for so long rushed over him: the screaming of the shells, the stiffness of his uniform, the fear, the falling and the darkness. Behind him, the monument called out to him, offering the serenity of silence and the strength of stone, but the candle flame still beckoned and he stood frozen, unable to go forward and unable to go back.

Far away he felt himself lifted as the voices that had begun his transformation spoke again.

"Be careful with his bones. They're fragile."

"I wonder if he has any relatives still living who might remember him."

"I doubt it, after all this time. But there might be family somewhere and a grave. People do that sometimes, you know. Just place a marker with a name on it to have a place to go."

He glanced about the rows of gravestones. Many of

them had fallen into disrepair as the people who'd once tended them had died in turn. The soldiers who lay beneath them had long since passed beyond the trees.

All save one.

He moved towards it, then crouching down, he stripped the moss away and read the words aloud.

"Private Arthur Townsend."

His own voice startled him for a moment; then he shook himself and bent to study the grave itself, seeing it as only he could see it. The soldier who slumbered in this place held on to memories so dear that he would not be moved no matter how beseechingly the candle beckoned. And stretching out into the distance, past the monument, he saw a line of equal strength that bound the living to the dead through memories too precious and too painful to be forgotten.

But as he watched, it wavered and he knew it would not bind them long. Death was searching for this final soldier and it would not be denied. A day, no more. The dead might refuse the candle flame but the living could not refuse the dead no matter how much strength they might command. No strength could overcome the strength of death.

He paused. No strength except the strength of stone.

He rose and, with a sudden urgency, passed through the cemetery's wrought-iron gates and set out walking, his boots making a soft *shush, shush* noise in the fine layer of snow upon the ground.

He walked all morning, barely pausing to register the changes in the world. The memories he carried were not the memories of shops and streets and he could not remember how the world had been before them enough to notice any change. No one remarked upon his presence and for a moment he doubted that he was even really there until he paused before a tavern window and peered in at his reflection with a frown.

He saw a young man, eighteen or nineteen years old, smooth cheeks, hair cut short, but grown out shaggy and uneven beneath his helmet's rim as if he'd had no time to care for it. Uniform tunic, belt, and trousers wrapped in linen up the calves, boots old but serviceable. Hair, and eyes, and face, and clothes the gray pallor of cold stone and expression: haunted. He shuddered but, as he turned away, he saw the candle flame and, with a new resolve, he set out walking once again.

He passed by people, young and old, some healthy and some ill, some carrying the memories of sacrifice and pain but none of them the one he sought and so he passed them by and came at last to a long, low building of gray brick painted white. Not a hospital, although it had the sense of one. The entrance door was locked, but as two women exited, chatting amiably together, he slipped inside a hushed and carpeted anteroom. Old men and women sat in wheelchairs, some talking loudly, some calling for a nurse, but most just staring into space, into the past. An old man sitting in a patch of sunlight, a blanket thrown over what once had been his legs, gestured to him.

"Are you Death?" he demanded when he approached him.

"No."

The old man's shoulders sagged. "I'm Clem and I'm dying. They don't think I know it, but I do. I can see it, that light out there. Can you see it? A single light, like a candle maybe?" Clem waved his hand before his face, then dropped it with a sigh. "Can you see it?" he repeated.

He looked into Clem's eyes, past the lines of battle, past the fallen, past the blood, and pain, and death, and saw the candle flame and nodded.

"I can see it."

"I can't reach it."

"That's because your memories won't let you go. You're holding on to them too tightly. Let them go and they'll let you go."

Clem gave a snort. "Easier said than done, boy. I've got nothing left but memories. My friends are all dead and my legs ache something awful in the night. They keep me up. They keep me remembering. Yeah, yeah, I know they're gone," he snapped. "I lost 'em in forty-three, but they still ache." He jerked the blanket up about his stomach.

"So why are you here?" he demanded. "You didn't come for me, not in those clothes, you didn't. You look like a picture of my old dad from the Great War and he died years ago."

"I'm looking for someone."

"Someone?"

"One of mine."

Clem snorted. "You won't find him. They're all gone. All of them. Most of mine are gone now, too."

"I will find him. I have to find him."

"You won't. I told you, they're all gone. Go look in a

cemetery, that's where they all are now. Bones, just bones." Clem fell back, panting slightly. "All," he muttered. "All but me. I'm tired, boy. I'm so damn tired, and I miss my friends."

The sense of urgency grew as the line wavered once again but the call of duty was still strong, and so he crouched before the aged soldier and took one hand in his, drawing out his memories of battle, one by one. "The candle flame is coming closer," he whispered. "Can you see it?"

Clem's haunted gaze drew inward. "Yes, but . . ."

"Hush. Can you hear the bugle sound the ending of the day?"

"Yes."

"And do you see them, the lines of the fallen, your fallen, moving off into the distance?"

"Yes."

"Follow them."

He left the old man's body slumped in his chair and walked away without looking back. Rooms marched along either side of a long, somberly painted hallway; bedrooms, some with two beds, some with four, not a hospital although he could sense that many of the people in the rooms were ill, and some were dying. At the far end of the hall, he turned and stared into a final room to see a wizened old woman nestled in a pile of brightly crocheted afghans staring back at him. He saw the trenches in her eyes and heard the hiss of gas and felt the fear and the resolve they shared and knew he'd found the one he sought.

Her rheumy eyes traveled down the length of him as he approached her bedside.

"Are you Death?" she asked as Clem had asked. "I saw Death on the TV once and he looked like you, a pretty boy in uniform."

He shook his head. "Not Death," he answered.

"Good, 'cause if you were, you could go take a flying leap," she snarled. "I'm not going anywhere." She crossed her arms and glared at him. "I can see that blasted candle shining in the darkness, just like in the old days," she stated. "You know. You were there. I can see you were. You got some mud and you built a little shelf and you pressed a candle stub in it and it held up good. In the dug-outs. You remember, don't you?"

"I remember." The tiny specks of light, the smell of petrol, and the odor of unwashed bodies. The faces in the darkness holding fear, and hope, and a dreadful, bone-numbing weariness that could never be forgotten.

She snapped her fingers at him impatiently and he returned his gaze to her.

"Stay outta there," she ordered. "No good can come from memories like that. You wanna see the dying all the time, hear the whizz-bangs and feel the cold mud seep into your bones forever?"

He shook his head. "No," he whispered.

"I should think not. Memories like that'll drive you mad. I oughtta know. I'm 107 last month. Got the letters from the government to prove it. All of them saying congratulations for not dying sooner." She laughed, a weak, raspy laugh that devolved into coughing. "That's all they know," she sputtered once she'd regained her breath. "Hundreds died, thousands, but I didn't. I promised Arthur that I wouldn't. I promised him I'd live." She stared off into space. "I promised him I'd live for both of us."

The line grew fainter and for a moment he feared she might reach out for the candle flame at last, but then she shook herself with a rough gesture.

"Fetch me the picture on the shelf up there and I'll tell you a secret I've never told anyone in near a century."

He brought down a small framed photograph so faded that he could hardly make out the figures standing grinning together, two young soldiers in brown woolen uniforms, arms slung companionably across each other's shoulders. He turned it over and peered at the fine, black writing.

"Arthur and Mark Townsend," he read out loud, "France, 1918."

She closed her eyes and he watched the memories flit across her face. "We were 15, both of us, in 1918," she whispered. "Only just and we couldn't wait no longer. We were powerfully afraid it would be all over before we had our chance to see it. Fools. Young fools, the pair of us, and I'm an old fool for remembering how important it all felt; how *necessary*. We *needed* to go, Artie and me, we felt it that strongly."

He nodded.

"Both our parents died of the fever just a month before and the bank took the farm for taxes. Bastards. There was nothing keeping us, so I cut my hair and Artie gave me some of his clothes to wear. We were that close in size. Twins we were, as alike as any brother and sister might be and tall for our age. We walked for three days to get to the recruitment center, and just before we went inside, we took some chalk and wrote the number 18 on the soles of our boots." She chuckled. "You remember that trick? Over 18?"

"I remember it."

"They were pretty desperate for troops by then and we went out fast. We didn't have much training, but then, we didn't need much. We both knew how to shoot already. Most farm kids did in those days. Not so much now. So much has changed. I guess it's for the better. That's what they tell me, anyway."

Her gaze grew far away. "The battles all had names, but I think they gave them names afterwards. It was all the same to us. There was mud everywhere so thick it would pull a body down right before your eyes and there was nothing you could do to save them." She hunkered in her blankets, her expression bleak. "I haven't thought about that time for many years. Haven't talked about it either. But you were there, you saw it, so you know. No one knows I was there, you see, no one, and I didn't tell no one neither, not even afterwards."

"All the battles had names," she repeated. "Named after the places they fought them at. Those that died there, well, the battles and the places became theirs for all eternity." She snorted. "I heard a minister say that once years ago. I suppose it's true. Artie's place was Ors. Did you see Ors?"

"I saw them all."

He closed his eyes as one single line of memories rushed over him. Lying on his belly in the darkness, unable to move his legs, unable to cry for help. Already the mud had a hold of him, pulling him towards his grave. One arm was trapped under his body wrapped in wire, but the other one was free enough to reach out towards the lights of camp so far away.

Too far away.

When he opened his eyes, she was watching him with a knowing expression.

"No one came," she said simply.

He shook his head. "No one knew I was there and no one could have made it even if they had. The shelling was too fierce."

The sound of it filled the room and he pressed his palms against his ears to block it out, but it was coming from inside, not outside, and so he dropped his hands again and saw her do the same. She'd heard it, she'd known it. There was no need to describe it.

"They came for Artie," she said after a moment. "The medics came for him, but it was too late. It had been too late right from the beginning. A shell took both his legs and he bled to death in my arms almost at once. But not before he made me promise to go on living. I held him and I promised and they came for him and carried him away."

She slumped, her energy spent. "I almost left the war right then," she said. "I could've; no one would've been the wiser, but I saw his body back to camp and went back out. I did my duty. We both did, though for the life of me now I can't imagine why. The next day I learned they'd signed the armistice. Years later than they should've. Bastards." She shook her head. "Matter of hours and he would've been safe." She swiped irritably at her eyes.

"I walked out after that," she said. "I found a house

and I broke in. I traded my uniform for a dress and a kerchief and I went back to camp as Margaret Townsend to claim my brother's body. They gave it to me easily enough; I looked so much like Mark. But they couldn't find Mark. They looked but they never found him. They thought he must have died somewhere out there." She gave a sad smile. "At least they never said I deserted. There were some that did desert, of course," she acknowledged. "But less than you might think."

"I know."

"Most of them just died," she continued as if she hadn't heard him. "Unseen in the mud, you know?" His throat ached as he nodded.

"I brought him home and I buried him and I turned my back on all of it. I never spoke of it, but I never forgot it, either. I married a fellow that had been too young to go, just like I had been. We had four children. The first boy was old enough to go when the call came around again but he wasn't right enough in the head for them to take him, bless him, but he was a good lad for all that. The others were too young. They had babies of their own and those babies've had more; just like they should. Just like Artie should have." She gestured at the collection of photographs and drawings on the wall above her bed. "None of them chose the life we chose. None of them had to, so maybe it was worth it after all. I don't know. But I lived, just like I promised him I would, and I never forgot him."

She peered up at him suddenly as if truly seeing him for the first time. "That bastard Death is coming for me now, whatever me and Artie might want, isn't it?" she asked.

He nodded.

"How long have I got?"

He glanced out the window although he already knew the answer. "A few hours, maybe less."

She gave him a shrewd look. "Is that why you're here? To make me accept that blasted candle?"

"No."

"Why then?"

He looked into her eyes, and past the trenches and the hiss of gas, past the fear and the resolve, he saw two grinning soldiers in brown woolen uniforms.

"I've come to bring you back to Artie."

"But Artie never went away," she said suspiciously. "I can feel him." She pressed her hand against her chest. "In here."

"I know."

They left her room together, an old woman in a pair of flowered pajamas and a young man in a worn brown uniform, boots leaving no more than shallow dents upon the carpet. The old men and women in the wheelchairs watched them go. Some smiled. Some frowned. Most continued to look inward to their own memories as they passed. They left the building unremarked but, as they stepped into the street, the cold wind caught them and she shivered.

"Is it far?" she asked.

He shook his head.

"Good, 'cause I'm too old and it's too cold to walk for long."

He shrugged out of his tunic, passed it over, and watched her fasten the brass buttons up her chest. He felt cold, then numb; looking down, he saw the beginnings of a dark red stain begin to trickle down the ruins of his shirt. Scraps of moldering wool began to unravel around his body and he felt the press of leather at his ribs and the bite of wire around his arm.

"Hurry," Margaret urged him, her white hair turning grey as his turned brown. "Before the bastard gets us both."

They ran.

The setting sun chased them all the way. She only stumbled once as her slippers caught on a jagged bit of pavement and he pulled his own boots off immediately. She stuffed her feet into them, staring down at him as he bent to wrap the linen around her calves.

"You'll soon be naked, boy," she noted, flicking the gathering snowflakes from her face.

Pulling off his helmet, he set it on her head. "I'll soon be bones," he answered weakly. As he rose, he swayed, and she threw her arm around his waist and pulled him upright. They broke into a shambling run. He felt his legs grow cold. He saw the candle burning brightly as the setting sun burned in the twilight and he stumbled as he felt the mud reach up and catch his legs. But this time someone came. A pair of strong arms pulled him forward and he lent his failing strength to them. The memory of the mud released him as Margaret Townsend pulled him onward.

They reached the cemetery gates just as the sun caressed the treetops. They passed the tombstones and markers; as her clothing stiffened as his softened; her arms grew stronger as his weakened. When they reached the monument, he sagged and she laid him down before it, staring upwards at the sky. She cradled him against her chest as she had cradled Arthur and he felt his journal press against his ribs, safe against the ravages of time.

"Are you Death?" he whispered.

She pushed her helmet back and grinned at him the cocksure grin of youth. "No," she answered. "I'm Private Mark Townsend, missing in action at the battle of Ors in 1918. Who are you?"

He smiled back at her. "I'm Private William Falkner, missing in action at the battle of Passchendaele in 1917," he answered. His eyelids fluttered and he fought to keep them open. "And found again," he finished dreamily. "In 2011."

"Do you see the candle burning?" she asked him.

"I do."

"Can you hear the bugle sound the ending of the day?"

He nodded.

"And do you see them, the lines of the fallen, our fallen, moving off into the distance?"

"Yes," he whispered.

"Follow them."

She left him lying before the monument and turned, stepping up onto the sentry box. The final memory they shared was of a team of diggers lifting the bones of a young soldier one by one, out of the earth. Scraps of cloth and rusted bits of wire followed and the remains of a leather journal and two brass buttons. She took the memory from him and released him to the candle flame.

Physical sensations left her slowly, so slowly that she had time to remark upon their passing. As the sun dipped below the horizon, she felt the serenity of silence and the strength of stone; watched Private William Falkner passed beyond the trees and felt her brother's arm drape companionably across her shoulders.

TEN THOUSAND COLD NIGHTS

Erik Scott de Bie

The time for words had ended—the time for swords begun.

The Master and the Rival studied one another. Both stood at the height of ability, and both knew of the other's skill. They were men of war—men of passion and anger thinly veiled in honor. Their deeds inspired songs and their swords carved legends.

They met in this place, beneath the blossoming cherry trees by the river, to enact the final test—to see which proved stronger.

Darkness traced one of the blades, and the wind split apart and whistled around the edge. The Master had slain uncounted men on such nights as this, and his sword had drunk of every felled foe. This was the Bloodsword, and it delighted in death.

The light of the setting sun caressed the other sword, and its reflection illumined the calm face of its wielder.

The Rival had killed men as well, but he had taken no joy in it. His steel was called Soulsword, and it wept at what was needful.

Time meant little to the warriors. The battle lasted hours in the space of a single moment.

They met, blades flashing. The dark sword struck relentlessly and the shining blade parried with a song of warfare. Steel rang in the night, each sword fighting to drown the other in its scream. They danced as the world crawled around them.

It ended as soon as it began. The Master fell to his knees.

"Why can I not beat you?" Blood trickled from his mouth. "I am the stronger." His murderous sword fell from his hand, into the river.

Cherry blossoms drifted down into the swift water, and as they touched the fallen blade, they split apart and dissolved into nothing. The sword drifted among a sea of slain beauty.

The Bloodsword languished for a time, lost and forgotten where it caught among the rushes near the sea. The blade would take no rust, and the water parted around it. Curious fish touched the sword and died, floating away in two pieces.

The Bloodsword hungered.

In autumn, leaves turned red as blood floated atop the water—the sword cut these as well. The winter snows fell, and boiled away atop the churning river.

Its Master had drawn it but not sated it, and it could not sleep.

The sword did not know its Master's name, but

names meant nothing to the sword—only simple truths. It knew the Master and the Rival: it remembered the one slain and the other victorious.

The Bloodsword hungered still.

In time, a fisherman's son found the sword in the river. Its handle bore no recognizable carvings, and the steel seemed impossibly pure.

The boy took the blade, and its darkness filled him as he touched it. The sword saw what was in his heart—lust, anger, inadequacy—and it promised vengeance for those things.

Afterward, finding the Rival took one day and night.

With the boy's body, the Bloodsword carved a swath of death and fire. No man could stand against it. The two of them destroyed village after village, slew challenger after challenger. Every wound the fisherman's son suffered spurred him to greater urgency. He bore a single word on his lips, set there by the sword: "Rival."

The boy and the sword found him after a day and night of carnage. He was a shadow of a man standing calmly against a field of fire and brandishing the Soulsword. The spirit of his blade spoke to the Bloodsword with familiar sadness.

The Bloodsword hungrily drove the boy to the Rival. The boy bled from dozens of wounds and fear filled his heart, but the sword compelled him.

They fought, and, inevitably, the boy died. In desperation, the Bloodsword claimed the boy's life.

It was not enough to assuage the terrible hunger.

The sword fell once again, discarded among the burning detritus of a dead city. It raged against its fate, to lie forsaken amongst the ashes.

The sword hungered still, but now it knew what was needed. In one day, it had found and faced the Rival. It could do the same again, if it had one day for its vengeance.

One day.

The skeleton of a city stood monument to the sword that could not be sated. None sought the lonely ruin by the sea. Tales of dark spirits frightened away travelers, who said that voices whispered amongst the stones, weaving tales of rage and death. They guarded a deadly treasure untouched by time.

Entombed, the Bloodsword hungered.

In time, a man braved the haunted crypts and defeated the spirits that roamed there. The sword sensed him but could not know him, for he did not claim it. Instead, he knelt before the fallen blade and whispered prayers to old gods, speaking of peace and honor. The darkness lifted from that place, leaving only the hungry sword.

The sword called to him in all the ways it could, promising power and skill if he would only wield it against the Rival.

The man took the blade then, but not as the sword wished. Instead, he bore it as a servant does a great treasure. He carried the sword to a shrine, where he cleaned it, washed it in blessed water, and prayed over its dark, folded steel. All the while, the sword raged against him—named his cowardice and threatened him—but the man would not be swayed. He set the sword upon an altar, and there it remained.

The sword hungered still.

One day.

The swords clashed again and again.

The power of the Bloodsword corrupted more men like the boy: monks and farmers, soldiers and nobles. Each took the sword for his own reasons, and each fed its undying hunger. None of them could sate the Bloodsword.

It wanted one man—the man who had defeated it when he should not have.

Again and again, the Soulsword came against the Bloodsword. The Rival faced them each time, and each time, the sword's chosen wielder failed. None could match the Rival. And every time, the Rival reclaimed the sword and returned it to its place in the shrine.

The sword hungered with a painful longing.

One day, it would find the right wielder.

One day.

In time, men came to pray over the sword. They filled the shrine, kneeling before the altar, and communed with what men cannot see. None of them touched the sword that could not sleep. It demanded—it begged—it *raged*—to no avail.

Every day, as light first filtered across the altar, a single monk came to cleanse the sword, and every day, the sword fought him. Called to him. Demanded of him.

Every day, the sword cut his cleaning cloth in two, and every day the monk brought a new one to wipe the blade. This he did for honor's sake. The sword did not need cleaning: dust split apart and fell away from the sword's flawless edge.

Every day, the monk bathed the blade in blessed water, which the sword also cut. The droplets fell in two upon the altar, never touching the blade that rejected them. The monk, fearful of the sword's hunger, took care never to touch it with his own hand.

Even after men stopped coming to pray over the sword, the monk still came to purify it. Soon, only they two occupied that place—caretaker and treasure.

The sword hungered not for cloth and water, but for flesh and blood. It existed only to kill, not to be cleaned and prayed over and displayed like a trophy.

It would have its vengeance, and one day was all it needed.

One day.

Then one day, the monk who tended the sword made a mistake. He had grown old and lost the deftness of youth. In wiping the blade, he touched the edge with his bare finger.

Instantly, the flesh split and blood welled. The man staggered away and fell. Red spattered his robe as the wound gushed. The man tried to rise but his body grew weak.

At long last, the Bloodsword bathed once again in that for which it hungered. In blood, there was power. The sword had learned, with countless wielders, how to use that power in a different way than before. No wielder had been worthy of its power, so it would have no wielder. It no longer had any need for one.

As the monk lay dying, the sword on the altar trembled. Its shaking grew, and it tumbled from its rack and clattered to the floor. There it danced, end to end and back, until finally it stood in stillness upon its point. Darkness swirled around it, tinged with blood—

And then it was a man.

A particular man: its only worthy wielder, whose face had been reflected in its steel countless times. Dark hair, pale skin, red eyes.

The Master.

The sword was wholly a man then, and saw the world as men did. Before it could take a single step, it—*he*—fell to his knees. He had his own blood, beating in his own veins. Pressure built in his chest as though he would explode, and finally it left in a great flood of air. Breath.

So many years of battle had taught him of men's strengths and weaknesses. He knew how they moved, how they fought—and now he knew how they breathed.

Soon, he would teach many how men died.

He rose, moved, and almost fell. He sought to learn the ways of men's bodies. He grunted and hissed—he strained and flexed. He learned.

In a moment, he knew everything there was to know about men's bodies. He knew how they moved and could be moved—how they could be killed.

The ways of men included more than movement: he explored his new senses as well. He smelled incense, which almost overwhelmed him with its sharp tang.

Beneath that smell, there was wood and pitch. And blood, of course—the monk had left a pool of it.

The sword-become-man moved to the monk on the floor and knelt with the grace of water flowing over stone. He opened his mouth, and it took a moment before he could make sounds emerge. He spoke with words he had known the Master to use.

"Where?" he asked. "Where is he?"

The monk said nothing, however. He was dead.

The Master had not realized this. He no longer sensed every drip of blood onto the ground or the ebbing of his victim's soul. A man's death felt different when he wore a man's body.

Good.

He left the shrine, and passed into the open air. The sun was rising, and the wind cut warmly into his face. Cherry trees flanked the entrance, and the scent and color of blossoms overwhelmed him. He heard a stream trickling past, so loud it thundered in his ears. The world outside had so much more in it than he had ever known as a sword.

A light rain fell upon his face. He looked up, marveling at the sensation of each individual drop breaking open on his skin. The rain caressed and seduced him, but he knew it could also drown him. Too much, and his life would end.

The world wanted to kill him, but he would kill the world if it stood in his way.

He saw lights in the distance—a village, just opening its doors to welcome the day. Men dwelt there—men to be killed.

He started forward, then realized he was naked,

with neither clothes nor sword. He turned back to the shrine.

The monk's robe would do. Only a single sleeve had touched the bloody pool. He dragged the body away from the blood and stripped the clothes. He was just sliding them on when he saw something at the altar.

It was a sword, and one he remembered well. The only sword ever to defeat him. The sword of the Rival: the Soulsword.

He strode forward and claimed the weapon for his own. The steel did nothing to protest—it could not speak to him when he was a man.

With this, he could draw the Rival. He could bring such dishonor to this sword that the Rival would surely come to face him. And even if he did not, destroying the Rival's sword would be like destroying him.

One day would be enough.

He slid the sheathed blade into his belt and turned toward the village.

He arrived at the village just as night fell. Shops closed their doors at the fall of darkness, and the lamplighters went about their business. Men and women walked briskly through the streets, talking and laughing.

The time it had taken him to walk through the forest prepared him somewhat. There he'd learned the smells of trees and of animals—their flesh and their leavings—and had realized not every sound was a threat. He'd learned to walk in silence, such that he could place his hand on a deer before it heard him.

The village was another matter.

Thousands of sounds and scents filled this place, making him dizzy. Flowers hung in windows overwhelmed him, and bread and roasting meat made his mouth wet and his midsection ache. The villagers kept pigs in their yards, which had a particular smell—tangy and rich. It all struck his senses so sharply he could barely see where he was going.

He passed among people and wanted to touch their clothes—to feel the different textures of the fabrics. He wanted to test their steel. He wanted to feel their blood on his hands.

He heard deprecating words and laughter. He turned and saw three young men looking at him. Two wore swords, while the third leaned on a spear. The biggest and strongest of them pointed and spoke, and the others laughed all the louder. They had seen him wandering like a dazed child. Though he knew few words, he understood well enough that it had cut like a blade.

He stepped toward them. "Apologize."

The two lessers looked to the leader, who scoffed. "Apologize for yourself, old man," he said. "Trouble your betters and you'll suffer for it."

"Calm," said another. "He's just lost and confused."

"Bah, he's an old man! Let him apologize!"

The Master looked around at the three. They were young and lazy, but they spoke in earnest. He could not walk away without a proper answer, so he searched his mind. He knew words of battle and of mockery—words meant to wound and provoke. He'd heard his Master issue a thousand challenges, and watched a thousand men lured from their guard. He remembered how to fight with his voice.

"My betters," he said, reciting an insult his Master had favored. "My betters do not eat themselves to death like pigs, then squat in the mud doing nothing of value."

Their faces flushed and their eyes grew wide. "How dare you!" they cried.

The Master's mind fell away as the leader came forward with an overhand strike. He moved without thought, drawing the Soulsword in a blur. Its steel glistened in the fading light. The man staggered as the sword sliced through tendon and bone, and his chest became a welling fountain of blood. He looked down, confused and horrified.

Even as his foe fell to the ground, the Master flowed into a parry that knocked the second attacker off-balance. He grasped this one by the wrist, spun him around like a shield, and stopped a seeking spear with his body.

The Master slashed down, opening the throat of the third attacker as the man struggled to pull his spear free of his friend's ribs. The man fell to his knees, and his head slid off.

Simple.

The Master stood with his attention fixed upon the sword in his hand, smeared with lifeblood. The blade held immense power. Paired, the Bloodsword and the Soulsword could not be defeated: the corpses of three men gave that testament.

Two, he corrected himself. The second of the youths was squirming, still alive. Blood turned his shirt to a sodden mess. He reached for it, and his fingers came away slick and trembling. He stared at his hand, disbelieving.

"This is death," the Master said, realizing he needed to explain.

The boy—he no longer seemed a man, but a pathetic boy—drew in a deep breath and coughed. Blood flew into the air and spattered the Master's hand.

"Why?" the boy asked. "Why?"

The Master pondered this.

"Why?" The boy's breathing grew heavy and he trembled.

"It is my nature." The Master raised the Soulsword high into the air. Blood dripped onto the boy's forehead and rolled down his cheek. "It is what I am."

There was acceptance on the boy's face. The Master put both hands on the hilt of the Soulsword, ready to thrust it into the boy's chest. Wind whispered around him.

Then he stopped.

A terrified crowd had formed around them to watch. By their eyes, they had never seen such impossible, ruthless skill. They were innocents, even if some of them wore steel. The boy at his feet was one such, the Master realized. It was in his clumsy movements and his pathetic cowardice. He thought the boy had never shed blood, either his own or that of a foe. He was a fool to carry a sword—they were all fools.

The crowd stared at him, and why not? His body was perfect in every muscle, unscathed by arrow or blade, newly born and fully formed. His skin was dark, his hair long, and his eyes crimson. He held in his hands the finest sword ever crafted by mortal hands, rivaled only by the Bloodsword—the only sword that truly mattered. *Himself.*

And yet, not all eyes fell upon him. One of the women stared instead at the boy on the ground with fear and longing. Misery surrounded the old woman and no matter how the Master willed her to face him, she would not meet his eye.

What was this hesitation? This cowardice?

His thirst for death was gone.

The Master turned his gaze to the sword, which quavered in his hand. He could not hold it still. "Why can I not beat you?" he asked. "I am stronger."

Finally, he lowered the sword and stepped away. The old woman ran forward and draped her arms around the boy's neck, sobbing. Others in the crowd cried out, the silence that had held them now broken.

Disgusted, confused, the Master returned to the forest.

The walk back to the shrine took the remainder of the night.

They followed him, of course. They brandished blades and shouted threats, but none dared cross steel with him. He lost them in the woods, amongst the paths and hiding places he had found that morn. The darkness grew deeper as midnight descended. He jumped at every rustling twig or leaf, raised his sword at every looming shadow.

He could not name the feeling that coiled around his heart and muddied his mind.

When rain began to fall, it obscured his tracks and

blurred his vision. He shivered in the cold, but the rain was a blessing. The men following him trailed off and turned back.

When finally he broke into the clearing that housed the shrine, light glowed in the window beneath the cherry trees. Water streamed from the roof and dripped from the blossoms. He stopped, although he had no sense of danger. He had slain the monk who tended the shrine. Who could be waiting for him?

The Rival. It could be no other.

The far horizon had begun to lighten. He had little time left—just enough to kill one man.

The doors stood open, and he padded through. Across the chamber, a single candle burned on the altar, casting dancing shadows. He stepped into its muddy radiance, keenly aware of the moisture pooled on his forehead and hands. He grasped the hilt of the Soulsword. Again, he entered the focus of the true swordsman: his mind fell away, and he raised his blade.

No Rival lurked in the corners of the shrine, nor near the altar. His breathing quickened as he stalked, cat-like, around the chamber, searching the shadows. He found only the monk, who reeked of death, and the candle. An empty sword rack stood upon the altar of cut stone.

Nothing else.

"Do you hide in the shadows, afraid to face me?" he called.

He searched again, but there was nothing in the corners, nothing in the rafters. He slashed his sword through the shadows, as if striking at invisible foes. The blade whined as it cut the air.

"Face me, coward," he said. "Face me!"

Finally, after his third search, he raised the sword over his head and hurled it through the air. The blade smashed off the wall and clattered to the floor, and the Master fell to his knees. Hot liquid streamed down his face, and he realized he was weeping.

He did not know what came to pass in that place, or why his body felt as it did.

He became aware of a presence then: a man who sat a few paces away, legs crossed, facing the altar. He wore a flawless white robe, which seemed luminous in the soft candlelight. How he had materialized, the Master did not know.

"Time has passed," he said. "I have spent it in contemplation, and I have not found what I sought. Have you?"

The Master recognized the reedy voice from long ago.

The Rival.

He looked to where he had hurled the Soulsword, and had risen half to his feet before he realized it was gone. His eyes traced the empty shrine. Had the Rival reclaimed his sword?

"Why are you here?" the Master asked. "Have you come to answer the dishonor I've given? Have you come to face me at last?"

"You summoned me, but not in the way you think," said the Rival. "Not through blood, as you were called, but through compassion."

The Master looked down at his hands curled into fists. The blood of the men he had killed had dried upon his skin, coating his hands black.

"Why couldn't I kill the boy?" he asked without knowing.

The Rival sat unmoving. "Ten thousand cold nights have passed since we faced each other beneath the cherry blossom trees—many times that," he said. "And in all those years, the world has changed and left men of war behind. They have no place in this world—you and I do not belong here."

"I am a *sword*," the Master said. "I am a tool by which men kill other men."

"You were," the Rival said. "But now you are a man, and you feel as other men do."

"What does that mean?"

Silence spread between them. The Rival sat in stillness, the Master in shivering unease.

Finally, the Master could stand it no longer. He jumped to his feet, fists clenched at his sides. "You dishonor me with your silence," he said.

The Rival remained placid. "I do you honor by my silence," he said. "You know the answer in your heart, even if you will not hear it."

He wiped sweat from his brow. The Master stood over the Rival, quivering with the urge to fight. His nails dug into his flesh, and fresh blood traced gleaming channels through the congealed stains.

More candles appeared out of the darkness, lit by no apparent cause.

"Face me," said the Master. "Face me, and finish that which we began. Or in the end, after I have desired this so long, do you prove a coward?"

The man looked at him, at last, and the Master drew back. The Rival was old—ancient beyond reckoning.

His hair and beard extended to the floor as he knelt, and the furrows on his face plunged like canyons into his flesh. His eyes gleamed white as the Master's burned red.

"Our fight is ended," he said. "It ended that night under the cherry blossoms—that night when our finest masters clashed—but it has taken both of us all this time to see it. We needed to walk as men, and so we have."

The Master wanted to rage. He wanted to spit in the Rival's face and deny him. He wanted to wage this war unto eternity. He *hungered*.

And yet.

The Rival rose and gazed out the window, where light spread into the world like a growing tide. He breathed a long sigh. "The night ends and the day begins," he said. "Will we continue this battle, or will we make an end of it?"

They stood facing one another as they had that night—as they had faced each other many times before and many times since. They had fought a battle that had never sated them, and now he saw that it never would. He had seen this when he stood over a foe and failed to slay him. He had seen this in the old woman's sadness, when the thirst for death had left him.

The Rival held out his hand.

The Master took it.

The next day, when the searching villagers came upon the old shrine, they found the body of an ancient monk inside, lying in a pool of congealed blood. They buried him beneath the cherry trees. The blossoms fell on the fresh earth of his grave.

A single candle guttered cn the altar, and none could say who had lit it.

They found two swords in the shrine, lying on the floor side-by-side, like companions. The men hesitated to touch them, knowing the legends of these blades, but a sense of peace surrounded them. The wounded boy, still coughing and shaking in his step, knelt to claim the black-hilted blade. He breathed easier, soothed by its touch.

The villagers returned the swords to their place of honor in the old shrine.

Then they knelt and prayed.

MORTALITY

Dylan Birtolo

"You have been chosen."

The words came to Deniel in his mind—a disembodied voice that filled his entire being with calm, happiness, and unquestioning loyalty. "How may I serve?"

"From sunrise to sunrise, you shall exist on earth and live as a man. During this time, you must not lose faith. Be an example for all who have lost their way."

"Thy will be done." Deniel bowed his head.

"Be strong, my child."

After hearing those words, Deniel was ripped away. He felt as if unseen ropes wrapped around his entire body and yanked him through the sky. They burned as they pulled, scorching his skin though leaving no marks. He wanted to scream, but clenched his jaw shut. He would be strong. He was worthy. The burning grew to an almost unbearable level.

As he fell, he imagined ghostly hands reaching into his body, gripping his heart, and tearing it out of his chest. Deniel shut his eyes, clenching them tight against the pain. He could feel the air rushing past him, and it offered no solace from the fiery intensity. Then it all stopped and he only felt air rushing past.

Then he hit the ground.

A large crack echoed in his head as Deniel collided with the pavement. A groan escaped from his lips as he finally released the tension in his jaw. After a few seconds, he opened his eyes and kept them squinted against the light of the afternoon sun. Rolling onto his back, he forced himself to look around. He was in an alley, near the back of it. Thankfully, it was abandoned.

He saw he was in a small crater. Inching his hands behind his back, he pushed himself up to a sitting position and let his head hang. The impact hadn't hurt him, at least not as far as he could tell. But he was sore; a sensation that was unusual. With another groan, he pushed himself up to a standing position.

He regretted the motion as his legs buckled and he had to put out an arm to catch himself on a nearby wall. Deniel looked down at his legs and their sudden betrayal. Putting his second hand on the wall for balance, he shook out one leg and then the other. It was almost a minute before he felt stable enough to stand up straight. Even so, he stumbled on the first step and put out his fingertips for balance. After that small mishap, he was able to walk towards the mouth of the alley.

The street beyond was a busy city street; cars inched along in traffic while they were passed by people walking on the sidewalks. Stores were open, some with wares available for display on the street. At the next corner, a man wearing three coats held a cardboard sign and a cup that he shook back and forth. The people on the street passed Deniel as if he were a normal part of the scenery. Being at the same level as so many humans made Deniel look at himself for the first time. He had been given suitable clothes: jeans, a shirt, a jacket, and a pair of shoes. The clothes felt confining, hugging his skin as he moved.

Taking a deep breath, Deniel stepped out into the stream of people and moved with them. He wandered down the street, looking around. He was not sure what he was looking for, but he knew he needed something. He needed to do something. As his mind stumbled over this, his body responded with its own answer; his stomach grumbled. It made Deniel stop in midstride and reach to his abdomen. The sound was followed with a sudden pang of hunger. To his left, he saw a street vendor selling hotdogs out of his cart. Deniel's mouth watered. He walked over and watched as a customer bought a hotdog and added a generous amount of toppings.

"Want a dog?" the vendor asked.

Deniel nodded.

"Two bucks." The man reached into his cart and pulled out a dog with a practiced motion. Before Deniel had a chance to check his pockets, the vendor had the hotdog sitting in a bun and napkin in his hand. Deniel checked all of his pockets, but found nothing.

"I'm sorry, I don't have any . . ."

"Then get outta here."

"Please, sir . . ."

"No dough, no dog. Beat it." The vendor turned his shoulder so that he no longer had to face Deniel and could offer his food to the woman standing on the other side of the cart.

Deniel continued to wander down the street, following the gentle flow of foot traffic. It seemed that with each step his stomach became increasingly insistent. It had passed beyond discomfort and crossed into pain. But with no money, how could he get food? Stealing was not an option. When he appealed to people for charity, most ignored him. Those who didn't, looked at him once, and then passed him by.

Up ahead, Deniel saw the towering spires of a cathedral, and it brought him comfort. Without realizing it, he straightened his spine as he altered his course in that direction. When he rounded the corner, Deniel saw it in all its majestic glory. It was a beautiful cathedral with a large central tower housing four bells. The doors stood open and even from this distance, Deniel could see into the nave. Warmth filled him, diminishing the awareness of his hunger.

Deniel entered the cathedral and walked towards one of the pews. Getting down on his knees, he prayed, losing himself in the words. He could not say how long he had been lost in prayer, but he felt a gentle hand on his shoulder.

"It's late, my son. Time for you to go home."

Deniel lifted his eyes and looked into the face of an elderly priest. "I can't go home."

"Oh, it can't be that bad."

Deniel stood up with a weak smile. "It's not that I don't want to go, I can't. Not yet."

Again, Deniel's stomach betrayed him and let out an audible rumble. This made the priest smile.

"I think you'll find that it's easier than you think. But let's at least get you a meal before you go. The sisters run a soup kitchen next door."

The priest escorted Deniel out of the cathedral, locking it up once they were outside. Deniel was surprised to see that night had fallen. He followed the priest to a small squat building next to the cathedral that was well lit. Several people were taking advantage of the sisters' hospitality and enjoying a warm meal. The priest brought Deniel up to get a meal and sat with him until he finished. They talked very little, but the priest insisted things were not as bad as they seemed and told Deniel to have faith. When he left, Deniel's stride was quick and strong.

Still not sure where he was going or what he was doing, Deniel wandered the streets following his instincts. With each passing hour, more buildings closed their doors and fewer cars appeared on the road. As he passed a small side street, Deniel heard something that made him stop.

"Gimme your money! And that briefcase, too!"

Deniel tensed and turned down the side street. Behind the corner of a building he saw two men. One of them cowered in a corner and fumbled in his pocket while the other looked on. The onlooker pointed a gun at the victim. Without hesitation, Deniel strode around the corner and advanced on the mugger.

"Leave that man alone!" Deniel shouted, making his voice as imposing as he could manage.

The mugger turned and snickered as he brought his gun around to point it at Deniel. "Or what? You ain't a cop. Gimme your money, too!"

Deniel jumped to the side, bursting into a run as soon as his feet hit the ground. The mugger fired his gun, but the shot went wide—straight through the space where Deniel had been. The mugger continued pulling the trigger as he swung his arm around towards Deniel. Another bullet soared well clear, but the third bit into Deniel's arm. He was dimly aware of a sharp burning sensation as it ripped through his skin. By then, they were within an arm's reach of each other.

The mugger tried to bring his weapon around and point it at Deniel's body, but Deniel shot his arm out and caught both of the mugger's hands in his one. He lifted up while still charging in and a fourth bullet soared into the sky. Deniel's knee came up and slammed into the mugger's side right in the ribs. The man expelled all his air at once and dropped the gun so that it clattered to the ground. He tried to stumble away, but Deniel kept a death-grip on his hands.

Ducking under the mugger's arms, Deniel spun around and drove his elbow into the mugger's back. He let go of the man's hands at the same time so that he stumbled forward and landed on the ground on his face. Deniel stood over him with his fists clenched at his sides. The mugger didn't even look at Deniel; he ran off so quickly that for the first few steps he staggered on all fours.

"Yeah! You better run!" the other man screamed as

he ran up beside Deniel and threw a rock at the retreating criminal. "Get out of my neighborhood!"

When he turned to face Deniel he was beaming. He held out his hand. "I can't thank you enough! You saved me. Thank you."

"I'm glad I could help. I was only doing what anyone would have done in the same situation."

The man let loose a short barking laugh. "You haven't been here long, have you? What's your name?"

"Deniel."

"Nice to meet you, Deniel. I'm Julian Blake. I owe you one." As he spoke he clapped Deniel in the arm where the wound was. Deniel hissed and brought his hand up to the wound. "Oh god, I'm sorry! I didn't know you were shot. Let me take a look."

Deniel complied, sitting down on the ground so that Julian could look at his arm. Julian helped Deniel take off the jacket and then lifted up the sleeve of the shirt. Deniel looked at his arm. He was bleeding. He couldn't stop staring at the blood as it slowly trickled down his arm. Those drops were his blood. His *human* blood.

"It's not too bad. Just a graze. Come on, let's go back to my place and I can stitch it up for you. Cheaper for you than taking you to a hospital and that way I can thank you properly."

Deniel shrugged back into his jacket, moving slowly as he slid it around his injured arm, "Thank you. But the police? There was gunfire."

Julian barked again. "Like I said, you're not from around here, are you? No sense in having you bleed out while we wait for them to show. I'm only just around the corner."

The two of them made their way to Julian's place. It was a small apartment with two locked doors at the entrance, one of which had bars. Julian led Deniel into the elevator and they got off at the twelfth floor. When they entered Julian's apartment, the smell of roasting ham filled the air. Julian called out to his wife as soon as he entered the door. A young woman walked around the corner to greet them. When she saw Deniel, she lowered her head and turned aside.

"We have company. Set out another place for dinner." His wife gave a quick nod and then disappeared back into the kitchen. "Don't mind Melanie. Come on, let's get you fixed up."

Julian took Deniel to a small study and had him sit down on a stool. He left the room and came back with a big white box labeled "Medical." Opening it up, he pulled out sutures, triple antibiotic ointment, and a small syringe filled with a clear fluid. After the initial pokes from the needle, Deniel felt nothing as Julian stitched his arm up. Once he was finished, he cleaned up the wound and then the two of them went back to the dining room. Melanie stood in the doorway to the kitchen. As soon as they entered she turned around and retreated to get the food. Julian and Deniel took their seats and Melanie came back with the ham, placing it in the center of the table. As she was putting it down, Deniel noticed that she had a large bruise on her left cheekbone.

"Are you all right, Miss Melanie?"

"Oh, yes. I'm fine. Just had an accident in the kitchen." When she spoke, her voice was barely above a whisper. She scampered back into the kitchen.

"Excuse me for a minute, Deniel. Help yourself to some food."

Julian got up from the table and disappeared in the kitchen. Deniel waited, not sure how long he should do so. It wasn't long before he heard shouting from the kitchen. It was subdued at first, but quickly grew in intensity. When he heard a crash of metal he bolted from his chair hard enough to knock it over. With two strides, he was through the door leading into the kitchen.

Melanie was on the floor in the corner and she held her hand to her face. A fresh red mark formed on her cheek. Julian stood over her with his hand over his head. Deniel caught the tail end of what he was shouting.

" . . . let him see you like that? Are you trying to make me look bad?"

Deniel lunged across the kitchen and grabbed Julian's wrist in his hand. He yanked back, forcing Julian to face him. He brought his other hand up in a cross punch, sending Julian reeling until he collided with the counter. He fumbled on it with both hands trying to stay upright. Melanie screamed and pushed herself further back into the corner.

"It is wrong to strike those who are defenseless. You should seek forgiveness."

Julian seemed to lose the capacity for language. Pushing off the counter, he drove himself right at Deniel. It was a clumsy attack, and Deniel faded back so that it passed several inches in front of his face. He pushed on the back of Julian's arm, using his own momentum against him to drive him into a wall. Deniel clenched his fists and narrowed his eyes as Julian turned around. He held a kitchen knife in his hand.

Taking a step forward, he slashed through the air. Deniel jumped back out of range. He dodged a second attack as the knife came back across his body. Julian lifted the blade and stabbed at Deniel's throat. Deniel stepped to the side and pivoted so that he could grab Julian's wrist. Before he had a chance to twist, Julian reached around and punched Deniel directly in his recently stitched wound. Deniel yelped as a flash of fire shot down through his fingers. He barely managed to twist away as the knife came across again. It scraped him across the chest, cutting through the shirt and just a bit of skin underneath.

Julian tried to stab again, and Deniel had little time to react. Thousands of years of training kicked in. He struck Julian's hand from the side, making the attack go wide. In one fluid motion, he struck Julian's elbow and used his other hand to guide the knife in a big circle. It came around and sunk deep into Julian's neck. His eyes went wide and he dropped to the ground, blood pooling underneath him.

Melanie screamed again between sobs. Deniel stood over the body, looking down at the corpse. His eyes slid from the corpse to focus on his right hand. It was covered in blood and he still held the knife in his hand. He backpedaled out of the kitchen, away from the body and the hysterical woman. He bumped into a chair and stumbled over it, falling to the floor and dropping the knife. He needed to get away. Picking himself up, he sprinted out of the apartment and made his way to the stairs. He bounded up the stairs four at a time on his way to the roof. When he reached the final platform, he burst through the door with his shoulder, only stopping when he was on the roof.

Deniel fell to his knees and looked up at the stars, half-hidden by clouds. They blurred in his vision as tears pooled and traced down his cheeks. Falling forward onto his forearms, he sobbed. What had he done? How could it have come to this? The man was a sinner, but he didn't deserve to die. Emotion overwhelmed him: despair like he had not felt in all his eons of existence. It was a human emotion and heartbreaking in its power.

The sound of sirens shook him from his sorrow. Standing, he shuffled over to the edge of the building. Looking down at the ground 15 stories below, he saw police cars at the front of the building—their telltale lights decorating the street in an almost festive glow. Feeling that overwhelming despair, Deniel climbed up to stand on the edge. He had failed. He was not worthy.

He fell forward, closing his eyes as he rushed to meet the ground.

With a gasp, Deniel woke up. He jerked to a sitting position and looked around. Everything was black. It wasn't dark; just black for as far as he could see. He heard the staccato tone of someone walking in boots on a hard floor. Deniel stood up and turned around. A meticulously groomed man walked towards him wearing a suit. He had a charming smile and eyes that seemed to glow of their own accord.

"Brother," the stranger said as he came forward and put a hand on Deniel's shoulder.

Deniel looked down and his shoulders sank. "I failed. I was not worthy. I died as a sinner and have fallen from grace." He sighed. "Are you here to gloat, Lucifer? To claim me as a trophy?"

The other man softened his features, pulled Deniel to his feet, and shook his head from side to side. "No, brother. You are no trophy and you did not fail."

"But I killed a human. He didn't deserve to die."

"What about the millions that you were commanded to kill? Did they deserve it?"

Deniel paused and looked up with his eyebrows furrowed together. "I don't know. They must have. Otherwise . . ."

There was a brief pause and then Lucifer finished the sentence for him. "Otherwise, He would have been wrong."

Deniel snapped his gaze to meet his brother's. "That's not possible."

"Are you sure?"

Deniel had no answer. His head swam in the possibility of what was being suggested.

Lucifer continued. "You have not failed. You just realized what I realized so many years ago."

"What is that?"

"Father can be wrong."

They stood there without saying anything, one providing comfort to the other through a gentle touch on the shoulder. After several breaths, Deniel reached up and put his hand on top of his brother's. He closed his eyes. In response, Lucifer stepped in and wrapped his arms around Deniel in a gentle embrace.

"Why was I tested?"

"It's the only way I could show you the truth. Living as a mortal, separated from His voice, you see the world as it truly is with all its faults and beauty. Father agreed to the test because He believes He is infallible."

With his eyes still closed and his voice a whisper, Deniel asked a question. "What do we do now?"

"Now we search for the truth without being blinded by the light, and try to help those that we can. Will you join me?"

"Yes."

THE DOG-CATCHER'S SONG

Tanith Lee

They were playing it on the radio, that first time I saw him.

He was by the highway. Just sitting there, and the sun was going west, shining back on him so he glowed like gold. He was a kind of a crossbreed, I guess, biggish built but lean, and his coat real good. I like animals. Always have. They can sometimes reach me where a human can't. That's wrong, maybe. Or maybe it ain't.

Now don't think I just pull over and run up to any animal I see. I know about rabies, even with the shots, and this was pretty wild, lonely country I was driving through; those long plains and mountains combed up on the backdrop, and maybe one thirsty tree per mile. But he had a collar and he looked in real good shape. Only thing was the way he just sat there.

So I pull up and roll down the window. I say to him, "Hey, boy, how y'doing? You okay there?"

He turned his head and looked right at me. He had one of those long noses. He had white teeth—no suspicion-making froth or nothing. And his eyes. Black. Great big eyes. I never saw eyes, any eyes, so damn sad.

First thing I did, I looked at his collar. Sure enough there's a tag on it. *Scott*, and an address. No place I heard of, but out there, no reason I would. I was making for Santa Zora with the delivery, and no need to get there until tomorrow. I left early, get bored waiting around, nervous, if I'm honest. I like to be doing something. Ever since Della. Since then.

Well, the dog seemed calm and together, but how'd I know what kind of trash might come along the road next. And anyhow, in another hour maybe it'd be jet black dark and only the stars for company. The back of the pickup had some space and the stuff I was carrying all boxed-up and waterproof. So I offered the dog a lift to the next town, which according to my info was only a few miles on. From there, I could get directions to the address he had and could drive the poor guy back to his folks.

He just jumped in the back of the pickup like he'd done that a hundred times already. He laid himself down and kind of sighed, the way a dog does. He shut those sad eyes of his, and we drove on, until the sun set chili-red and turned the mountains into crimson glass.

In the town main street I found a guy who knew the way to the address on the tag.

I bought a plastic bowl and a bottle of water, and let

the golden dog take a drink. He was thirsty as those desert trees.

We cut off along this dirt road that was full of ruts and stones, and I could hear my cargo complain a tad, but the dog seemed to be sleeping. Took me another half hour. The stars were lit up by then. It was a long, low, white house with a flat roof and some kind of palm trees grew there. Had a swimming pool, too, in the backyard. The other houses around were sort of the same. When I got out, I saw the dog was awake. He was sitting there, looking at the house.

I thought, I guess he knows he's home. But he didn't make a move or a sound. So I thought, hell, they'd maybe just gotten him and he didn't know it yet. Or maybe he does a bit and that's confusing him. "Hey, boy," I said to him, putting my hand on his head, gentle, you got to be gentle, "hey, gonna be fine."

I go to the door and knock. A little round Spanish woman answers.

I say I need to speak to Mr. Scott.

She looks worried. But then her eyes slide past me and she sees the golden dog in the house lights. She sputters out something in Spanish and makes the sign of the cross over herself and then she slams the door shut. I hear her running back inside the house along the tiled hallway. I stand there wondering if maybe I should beat it. Then the door opens again and now there is a tall, well-built guy, thirty-five or so. *He* looks instantly right past me. He's still looking past, in a scary, blank kind of way, when I say, "Mr. Scott?" At which he goes red under his tan and glares at *me*.

"That isn't my name."

"Not Scott?" I ask, thinking maybe the feller in town gave me the wrong directions.

But this man says, "My name's McCall. *Scott*, for the sake of—Scott is the name of that—the *dog*."

I laugh, seeing the dumb but quite logical mistake I made. "But he's your dog," I try then. "I found him out on Route—"

"I don't care where in the *hell* you found him," the man says, cracking his sentences out at me like rounds from a gun. "Get him offa this property. Take him *outta* here. Do you get me? Yeah? Fucking get lost. *Both* of you."

"But why? What—"

And then there is this girl, running out toward the door. She's about seventeen, young and sweet, slim, with a pale white skin despite the desert, and long, dark, curling hair and great big dark eyes—and the thing that comes to me is, crazily, how like the eyes of the dog hers are—huge, dark, *sad*.

"Rosalie," cracks out the man, "leave this to me."

"But Dad—is it—*oh*," she sighs, stalling just behind him. And the big black eyes are on the pickup, on the dog, and her eyes are raining as it never would rain out here, but for human tears. "Dad," she weeps. "Oh Dad, make it go."

"You heard her," he snarls. He puts his arm around her and she buries her face in his shirt. "S'okay, honey. *Go on*," he adds to me. "Take that—*thing*—and beat it back to hell." And then a change comes over his face. He says, "No, wait there."

Turning he bellows behind him, something in Spanish. It sounds like something about paper, or a letter; my Spanish ain't that good. But the round woman suddenly comes rushing back and in her hands is a folder and she pushes it at him and he shoves it against my chest, so I kind of grab it, not meaning to. The next second the door is slammed again and through it he yells at me, "Read that, you idiot. Don't come back or I'll see you in the jail. You hear me?"

"Sure," I say softly to the door.

Crickets, which have been quiet as stones, start their singing again as I head back to the pickup. The dog is lying in back, his head turned away from the house.

I need a damn beer.

We went to a diner, and like before, the dog sat quiet outside in the pickup. When I was done, I brought him out some of the steak in a napkin, and poured him more water. He ate and drank like a machine, like a robot that somehow still needs food. Then he lay back down. He put his long golden head on his long gold paws and closed his sad, dark eyes. I drove someplace just off the road and parked.

And then I opened the folder.

I don't like reading. It never holds me, not now. Though when I was younger, with Della, I'd read whole books.

In the folder were these two things: a cell phone, a model like the kids want to have, takes pictures and plays music, that kind of thing; and some sheets of paper. They were printed off a computer.

I sat and stared at the paper. And then put it down, because the words wouldn't stick together. Then I tried the phone. But something had gone wacky with it; it'd only make a kind of buzz, and then show me just these two pictures. One was out front of the low white house with the palms. Nothing in this picture but the dog. The golden dog. He was sitting on the dry front lawn, slim and shining, and his tongue lolled out, and his eyes all big and bright . . . and happy. It was the same dog, with different happy eyes. And then the second picture would snap on. This one was taken at the back of the house, right by the sky-blue bowl of pool. The dog wasn't in this picture. Only . . .

Only the moment I saw it first, this second shot, I looked and looked at it. And after I did that maybe seven, eight, nine times, I turned off the phone and picked up the papers again. And read them.

I don't know how to properly start this. So I'll simply begin. I'll be totally honest. Or there's no point.

I remembered everything when I woke. But somehow I wasn't fazed. It didn't really affect me. Which is mad, but that's the only way I can put it. Or the only way I can, here. There isn't much time now. I know that. Or much space, come to that. This was all the paper I could find, to print this out.

Please try to believe what I say.

Basically, yesterday—and all the days, weeks, the entire three-and-a-half years before—I was a dog. I forget the name of the breed. Funny I don't recollect, when I seem to remember so much else. And to know. I can read and write for example—self-evidently. I can use a computer, just like, if I wanted, I could make a sandwich, and eat it, without a single eyebrow being raised. I mean, how is that possible? And I can talk. From the moment I opened my eyes this morning, when I stretched and stood up, stood up that is the way a young man would do, and not as a dog, from then I knew all these things, had all these human skills. I don't know why.

But then, I don't either know why I turned from being a dog into being a man. Just knew I had done. Also, I knew how to operate the human body I was in, just as if I'd done it for seventeen years. I knew and recalled how it had been when I was the dog—only, weirdly, at once removed. The dog, to me, had become, instantaneously with the transformation, he. Not I.

I can confirm, I don't think or feel or react like a dog, now. My emotions are a man's. A young man's. How can this be? I've no notion.

It's the same with the other strangeness. Like this truly peculiar fact—I seem to remember having read certain books—say Ray Bradbury's *Fahrenheit 451*, or listened to pieces of music: Rachmaninov's 2nd Piano Concerto, Panic! At the Disco's song "I Write Sins Not Tragedies."

How is that? Did the dog get read to? Get music played him? Come to that, did he watch them use the computer? I don't know.

How can I? Every minute of this day I've moved farther and farther from being the dog. Though I still know the people I'd known as the dog. Oh yes. But he wasn't me. I'm not him.

So I guess I'm just going to have to leave that as it stands. I can't add anything to it. I don't have the answer. Or no answer that is sane. As I don't have—never did, never will—any choice.

Mornings, Concha gets up at about five AM. She is the Mc-Calls' maid-of-all-work. Thing is, she undoes the kitchen door that opens on the backyard, which lets out the dog. That morning (today), Concha came down and undid the door. At that point the dog, if still asleep, generally sprang up and bounded out, racing up and down the lawn, sniffing and rolling, staring in the pool, gazing up at birds, or any neighborhood cats. Today, though, the dog didn't wake straight off. He lay there sleeping, it seemed, just twitching a bit, perhaps. She saw nothing to concern her in this, put on the coffee and set out the ironing.

Concha always irons in the mornings, before any of the family drift down around seven. This is because she often irons the clean clothes of her three sons, along with the family stuff. One of these sons is eighteen. Lucky for me.

I came to when she'd gone off to the bathroom, which regularly happens after her first mug of coffee. (How do I know? Because the dog had seen it day after day for almost two years.) And that is when I *woke*. When I woke as *me*, how I am now. The clock on the wall showed 5:30 AM. And the morning light showed me myself, young, male, human, and naked, lying out from the dog basket on the tiled floor.

I didn't have a second's disorientating doubt. I got myself to my (man's) feet. I grabbed a pair of jeans, underpants, a white shirt, and—*nearly* like the dog I'd been—rushed out into the yard. There was a cluster of palm trees. In there I dressed myself. (How did I know? *Instinct?*) And here is the other weird thing. Before I woke, just as I became human, I'd had access to some kind of—*psychic?*—bathroom. I'd done all I'd needed to, and was now showered clean, had used some okay deodorant, washed my hair. I'd brushed my teeth. The taste of mint mouthwash wasn't alien at all.

Concha came back soon after. I'd been given just enough

time. She called for me (the dog-me). "Scott! *Iprisa*, Scott!"
But he didn't, *I* didn't, always come when called. Depended
how interesting the morning backyard was that day. She'd
gotten upset though when she couldn't figure where the
extra clothes had gone to. Then I heard her tell herself, in
Spanish, which I partly understood, as the dog probably
learned to, that she was *idiota* for leaving them behind yesterday, when she'd visited her sons.

I'd gone wandering by then. I'd gotten over the low wall. I
investigated adjacent spaces, paths, walls, the road. A mail-
man passed me and waved. I waved back. I was just somebody's teenage son he must have met before, clean, good
haircut (it is, I've seen it) dressed casual the way kids dress
from well-off homes; a friendly, well-raised boy.

I don't know what I might have done. Or I guess I do
know. I just had a walk and rambled back. Like a dog does, if
he likes the house where he belongs. And this time the sun
was an inch or so higher. I could smell cooked eggs and ba-
gels. And the . . . I could hear her voice. I knew it. *He* did.

Rosalie.

"Dad? Wonder where Scott is—"

I stayed by the palms. I never felt that before. The way a
human heart can seem to stop, but it never has. And then it
beats like a drum.

When finally she came out to look for me (for the dog) she
had on her bathing suit. She had a day at home, no school,
and Dad had already taken off for town. I'd heard the car.

Her suit was pool-blue. She doesn't tan, it never takes.
She has great skin. That had never mattered. Now it did.
Everything about her. She was lovely.

She glanced around and called out "Scott?" a couple

times. Then she shrugged. She dived into the pool. Cleaved the sapphire surface with hardly a ripple. Her wet hair spread rich black. When she came out, she *shook* herself. Waterdrops scattered like pearls from some necklace I must once have seen. Did she learn to shake off water like that from *him*? The one I'd been—

That was when she saw me.

She stopped still.

I thought, she'll scream for Concha. But she didn't.

"Who are you?" she asked, dead neutral.

"Excuse me," I said, "I came in from the front, mistook the house—" They are alike here, to the human eye.

She didn't look scared. Her eyes had opened wide as wide was all, but no fear in them.

I said, "We moved in around a week ago—that new place up the side track." The dog had a memory of that from previous wanderings.

She nodded. She said, "So who are you looking for? I know most of the people around here."

That music, the book, started swirling in my brain, it was all I could think of to coin some—really stupid—name. "Uh—Disco Bradbury," I said.

She looked blank. The intelligent response.

"No, never heard of him."

"Oh, okay. Well I guess I have it wrong. Guy from school, thought he lived here, meant to look him up—"

She said then, "What's your name?"

"Scott." I said it before I could hold it back.

And her dark eyes went even wider as she laughed. "That's the name of my *dog!*"

"Oh boy. Hmm. Should I be destroyed or pleased?"

"Pleased. He's great. Only—" she looked around now, "he's gone slightly missing . . ."

"What does he look like?" She told me. "I think I *saw* a dog like that," I said. I described it as a dog trotting along one of the paths down the block, causing no trouble.

She said he never did, but still he shouldn't be out there. But yes, it had happened before. And so I said, if she wanted I would go try to catch him. She said that it was fine and he always comes back, but maybe we could both go. She'd just go change. Or would I like a cup of coffee first, Concha had just made a fresh pot. She laughed again, pretty, and like the way I hadn't been able to not answer. "*Scott*," she couldn't seem not to say, "You're just his color scheme, you know. Your tan and your hair. You have *great* hair." Then she blushed. It was beautiful.

Would you believe, Concha liked me too. I think so. But I had to make up a whole history of really terrific if slightly forgetful parents to satisfy her. I longed for the old novels I'd somehow read, where you could be a man at fifteen, or younger, and no one expected you to still be attached to a family, collar and leash, for your own protection and happiness.

The dog had loved Rosalie. And she'd loved—*loved*—him. Inside one quarter hour I knew that I, whoever, whatever I was, loved Rosalie too. It doesn't rattle me to say it, even now, with the sun only about an hour off rising for another morning. I loved, I *love* her. The way only one human can love another. I want to know her. Get to know her really slowly, gently, intensely. I want time—a year, two years. Moment by moment, day by day. Until that perfect season, some unearthly hour—and then. Oh, yes. Time. I want time. Wanted.

She took a picture of me on her phone, in the backyard. I didn't realize she did this until she'd done it. "Is that okay?" she asked me. She blushed again. She showed me the photo and I looked at it with some interest. Could I be objective? Who knows? I was tall, fit and athletic-looking for seventeen, and very tanned, like she said, and my hair was thick and shiny and the exact color of the dog's coat. And my eyes were dark, like hers.

We went looking for the dog. It was getting hot, but what did we care? We went by the parched lawns and under the palms and through a plaza with some stores. Lots of people. Plenty of them she seemed to know, and she introduced me sometimes, the new guy just moved in. We asked if anyone had seen the dog. Nobody had. (Some surprise, of course they hadn't, had they? The dog was standing in front of them. Only he wasn't.)

Finally, we bought some Cokes—or she did, no coins in my pockets. We stood in the shade under a palm, and her eyes went wet. "He's never been gone so long."

I took her hand. She let me. "Listen," I said, "I know he's okay."

"How do you *know*?"

"He is. I just do. Rosalie, he's fine. I wouldn't say that if I didn't—sorry, I can't explain."

"You can see things, feel things other people can't? Sort of psychic?" she asked, hopefully.

"If you like."

She smiled. She trusted me. Her hand in mine. We didn't let go until some more of the neighborhood came walking by.

I wish I could have stopped time. Just stood forever holding her hand. For the very first time I wondered maybe if this is why I'd—*he*—had changed. Like—what's that story—the guy who's a frog, but when the princess kisses him he becomes a man.

That was only this afternoon. Less than fifteen hours ago.

We went back to the house and ate a sandwich. Rosalie thought she should call someone about the dog. Concha said "Wait 'til Mr. McCall comes back." That would be around evening time.

So she and I sat on the back porch. You know, she didn't really get that uptight about the dog. As if in some way she *knew* what really happened. We talked. She told me a lot about herself, things obviously the dog hadn't understood. About her mother, some minor actress, who'd taken herself off to L.A. about three years before and now only sent them postcards. I didn't hear it all. I just wanted to listen to her voice. I think we slept? Or only I did. Suddenly, there were blue shadows hanging veils along the yard fence. I could hear crickets practicing, then a sprinkler coming on someplace. And a car.

"There's Dad," she said.

I ought to leave now. But I didn't. I said, "Will he mind me being here?"

She said no. And I thought, even if he does, I'm already part of the family. I was very sure, confident. Yet as I waited, standing by then, the shadows were knotting themselves like vines around the wall and trees. Then I knew it—at about 5:15 AM that same moment when, today, I'd switched from dog to man, tomorrow, that would be the moment *I switched back*. I turned to frozen stone. I don't know why it came to me right then. Or why, if I could realize at all, I hadn't gotten wise to it before. It was—the *light*, the *change* of the light. I started to shake. I wanted to take to my heels. Run away fast as I could. From the house, from her, from every other thing. From *tomorrow*. I was *me* now. *Me*. I couldn't go *back*.

That was when he came out on the porch, Mr. McCall, with his daughter, the girl I loved.

"So," he said, glaring at me, his shades pushed up on his head and his eyes squinting against the sidelong sun. "*So*. Who the hell are you?"

"Dad! He's called Scott." Rosalie said, soft and anxious behind him. I couldn't form words. My brain was ringing. Was I going to *bark* at him? He'd liked me as a dog. The only other male thing, maybe, he *would* like, after his wife took off.

"Yeah, I know he *said* his name is 'Scott.' I have that correctly, do I, boy?"

"Yes, sir," I cautiously managed.

"And that's the dog's name, right? Perhaps you think that's funny, huh?"

"No, sir. It just happens I have the same name as your dog."

"Okay, feller. Where did you hide the dog?"

That threw me, even in the state I was. I think my mouth fell open. "*What?*"

"You heard me. You've hung around, seen the dog, gotten the name, taken him off. So what—you're holding my dog to ransom, right?"

"Dad—Scott lives just up—"

"No, he fucking doesn't. That place is still empty. So what's his game? The hell with this, I'm calling the cops."

At which point he felt after his cell phone, found he'd left it in the car or the house, and went a worse red before stalking back inside.

Rosalie came at me like a soft beating storm.

"I'm *sorry*, Scott—oh, he's been like this since Mom—

look, you'd better go—I'll talk to him. He's not *really* like this—but go—just go." She was holding onto me, even as she pushed me around the side of the house and out along the path to the front gate. "Look, come back around 11— can you? He has to go to sleep early; he has an early start tomorrow. When that happens he takes a pill at night. Come back at 11? Oh, Scott—maybe—please run!"

I must have said yes. She let go of me. I turned and belted up the avenue, under all the palms in their knots of dying dark blue and dark yellow light. About half a mile on I slowed, and saw I'd taken the exact right direction if I really had been living in that vacant property up the side track. And something in all of that made me double over wheezing with laughter. There was an open space there, and some other type of trees than a palm, with thick leaves. When I stopped laughing I leaned on one of them and cried. Young men cry, men cry. Dogs cry, only you don't see it. They cry inside.

I printed this out as I wrote it, and there's hardly any paper left. I better be quick. No paper, no time. The sky out the window has that hollow look comes on before first light.

I met her at the front gate where there was a handy palm to hide me. But the lamps were off in the house and in most places around. Oh, Rosalie. The starlight was sharp as steel and you beautiful in it. I can say that now. I couldn't say it to you then.

You—she—told me Dad didn't call the cops. He'd had a malt whisky and calmed down, and said maybe he shouldn't jump to conclusions. And yes, the house up the hill *might* have a new family in, now he recalled. Which was something I knew too, by then, having sat quite close to that house until the TV in their front room showed me it was 10:30, and I walked back down to Rosalie.

But after she told me all this, apologizing, so soft and kind to me, I had to go ruin it all. Again, no choice.

"Rosalie, I'm sorry. I didn't lie about the dog—I never took him—but I did lie about *me*." Her wide, night-dark eyes. I said, "Look, I can't go into it now—but, put it this way, I lost my home in a real strange way—no, just listen, Rosalie, please. That happened. And something—horrible—is going to happen tomorrow, too. No. You can't do a thing. *I* can't. And I can't—I don't even know how to say—but oh God, I'm scared, Rosalie, I'm so damned scared." And then she put her arms—your arms—around me and held me. I can't remember what we said.

I guess it's been said all over the earth, a billion trillion times and more, one human to another. Then we went inside, quiet and careful of her father, and Concha, passing their bedrooms like shadows. Rosalie's room was at the back and there was one lamp turned way down. You trusted me fully and you could. You—*knew*—I wouldn't harm you, not in any way. I'd have given my life for you. And somehow you saw that. We didn't have the love we'd had when I was him. But now—the love two people can have, sometimes. If only for twenty-four hours. That kind of a love doesn't always have to be tried and proven. We didn't even kiss. Just held each other a while, like outside.

In the end—it was just on midnight—she lay down on the bed. She was too worn out. But I went to her computer, like she told me I could. I said, didn't I, I'd try and explain it all, clear and easy, so you'd understand. But that's been so hard, Rosalie, because *I* don't understand. That's why I couldn't say it face to face. All I know is—around 5:15 tomorrow, I'll change again. I'll go back. I'll be your golden dog. No choice, no chance. I should run—before you see it *happen*. I don't know what you'll do, how it'll affect you.

You'll scream maybe, the world disintegrating for you. It could make you insane, break you in pieces, and your dad will say I played some trick, drugs maybe, then chickened out and returned the dog, who then will be me.

But I can't leave you. It's too late. I have to print out this final page. And I'm so tired I can barely see—except I can see you. Sleeping, silent, your lovely hair spilled on the pillow like the core of night just left behind. I want to look at you until my eyes close. Until the end.

I love you, Rosalie. I always will. I think *that* is what worked the crazy spell on me. Like in the story. Even though we never kissed. I love you, Rosalie. Good-bye.

When I finish reading those papers I sit awhile, there in the cab of the pickup.

Then I get out and go around, and he's just laying there, the dog. But his eyes are open. I say, "Scott, you wanna come in front with me? I'd like your company."

For a minute he doesn't move. Then he pulls himself up, slow, like an *old* dog does. Then he jumps out and comes around, and we both get up in the cab.

"Guess I'll sleep here tonight," I say. "Done it before. Save myself a pocketful of dollars. You okay with that? Then tomorrow we'll take those tables on to Santa Zora."

He sits, looking out at the desert, the highway and the hot stars. Then he lies along the seat. I reached out and touched him, smoothed his forehead. After awhile he shut his eyes.

"I don't know if you can understand me," I say. "Most the time I don't think anyone understands anyone else that much. But I'd like your company, if you'd care to stay. I'm just a delivery man; we'll eat regular. We can work something out, see how we go. Let's sleep now."

He did sleep, of course. An animal always can, even when they hurt real bad. It's a gift we lost, most of us, when we climbed up on our hind legs and started to think about every darn thing.

When Della left me she sat in our kitchen with me for hours and cried her heart out. Said she'd fallen for another guy, couldn't stay. I never cried until she was good and gone. That was close on five years ago. When we first met, we used to like that song. We were younger then and the song popular, though now you don't often hear it. I mean the song they played on the radio when I saw Scott by the road.

I guess he must've run away. Or they chased him away. His Rosalie hysterical and sobbing—God knows, like he said, what she'd seen happen when he altered back. And her father threatening, too shit-scared maybe even to try reading what Scott wrote on the computer. Just wiped it. Yet McCall kept the printout. Why's that? Like he had to pass it on, like it was some curse in runes. And the photographs. Scott as a young dog. Scott as a young man. They say it's around five years, don't they, an animal year to a human one. Three and a half as a dog must be seventeen for a man. Left to himself now, the dog will live a decent stretch, until he's twelve maybe, fourteen—in his 60s, 70s. But dogs can die of grief. Birds do, too. Even cats sometimes do. Even people.

He slept and I watched the stars rotating slow over the sky, like they show you in the planetarium. And the words of that song went on and on through my head. "The Dog-Catcher's Song." It was kind of like that other one, way back, "The Wichita Linesman," the guy fixing the phone lines for the county, and all he can think of is the woman he needs. And the Dog-Catcher is the same. He says, this ain't love to catch and shut them in the pound. But now she's left him, his heart's in the pound, even though he's running free. Like Scott and me. Hearts shut in the pound. No, this ain't love.

MORTAL MIX-UP

Laura Resnick

I awoke to the feel of sunlight gently kissing my face, bathing me in the warm glow of morning rays.

That was my first clue that something was wrong.

Seeking the safety of darkness, the reassuring cloak of shadow and gloom, I leapt from the bed and—

Wait a minute . . .

Bed? *Bed!*

"Where's my coffin?" I cried.

I looked around in frantic confusion. I didn't recognize anything I saw. The very place itself was completely foreign to me. I was in a room of modest proportions, with purple walls, one large window—through which sunlight *blazed*—and a few pieces of generic furniture that were mostly hidden beneath a bewildering profusion of rumpled clothes, scattered magazines, stuffed animals, jewelry, cosmetics, and personal electronic devices—a cell phone, an MP3 player, a netbook, a GPS device, and a camera.

There was a dresser, with several of its drawers open and clothes spilling out of them. Atop the dresser there were candles, several little statues, a mirror, a number of framed photographs, more jewelry, some weeds, a bowl of ashes (ashes?), a few books, and a cowbell. The large piece of furniture I was crouching behind as I hid from the terminal rays of the sun was . . . a twin bed, I realized. Moments ago, I had been asleep in it.

I was alone in a stranger's bedroom with no memory of how I had gotten here and no idea what I was doing here.

And it was *daylight*. I was trapped. Wherever I was, it was too late to return now to the safety of my lair and the comfort of my coffin. I would have to wait until nightfall to leave this unfamiliar room and make my way home.

Unless . . . unless I was a prisoner here? Wherever "here" was. Had I been abducted? Was I in danger from something besides the sunlight?

I thought back to the last thing I could remember before waking up in this messy and (frankly) rather garish bedroom. My current paramour César and I had shared a quick bite in an alley next to a club in the East Village. I had become lightheaded soon afterwards, since we'd had the misfortune to eat someone who was exceedingly drunk. This happens all too often, since the inebriated are far more likely than the sober to stumble off alone in the dark and enter the immortal embrace of a hungry stranger. However, at least someone who's pissed as a newt is unlikely to remember what happened, or even to remember meeting us; this is convenient, since it avoids the need for awkward explanations, especially if we meet again.

In any case, this woman had been *so* drunk that I didn't feel very good after feeding from her. I had decided to return to my coffin while the night was still young—and to go there *alone*, to César's flatteringly evident disappointment—to sleep it off.

Was our prey so drunk that her blood made me unable to remember what had happened thereafter?

I distinctly recalled going back to my comfortable lair in the subterranean tunnels beneath a Columbia University dormitory (warm in the winter, decently ventilated in the summer, and always plenty to eat if I don't feel like venturing far from home). Once there, I had relaxed for a while by watching my DVD of *Burlesque* (Cher, that great diva, is one of the few mortals I'd consider turning, if we ever meet); but the lightheadedness I'd felt ever since consuming that clubber turned into limb-heavy fatigue, and I soon retired to my coffin, where I sank into slumber.

Obviously, something else had happened—such as my being abducted—but it had evidently happened after I fell asleep. The question was: how could I have slept through being removed from my coffin and transported to this purple room? Indeed, how could I have slept through anyone entering my lair or opening my coffin lid? I have the keen senses of any normal vampire and would certainly have sensed such an intrusion, even in my sleep. So what on earth had happened?

I tensed as I heard a faint thud coming from somewhere else inside this building. A door closing? The sound was followed by footsteps. My abductor was approaching this room! My heart pounded as anxiety gripped me—

Wait a minute. My *heart* was pounding?

I hadn't had a heartbeat since being turned in 1927, inside the Biograph Theater in Chicago.

At the same moment that this bizarre realization paralyzed me with shock, there was a knock on the door, and then it opened. A middle-aged woman wearing a bathrobe took a couple of steps into the room, saw me, and paused in obvious surprise.

"What are you doing cowering on the floor like that?" she said with a puzzled frown.

I stared at her in mute confusion, listening to the peculiar sound of my heart beating and wondering who she was—and also how such an innocuous-looking person had infiltrated my lair, kidnapped me, and transported me to this messy prison.

"Did you have a bad dream?" she asked.

"I—I—" I couldn't think clearly enough to focus on the obvious question I should be asking: *Who are you and why have you brought me here?*

"Or are you looking for your shoes?" Her face cleared and she shook her head. "How many times do I have to tell you? *Clean your room.*"

"I beg your pardon?" I blurted.

"Well, you're up, anyhow," she said. "Do *not* get back into bed. Do *not* go back to sleep. Breakfast in twenty minutes."

I stared at her.

"Margot, do you hear me?" she prodded.

"Huh?"

"And the answer on that gold tube-top is still 'no,' so don't even *think* about coming downstairs in that thing."

"What?"

"No!" she snapped. "We are *not* going around and around about this again. Don't test me, young lady. Not unless you want me to let your father start setting the rules about this. Then you'll be wearing a nun's habit to school every day!"

She closed the door and stalked off. I continued crouching (I was *crouching*, not cowering) beside the bed, more confused than ever.

However . . . I had been mortal once, long ago, and I had been a daughter. There was, I realized, something monstrously familiar about this woman's attitude and tone. A horrible, dark suspicion was starting to fill my being.

I looked down at the hands that clutched the (utterly tasteless) bedspread that was spilling over the side of the mattress. I didn't recognize them; they were short-fingered and tan, quite unlike my long, slender, pale hands. And the nails were painted black.

I would never in a million years wear black nail polish. And as an immortal, I mean that literally.

"Oh, *no*."

As I said those words, I realized that even my voice sounded unfamiliar. It was nasal and a little high-pitched, quite unlike my own husky contralto.

I looked down at my body and saw that it was *not* mine. It was a stranger's body. Shorter than my body. It was also—I ran my hands over it, rather impressed for a moment—more buxom and curvaceous than my own slender frame.

From the corner of my eye, I glimpsed blonde hair. I pulled it away from my face and looked at it, so different from my own coal-black tresses.

"No!"

But my protest was pointless. Realistically, there was no denying that I was in a stranger's body. A *mortal's* body, I surmised, based on the way my heart continued pounding in response to my agitated emotions.

That *heart* . . . What a distracting sensation! *Ker-thud, ker-thud, ker-thud.* It was like having a three-legged rabbit running around inside my thorax. How on earth did mortals think with this giant muscle jumping away noisily in their chests? Or with this roaring of blood in their ears? It was making such a racket, I could scarcely hear my own thoughts.

My chest was by now rising and falling rapidly in agitation, and there was a repetitious gushing noise that was also distracting me. I froze when I realized what this was: breathing.

I hadn't breathed in more than eighty years. Not since drinking the immortal blood of my dark sire in Chicago and reawakening as a creature of the night by the light of the full moon.

(Those were the days. No one really turns a mortal in *style* anymore.)

I had forgotten how much energy breathing required. Now that I was doing it, I found it so demanding, it was hard to concentrate on anything else. No matter how much air I got, I still wanted more. No sooner did I expel one breath than my body—no, *this* body—craved another. And another. And another after that! If this body couldn't be sated, I thought with mounting irritation, this breathing could go on *all day*.

Then I remembered that breathing did indeed go on all day. And got particularly noisy during sex, too. (I never missed mortality after being turned.)

Thinking of sex made me think of César. He would help me.

But . . . help me with what?

All I knew right now was that I had gone to bed in my own home and body, and I seemed to have woken up in the home and body of someone else—an adolescent girl with deplorable taste, if my instincts were serving me well.

There must be some explanation for this bizarre circumstance. I had already discarded the notion that I might be having a nightmare; these repulsive physiological functions I was experiencing were too real for that to be the case. In fact . . . I realized with revulsion that I needed to find a toilet.

"Oh, hell," I muttered.

I rose from my crouched position, flinched when a ray of sunlight touched my skin and then stared in wonder and amazement when *nothing* happened. The sunlight did not harm me, let alone incinerate and destroy me.

Bizarre.

I was truly mortal now—or at least, this body certainly was. Therefore, I had to get rid of it immediately and return to my own without a moment's delay.

But first, I needed to find the damn bathroom in this place.

I exited the bedroom and roamed the hallway unrestricted, opening and closing doors until I found the tiled cubicle which I sought. I entered the room—then gasped and flinched when I saw someone else in there with me. An instant later, I realized I was not seeing someone else; I was looking at a mirror.

I hadn't seen my reflection since 1927.

And I *still* wasn't seeing my reflection. I was gazing at the reflection of the girl whom the mother had called "Margot" a few minutes ago.

She was a pretty girl, albeit in a bland, vacuous way. Her skin bore a golden tan, her eyes were blue, her teeth were white and straight, her shoulder-length hair was blonde and parted in the middle. She looked a little oily, and I realized after pondering this that she needed to be washed after I relieved her bladder.

Based on the foul taste in Margot's mouth, I ascertained that her teeth would have to be brushed, too. (Yes, it was all coming back to me now. There was no end to the long list of tedious maintenance tasks involved in maintaining a mortal body.)

Vampire hygiene needs are minimal compared to those of mortals, but César enjoys showers and shampoo for sexual purposes, so I had some familiarity with using them—though washing all that hair and that whole body (and doing so without any assistance from César) took some time. Brushing Margot's teeth was more of a challenge, since I hadn't done anything like this in many decades and had completely forgotten how. But I managed as best I could, by imitating what I had seen actors do in films. (I'm a huge movie fan. Though *vampire* films, to be candid, just make me want to chew vigorously on everyone who's involved in making them.)

As I returned to the purple bedroom, I heard the mother calling from the lower level of the house, "Margot! Breakfast!"

Margot's stomach rumbled. I realized I was famished. I wondered how much Margot's mother would object to being bitten by (from her perspective) her daughter.

"Margot!"

"Coming!" I called.

I searched the room for garments. I found what appeared to be a very large gold lamé headband. After experimenting with it, I realized that it must be the tube-top her mother had warned her not to wear. I cast it aside. I had no desire to enter into a fruitless sartorial debate while trapped in this body, so I sought clothing that I thought would conform to the mother's ideas of appropriate adolescent fashion. It wasn't easy. Based on the jumbled clothing I kept examining and discarding, Margot evidently aspired to be a streetwalker when she finished school and habitually dressed herself in eager anticipation of entering that profession.

I finally found a pair of sweatpants and a baggy shirt that completely concealed Margot's curves. Thinking these items would surely win approval from the girl's maternal parent, I donned them while responding to yet another summons from downstairs. Then I left the bedroom and descended the stairs in search of the kitchen, all the while trying to think of an argument that would convince the mother to allow me to sink Margot's teeth into one of her arteries.

I recoiled from the smell of mortal food when I entered the kitchen, then realized with consternation how inadequate Margot's senses were. I had not scented the disgusting odors of fruit salad and waffles until being *in the same room* with them. Margot's stomach rumbled, as if favorably stimulated by the stench. As one who finds carbohydrates particularly revolting, I tried not to gag at the sight of the food sitting on the plate on the kitchen table.

"Your waffles are cold," said the mother, with her back turned toward me as she occupied herself with cutting up a cantaloupe on the kitchen counter.

I remained motionless in the doorway, not sure how to proceed.

"Sit down and eat, Margot. You took *forever* in the bathroom, so you've only got about five minutes left before you have to leave." She paused in her task and turned to look at me—and froze with the knife in her hand, her expression a mixture of surprise and skepticism as she studied my clothing. "You're wearing *that* to school today?"

"Huh?" I said, staring hungrily at her carotid artery. Or, rather, at where I knew it must be; Margot's human senses were so feeble, I had to guess at its probable location, rather than seeing and sensing the warm, sensual pulse of blood flowing there.

"If this is some sort of attempt at reverse psychology," the mother said as she returned to cutting up that odorous fruit, "it won't work. If you want to be a frump, *be* a frump. It will not change my mind about that gold tube-top."

"All right," I said, not knowing what else to say.

"And another thing, young lady—ouch!"

She dropped the knife with a clatter and grabbed her wrist as she held up her hand. I saw that she had cut her finger. Blood was dribbling down the digit and toward her wrist.

Seizing the moment, I crossed the room swiftly, grabbed her hand, and stuck her bleeding finger into my mouth, sucking hard.

An instant later, I spat it out with a cry of disgust and made a face.

The mother gave me a strange look, turned on the faucet in the sink, and held her finger under the running water. I felt queasy as I watched the blood and water mix.

I blurted in appalled wonder, "That was awful."

"No argument here," she muttered. "What were you *thinking?*"

The blood was bland and unappetizing, save for a slightly chemical taste that remained in my mouth and made me feel rather nauseated. Its texture had seemed slimy rather than sensual as it touched my tongue. And the feel of the live finger twitching reflexively in my mouth had been unbelievably revolting, rather than arousing and satisfying.

Weird.

"I'm hungry," I said in response to her quizzical expression as she turned off the water and held up her bleeding finger. I discovered that I now found the sight of blood distressing and wanted to look away.

"Then sit down and eat your breakfast," she said in exasperation. "You've only got a couple of minutes left."

I glanced doubtfully at the plate on the table—and felt Margot's stomach rumble again. My mouth was suddenly wet, flooded with saliva.

I made a face and wondered how severely I would be reprimanded if I spat in this kitchen.

"Now what?"

I had a vague sense memory, from another lifetime, which suggested to me that this messy-mouth incident was a response to the smell and site of the food items on the table, and that it signaled this body's desire to consume the fruit and waffles.

But a vampire has to draw the line somewhere, and this was clearly the place. Whatever Margot's body might want, *I* found few things in this world more viscerally disgusting than refined carbohydrates. The very idea of consuming those golden waffles made me start gagging.

"Margot?" the mother said.

"I don't want breakfast," I said faintly, terrified that I was about to be subjected to yet another all-too-human experience, namely *vomiting*.

Now she looked at me with concern. She put her uninjured hand on my forehead, then on my cheek. "Your temperature feels normal. But you do look a little odd." She glanced over my outfit again. "And you obviously didn't feel up to making an effort today." After a moment, she said, "Are you sure you don't want something to eat?"

My glance fell on her other hand. When I saw the blood seeping from the cut, I gagged again as I recalled sticking that appendage into my mouth.

"If you feel this bad," she said, "I don't think you

should go to school today. I want you to go back up-stairs and lie down."

"What? No!" I wanted to escape this house and start seeking answers to my dilemma, not remain in Margot's bedroom doing nothing.

"If the very thought of eating makes you gag, you might be coming down with something, and you shouldn't be in school. Now go upstairs and lie down." When I tried to protest, she spoke in a voice I found hard to deny, "No arguments, young lady. Upstairs. Now."

I sighed in defeat, then turned and walked out of the kitchen and toward the stairs. My mood improved as I realized that this was probably a better plan, any-how. The school, rife with adolescent bodies and hor-mones, would probably overload Margot's senses to such an extent that I couldn't possibly focus on my problem (figuring out how to return to my own exis-tence); I would also be overwhelmed by the challenge of masquerading as Margot amidst her peers and in her regular lifestyle. At least in her bedroom, I'd have solitude in which to think.

"You don't need to escort me," I said when I real-ized the mother was following me up the steps. "I'm going to, er, my room."

"*I'm* going to the bathroom," she said. "I need to put a bandage on this cut."

I proceeded to the purple bedroom. She proceeded down the hallway to the bathroom. Only moments after I closed the bedroom door, I heard her shrieking at me about the mess I had made in the bathroom.

Unaccustomed as I was to human hygienic require-ments, I probably had indeed left the bathroom in disarray. I considered apologizing . . . but given the state of Margot's room, I suspected her mother was accustomed to finding the bathroom in unacceptable condition after Margot used it. So I said nothing.

I sat down on the unmade bed and considered my situation. Since I was in Margot's body and living her life in a suburban home (New Jersey? Westchester County? Long Island?), I thought the most logical prospect for what had happened to *my* body was that Margot currently inhabited it.

On that basis, confronting Margot-in-my-body was obviously the first step to take toward resolving this peculiar situation. What I should do, I decided, is call myself. I remembered seeing Margot's cell phone earlier, somewhere amidst the jumbled mess of her possessions. As I heard the mother descending the steps to return to the first floor of the house, I started searching the room for the cell. A few moments later, I heard music. A vapid pop rock song that I didn't recognize. I wondered why that music had suddenly started playing—then realized it must be Margot's ring tone. And the noise was coming from beneath the discarded gold lamé tube-top. I tossed the garment aside, seized the phone, checked the LCD panel—and recognized César's cell phone number.

I answered the call immediately. "César?"

"Yes, *chérie*." César said. "Is that you?"

"Yes! How did you get this number?" I asked. "What's going on? Where are you?"

"I'm at your place. Or, to be strictly accurate, I'm in the basement laundry room directly above your place." Cell phones didn't get a signal in my lair. "I came here shortly before dawn, hoping you were feeling better by then and would welcome a little company. Instead of you, I found someone in your coffin who looks, sounds, and smells exactly like you, but who is most certainly *not* you."

"Is her name Margot?" I asked anxiously.

"Indeed. And I would have called you sooner, but it's taken me since dawn to get her to stop shrieking, jabbering, cowering, and wailing. Whatever she was expecting when she started playing around with black magic, it evidently wasn't to wake up in a coffin underground to find a vampire trying to have sex with her. I think she's going to need a lot therapy after we get her back into her own body."

"*That's* how we wound up switching bodies?" I was aghast. "This girl was playing with black magic?"

"Yes. Though it's taken me some time to get a coherent explanation from her. Just listen to her babbling and weeping," he said with a sigh.

"I don't hear anything," I said. "Mortal senses."

"Oh, dear. Of course."

"But why *me?* I don't know this girl. I've never met her. I've never bitten her." I'd seen her face in the mirror this morning. I would recognize her if I had snacked on her.

"Apparently there's a self-proclaimed vampire living in this dormitory directly above you."

"Oh, no." One of *those.*

"She's a girl from Margot's town in New Jersey, one year older, now a student here. And for whatever reason, Margot wants her body, her boyfriend, and her life. But the body-swapping spell she cast and aimed in this general direction was—"

"Was aimed at a *real* vampire," I said in exasperation. "And so, sleeping innocently in the same area last night, and being the only real vampire there, I got the whammy."

"Precisely."

"Hell and damnation! I could just eat Margot's eyeballs for this." As soon as I said it, I felt queasy again. "César, I have got to get out of this body. You have no idea how disgusting being mortal is."

"Oh, believe me, *ma chére,* I remember. In fact, I even had acne when I was mortal. Can you *imagine?*"

"Let's not reminisce."

"Fortunately, Margot thinks we can reverse this."

"She thinks? *Thinks?* She'd *better* reverse it, or I swear I will feed her mother to you while I make her watch! I'll—"

"Calm yourself, *ma belle.* If it's any consolation, the experiences of the past few hours have terrified her so much, I think it may reduce her mortal lifespan by ten years."

"Given what her mortality is like, that really isn't much consolation," I said. "So, how does she *think* we can reverse this?"

"In her bedroom, there should be some candles, some idols, a bell, and some henbane, which looks a bit like—"

"Like a weed?" I said, moving toward the dresser, where all of these props were laid out.

"Yes! You've found it?"

"I've found *all* of it." I eyed the bowl of ashes I had noticed earlier. "She performed a ritual that involved chanting to these idols, ringing the bell, and burning the henbane? And—poof!—I woke up human."

"That's it, more or less."

"It's outrageous. She has no right to play with my existence this way."

"I think she has come to full and sober realization of that fact," César assured me. "And she has already experienced her punishment, in the form of shock and fear which will remain fresh in her mind for years to come. Thus, all that remains, my dear, is for us to enact the ritual and get you back where you belong."

Margot's heart was pounding again. God, it was annoying. With a distraction like this clouding my mind, I really hoped I would be able to competently conduct—of all the idiotic things—a black magic ritual for mutually reciprocal incorporeal translocation without winding up in the body of a poodle.

I lighted the candles, took a few breaths (how laborious—*breathing*), and said into the phone, "I'm ready. What do I do?"

"I'll put her on the phone so she can walk you through it," César said. "The next time I speak with you, I hope it will be face to face—*your* face. Good luck!"

A moment later, she said, "Hello?"

I told her I had the materials ready and asked for the first step in casting the spell.

She said, "God, your voice sounds so nasal!"

"It's *your* voice," I replied through clenched teeth. "Now how do I start the spell?"

"Your clothes are cool," she said.

Based on the evidence of her taste which I had seen today, I realized I would need to seriously rethink my look once I got back into my body.

"But, God, your skin is like *ice*," she said. "So is your boyfriend's. And it grosses me out that I wanted to bite the neck and suck the blood of the girl who was just in here doing her laundry. I mean, I know it's instinct and you can't really help it, but *still*."

"Then let's hasten your return to your own body," I said. "What do I do first?"

She walked me through a reversal-version of the black magic spell that had caused this outrage in the first place. It was fairly standard stuff, though the difficulty of breathing and chanting at the same time tripped me up, so I had to give it a few tries before I finally got it right.

After some dark whirling and flashing lights, I found myself sitting in my lovely, pale, cold, bloodthirsty body in the laundry room of the dormitory beneath which I keep my lair.

"*Ma chére?*"

I lifted my head and saw my handsome César gazing anxiously at me. "It's me," I assured him.

He made a little sound of relief and embraced me. I kissed him, enjoying the cold feel of his lips pressed against mine. From the corner of my eye, I could see and sense the pulsing jugular vein of the college student who pretended not to notice our embrace while he folded his whites.

"It's so good to be back where I belong." I said.

Holding hands, we adjourned to the forgotten underground passages in the building which I used to access my lair by day. Once safely ensconced in my coffin, we engaged in a satisfying bout of vampire sex—which, like everything else in my undead experience, is so much better than it was when I was mortal.

BAND OF BRONZE

Jean Rabe

"Thou knotty-pated execrable wretch!"

I watched Bill grab the purse snatcher by the wrist, his iron grip snapping bones and causing the thief to howl in pain and drop his foul-gotten gains.

"Thou warped elf-skinned puttock!" Bill continued, as he twisted the snatcher's limb backward and—I'm guessing accidentally—cracked the snatcher's ulna. The thief howled louder and Bill had to shout to be heard above the wail. "Thou churlish fool-born malt-worm! Thou—"

"Enough with the Elizabethan curses, Bill." I nudged his foot with mine. "He gets the message. He shouldn't've pinched the dame's pocketbook. I bet if you break his other arm, he'll never pinch anything again." Somewhat to my surprise, Bill did just that, and the snatcher mercifully collapsed into uncon-sciousness.

The throng that had gathered on this warm summer day—the young lady whose purse had just been rescued, a scattering of tourists snapping pictures, businessmen on their lunch break, a homeless gent stinking to that proverbial high-heaven, and a trio of daycare workers herding a flock of toddlers—broke into applause.

"Let's get out of here, Bill, before the cops show up."

He returned the purse with a flourish, bowing and kissing the woman's hand.

She grinned coyly.

"The robbed that smiles steals something from the thief," he said.

She cocked her head, not understanding.

"*Othello*," Bill supplied. "Act I, scene III. The robbed that—"

"C'mon, Bill, we gotta go."

Bill reluctantly followed me, as did One-from-Seven and an ugly duck. We cut down a bike trail into a more heavily wooded section thick with lofty pin oaks, where everything seemed oddly quiet. I loved this part of the park, not far from Belevedere Castle. I couldn't smell Manhattan's pollution here, too far from the cars belching exhaust, but I could detect a trace of manure, a by-product of the popular carriage rides. And when the wind shifted, like it was doing now, there were scents supplied by the hot dog carts and churro vendors, and let's not forget the hint of burning salt from the pretzel hawkers.

Bill was spouting again. Distracted, I'd missed the first bit. ". . . villains on necessity; fools by heavenly compulsion; knaves, thieves, and treachers by spherical predominance; drunkards, liars—"

"What?" I stared up into his unblinking eyes.

"From *King Lear*," he said.

"Great. Remind me never to animate you again. Ever." So maybe this year I didn't choose wisely. Maybe this year my moniker fit. This year I picked Bill—William Shakespeare. Coaxed him down from his stone pedestal southeast of Sheep's Meadow. Heard he'd been up there since 1864, and paid for by money raised from a benefit performance of his play *Julius Caesar*. He'd been sculpted by John Quincy Adams Ward. There were three other pieces by Ward in Central Park. I should've picked one of them, but I'd thought Bill was dressed interestingly enough to share my company, though a little out-of-date. Should've realized his speech would be out-of-date, too. At least he spoke some form of English.

With us was One-from-Seven. I don't know what else to call him, as he won't tell me his name . . . hasn't said a single word so far. I suppose I could call him Soldier Boy or Hey You, but I like the sound of One-from-Seven better. I plucked him out of the 107th Infantry memorial. There were seven fellows there, representing what was originally called the Seventh Regiment of New York during World War I. I'd animated the one in the center a couple of years past, and he'd told me their unit saw heavy action in France, nearly six hundred of them dying before November 1918 came to an end. The memorial was unveiled in 1927, not far from the perimeter wall of the park by Fifth Avenue and 67th. The soldier all the way on the right, One-from-Seven, carried two Mills bombs and had been supporting the wounded guy next to him. I picked One-from-Seven because I thought the bombs might come in handy later today.

Last was the duck.

I'd animated the statue of Hans Christian Anderson, the famous fairy-tale author. The duck, representing *The Ugly Duckling*, one of his most notable pieces, and thereby a part of the bronze display, was an impulse to bring to life. They were cast at the Modern Art Foundry in Queens, so you'd think Hans would have spoken English, right? No, Danish. We couldn't communicate; I couldn't get across what we all needed to accomplish this day, and so he'd wandered off, probably looking for tourists from Denmark to read to. The duck stayed with me.

Bill was babbling again.

"What? I missed that."

"I sayeth: the world is grown so bad, that wrens make prey where eagles dare not perch."

Both of my eyebrows rose.

"Act I, scene III, *Richard III*."

"Well, I guess you got the gist of it. Things are bad in the park, which is why I used my magic to give you guys flesh so you could help me clean it up." I watched a crow leap from a branch overhead and saw One-from-Seven shrink for cover. "Gangs and drugs are the worst of it, and that's usually at night. But overall, things are not nearly as bad as they used to be. I mean, a handful of years ago I would spend an entire morning catching muggers and kids toting cans of spray paint. But today . . . until that snatcher you nabbed, Bill, we've spent all our so-to-speak waking hours picking up trash in the North Meadow and the Great Hill and waving to the joggers. The park's a great place, safe, really, given the size of it and the number of people who come here every day."

"Sir Hatter—"

"And after the sun goes down, let me tell you, the scores of hookers I used to . . ." I saw the look of incredulity on his face. "Hookers . . . streetwalkers, prostitutes, hos . . . whores, you know . . ." I did a little bump and grind.

"Ah." Bill understood. "Fulsome wenches, callets."

"There were plenty of callets. I guess for the most part they're plying their trade elsewhere."

"Sir Hatter—"

"Mad, please," I said. "I'm not much for last names, Bill."

"Sir Mad—"

Another bird took flight, this a fat jay, and One-from-Seven sought cover beneath a low bald cypress branch.

"Prithee, let us endeavor to stop another micher, Sir Mad."

"Yeah, let's be about it." Bill fell in step at my shoulder, then marched One-from-Seven. The ugly duck waddled quickly to catch up.

Our meandering course took us across the Great Lawn and past the Delacorte Theater, where I directed Bill's attention to the sculpture of Romeo and Juliet, locked forever in a bronze embrace.

"It is the east," Bill said.

"And Juliet is the sun," I finished. "Act II, if memory

serves." I'd seen the play performed in the park a decade past, and sensed it played in years after that. I was connected to this park.

We hadn't traveled more than a dozen yards beyond that when Bill waylaid a pickpocket and returned the wallet to its grateful owner.

"Thou ruttish onion-eyed pigeon-egg," Bill called the thief before literally ripping his arm out of the socket. We quickly moved along before he could do something to the teen's remaining body parts.

In the shadow of the Obelisk we helped an elderly woman regain her errant Maltese. She stared wide-eyed at us, pointing at my colorful garb and then Bill's out-of-date duds, her gaze dropping to the Mills bombs in One-from-Seven's hands, her mouth subsequently opening, but fortunately nothing other than a barely audible "Thank you" coming out. It was the first time today—I didn't count the after-dawn jogger ogling us over by the Jacqueline Kennedy Onassis Reservoir—that someone thought us dressed strangely. Through the years I've learned that most people don't give me and whoever I pick as my companions a second glance. This is New York, after all.

Next we chased a pair of persistent beggars away from a priggish-looking woman feeding a gaggle of pigeons.

"Thou adulterate motley-minded scurvy knaves!" Bill shouted after the pair, nearly grabbing the slower of the two by the arm.

One-from-Seven kept his distance, his terrified gaze locked onto the pigeons cooing prettily and strutting in front of the park bench. I understood the soldier's fear of fowl, but I didn't share it. My hat is tall, the brim broad, and so when I am bronze no poop plops on my shoulders or onto the lips of my overly wide grin. Lacking a helmet, One-from-Seven does not have such protection.

Just north of The Ramble, we came across a drunk trying to make off with someone's ten-speed.

"Thou loutish dizzy-eyed haggard," Bill called him.

The drunk rocked back and forth on the balls of his feet, fingers playing with the lock he'd managed to work free from the rear tire.

"Thou unmuzzled shard-borne bear-whelp," Bill pronounced. "Thou accursed earth-vexing clotpole."

The drunk belched loudly and glared defiantly.

The duck quacked menacingly.

Bill broke both the man's arms.

I was beginning to see a pattern in how Bill dealt with ne'er-do-wells, and so I moseyed us along. It wouldn't do for us to get arrested. We could only spend twenty-four hours in skin, and we'd turn back into our bronze selves a little after midnight. Whatever would the cops do with Central Park sculptures in lock-up?

I took my troops past the Boat House, and Bill, One-from-Seven, and I stopped to pick up fast food wrappers and Styrofoam cups while the duck enjoyed itself in the lake. The sun was angling lower, and it sent motes of molten yellow dancing across the water. It looked like a pirate had cast out a sack of doubloons, all of them floating.

The park was the best part of this massive city, as far as I was concerned. A half-dozen decades past, I'd spent my twenty-four tooling around the streets of Manhattan, nothing more than a lookee-loo taking in all the noise, color, and constant rush-rush-rush of people essentially going nowhere. Through the years the city has only gotten louder. But the park . . . ah, Central Park has remained a constant. It is sweet-smelling grass and a hint of simpler things and times. It is dogs and children, picnics with strawberry wine, lovers kissing, old men playing chess, and friends sharing conversation. It is the polished, red shiny bit of skin on the Big Apple, a blessed respite from the cacophony that surrounds it. It is my home, and I have no plans to leave it ever again. So I've vowed to help keep it clean . . . at least for a twenty-four hour stretch, and hopefully my deeds will have some impact well beyond these hours.

I figure if any purse snatchers read the newspaper tomorrow or listened to the evening news they'll think twice about trying to get a five-finger discount in my park.

Yeah, my park.

Near the Conservatory Pond—where the ugly duck decided to take another dip—I took Bill and One-from-Seven to see my crib, the spot where I'm forced to spend the other three hundred and sixty-four days.

"Yon statues are so—"

"Shiny? Yeah, they are that. Me, too, when I'm hanging with them." The Alice in Wonderland statue, not far from East 74th in this part of the park, is a favorite with the children. There's Alice on a giant mushroom, fingers stretched out toward the pocket watch the White Rabbit has. The Cheshire Cat—who I animated a few years back and who disappeared on me for the rest of the day—peers over her shoulder. The dormouse and I—except for today—flank Alice. I'm sculpted with a crazed shit-eating grin splayed on my face, but never smile when I'm in skin. Gotta give the face muscles a rest. A fellow named George Delacorte Jr. had the Alice piece made in the 1959 in honor of his late wife, Margarita. The ensemble was shaped by José de Creeft, who on a blessed whim put magic in me. Old de Creeft was a wizard as well as an artist and gave me the gift to spring to life once a year, for a day at a time, and to bring four others with me. I suspect he figured I'd bring Alice—who supposedly looked like de Creeft's daughter—Cheshire, the dormouse, and Rabbit. Excepting for Cheshire those years back, I'd made my choices from elsewhere in the park.

"Why art they so—"

"They're shiny 'cause the kids can't keep their hands off 'em. Shiny from thousands of oily fingers that have polished the bronze to that patina."

"It fairly glows," Bill said. "Beautiful."

"Yeah, it is that, ain't it?"

The duck quacked.

One-from-Seven didn't say anything.

Plaques around the sculpture were filled with inscriptions from Lewis Carroll's book. Bill went from one to the next, intently reading. He scratched his head when he came to a poem chiseled in the granite circle that surrounded the work.

The bard cleared his throat and recited: "Twas brillig, and the slithy toves did gyre and gimble in the wabe."

"It's from 'Jabberwocky'," I explained, as I stooped to pick up an empty soda can.

Bill managed to break the arms of another purse snatcher before sunset. But we had more important villains to deal with.

Bill cleared his throat: "In peace nothing so becomes a man as modest stillness and humility; but when the blast of war blows in our ears, then imitate the action of the tiger; stiffen the sinews, disguise fair nature with hard favored rage—" He paused. "*The Cronicle History of Henry the Fifth.*"

"Well, let's go imitate that tiger, shall we? I promise it won't be easy." They followed me back toward the castle. "The purse snatchers, the drunk, the guys pestering the woman feeding the pigeons, that was nothing compared to what's ahead of us."

The shadows were stretching long, giving us some cover. The park and I were connected, and so I knew there were a few more cops than usual on horseback and on foot . . . probably looking for whoever was breaking arms. I didn't want them to stop us; I had plans. Part of me didn't think they were looking too hard, though; no innocent folks had been injured, after all.

"Thou has in mind?" Bill prodded as we cut down a path lined with ginkgos, English and American elms, and hornbeams.

"Remember how I said things have gotten much better here?"

He nodded, as did One-from-Seven.

The duck quacked.

"And that there were some problems with drugs and gangs . . . that would be the Crips and Bloods."

"Montagues and Capulets?"

"Uh, not exactly." The path narrowed here and the shadows swallowed us. Park lights were coming on, and their glows showed through gaps in the branches. The scents from the food vendors were all but gone, most of the carts packed up. The park stayed open to midnight, but unless there was a concert or something else going on, most of the cart owners went home after sunset. "Anyway, the whole city's been cleaning up its act, but gangs and drugs are still—"

"Vexing, Sir Mad?" He drew his lips into a thin line. "Pragging rump-fed miscreants?"

"You have a way with words, Bill." I stopped when One-from-Seven flattened himself against the trunk of a tall elm. The sky was suddenly filled with birds. When the flock passed, we resumed our course. "I can sense things in the park. Even when I'm bronze I can feel what's going on. I relish that, most of the time, 'cause mostly what I feel is an infectious joy. People tend to be happy when they're on the grass."

"But the miscreants?" Bill pressed.

"No joy from them. Greed, anger, all sorts of troubling thoughts. Hate. I can sense all those things, too. It's a real mix of emotions. A nasty head-trip."

"Is that why thou art called Mad?"

I shrugged. "Oh, there's some happiness in the . . . miscreants . . . as they like taking people's money, getting high, and their emotions spike when they've made an impressive deal, scored something, beaten a rival gang member to a bloody pulp. But it's not the same joy as the good people of the city feel and that pulses through the ground and into my sculpted feet." I paused as a sandhill crane passed by overhead and One-from-Seven cowered. "This park . . . this magnificent place . . . is the real heart of the city."

Bill put a sympathetic hand on my arm.

"And those . . . pragging rump-fed miscreants . . . are twisting it."

I knew the worst of them conducted their deals near the castle, in the shadows where the park lights didn't reach, and late in the evening when the dark hid their features and their vile transactions. Heroin and cocaine mostly, the park's heartbeat told me, and the people who traveled in this part of the park at night were looking to sell or buy.

I explained to Bill and One-from-Seven that we were aiming to stop them.

"They might have guns," I warned them, not bothering to explain that to Bill. "Semi-automatics, switchblades, you-name-it. And we're flesh right now. They can hurt us. I got cut up pretty bad when we went after a couple of them last summer." I touched the brim of my hat. "It was me and Christopher Columbus, Daniel Webster, and Duke Ellington. We came out of it all right, though. Managed to catch two dealers and chase off the third and their customers."

The wind picked up, and the trees rustled. Faintly I heard a car horn and music, some bluesy piece featuring a soprano sax. After a few moments, the music faded. We were deeper in the trees.

"At the end of this path. I can feel them. More of them than last year. Something big is going down. There's only a few of us, and—"

"We few," Bill said, as we crested the rise and the castle came into view. "We happy few, we band of bronze. From now until the end of the world, we shall be remembered. For he today that sheds his blood with me, shall be my brother; be ne'er so vile, this day shall gentle his condition. And gentlemen in New York City now abed, shall think themselves accursed they were not here, and hold their manhoods cheap whiles any speaks, that fought with us upon this midsummer's night."

There were eighteen of them . . . Crips . . . pacing, talking, waiting . . . for what? Drug dealers didn't travel in such numbers—there were three last year in this very spot. We couldn't take eighteen. Nineteen; one came around the corner, zipping up his pants. What were they waiting for?

I touched Bill's arm and whispered. "The odds. We can't do this." I gestured for us to go back the way we came. Maybe next year the numbers would be—

"We happy few."

I sucked in a breath of surprise. The words were One-from-Seven's.

"We band of bronze. For he today that sheds blood with me—" And then One-from-Seven was away, rushing toward the gang, right hand pulling back, fingers fumbling with the cork and pin of the Mills bomb. It was an early-version hand grenade, heavy, and after he lobbed it he flattened himself against the ground. I heard a whistle and sensed it hit the grass. It was so dark, I couldn't tell just where it landed.

I blinked as the ground erupted, clumps of earth and pieces of gang members showering up. The duck waddled forward, quacking in challenge. Bill charged just as One-from-Seven got to his feet and hurled his second bomb. "Get down!" he hollered.

Bill dropped in response and I skittered fast, passing by the duck. One-from-Seven found cover behind a tree. There was the whistle and the thud that I felt more than heard, shouts from the Crips, then another explosion. My face was wet. I brushed it away—blood.

"Though abominable doghearted hedge-pig!" Bill cried as he met the charge of one of the four survivors. My feet churned across the loam to close the distance just as Bill broke the arm that held a switchblade. I'd nearly reached Bill's side when he snapped the ganger's neck and dropped him. Then both of us dropped to our knees just as a semi-automatic sprayed the air where our heads had been.

One-from-Seven drove forward, knocking down the one with the gun and wrestling the weapon away. Bill and I raced toward the two remaining, who were both fumbling to pull pistols.

"Thou viperous white-livered infection!" Bill took down the closest, wrapping his arms around the ganger's waist. There was a sickening crunch as the Crip's back broke, the scream dying with him.

I was on the other, nimbly vaulting over the fallen form of one of the Crips done in by a Mills bomb. He aimed the gun at me, but it was shaking. His hand was trembling and his pock-marked face was spotted with his fellow's blood.

"Surrender," I offered.

The gun started to lower as Bill moved in.

"Thou qualling pumpion," Bill declared as his hands grabbed the ganger's head and twisted.

I'd heard enough Shakespeare plays in the park to know they were filled with bloodshed . . . *Julius Caesar*, *Hamlet*, *Romeo and Juliet*. Bill had a vicious streak that served us well tonight.

"That'll about do it," I said.

One-from-Seven proved I was wrong. Our soldier was armed, a semi-automatic in his left hand and a pistol he'd picked up off one of the other bodies in his right. He fired both in a sweeping pattern, some of the bullets biting into the ground, but others into the legs of a group of Bloods. I was right; the nineteen Crips had been waiting for something. There was going to be some sort of . . . rumble . . . was the term I'd settled on as Bill and I sought cover around the corner of the castle. I'd thought a drug deal was going down. The drug deals must be happening elsewhere; I'd concentrate on finding out just where after we cleaned up this mess.

"To be, or not to be: that is the question: whether' tis nobler in the mind to suffer the slings and arrows of outrageous fortune, or to take arms against a sea of troubles. And by opposing end them? To die—" Bill's *Hamlet* speech was cut off by a burst of automatic weapon fire; some of the approaching Bloods were returning One-from-Seven's fire. "—to sleep: perchance to dream: ay, there's the rub. For in that sleep of death what dreams may come when we have shuffled off this mortal coil."

The Bloods continued to fire, but most of them ran. One-from-Seven made quick work of the ones who tried to fight back. He'd been sculpted to represent a seasoned veteran, and so somehow he had all the skills of a New Yorker who saw action in France during World War I. The Bloods didn't stand a chance. When One-from-Seven ran out of ammunition, he rolled from one body to the next, grabbing up more guns and firing them from the cover of corpses.

I'd chosen wisely after all, this year. My band of bronze had slain the nineteen Crips, as well as eleven Bloods. Only nine Bloods lay on the field by the castle, but One-from-Seven tracked two that had fled and cut them down.

Our deeds would extend beyond this day, I was certain. There would be news coverage, and word would spread about the carnage. The gangs might stay away from my park for a long while. I know that all life is supposedly sacred, but I care not a whit about ending the life—or, rather having one of my fine fellows doing it—of some soul who threatens to sully my park.

We had just enough time to nab a dealer selling heroin before we had to resume our resting spots. We escorted the duck back first, carried him, actually. He'd been hit by a stray bullet, and he died in my hands as I laid him at the feet of Hans Christian Anderson, who had returned while we were on patrol. He looked incredulously at us and said something in Danish.

One-from-Seven was next. He dutifully climbed back up on his pedestal and arranged himself so he was again supporting his wounded comrade. He had a helmet, not a military one that fit with his fellow's but rather a motorcycle helmet that he'd picked off one of the gangers. In place of the Mills bombs he had a pistol in each hand, oddly modern. I hoped no one would notice.

"Anton," he said. "My name is Anton."

"Good night, Anton," I returned.

"When shall we three meet again—in thunder, lightning, or in rain?" Bill posed, looking up into Anton's stoic face. "When the hurlyburly's done. When the battle's lost and won."

"From *Macbeth*," Anton supplied.

"Next year," I told Anton. "I'll come get you."

I escorted Bill back to his pedestal. "Parting is such sweet sorrow," I said.

In the gleam of a park light I saw his eyes twinkle. "We are such stuff as dreams are made of," he returned as he climbed up and resumed his classic pose. "And our little life is rounded with a sleep."

"Sleep well, my friend. I will see you again on another midsummer night." I doffed my hat and bowed to him, and then I scampered back to Alice. "I am the stuff of dreams," I told her, knowing full well she couldn't hear me. I felt my limbs stiffen and grow cold. I sensed the police swarming over the battlefield around the castle. Of my own volition I displayed a wide shit-eating grin.

ZOMBIE INTERRUPTED

Tim Waggoner

Author's note: This *Nekropolis* story takes place between the novels *Dead Streets* and *Dark War.*

I made my way down a sidewalk in Ruination Row, moving with a stiff-legged gait that was only a little faster than standing still. It had been a couple weeks since my last round of preservative spells, and I was overdue for a little freshening up. One of the nice things about being a zombie is that, when your bouquet begins to ripen, people give you a wide berth, so I didn't have to worry about shoving my way through the crowd of pedestrians. The Darkfolk that had come to patronize the less-than-savory businesses in the Row stepped aside as I approached, the Bloodborn and Lykes grimacing as their heightened sense of smell picked up my scent.

"Goddamn deader," a genetically altered Lyke

growled as I approached. She looked like a cross between a leopard and an alligator, and she snarled and elbowed me hard in the side as I passed her. The blow didn't hurt—I hadn't experienced pain since the day I became a zombie—but the force of it sent me stumbling sideways into an alley. I tried to keep my balance, but even when I'm at my freshest, I'm not exactly the epitome of grace, and I stumbled and fell into a pile of trash—which wasn't difficult to do since the alley was crammed full of the stuff. Besides the usual crumpled fast-food wrappers, discarded newspapers, cardboard boxes, and empty beer bottles, there were chunks of meat, splintered lengths of bone, and various disgusting-looking pools of liquid spread about that, one way or another, had probably been inside a body at one point. The stench had to have been horrendous, but my sense of smell is as dead as the rest of me, and I was rarely as grateful for that as I was right then.

I rose to my feet with a series of stiff, jerky movements and brushed the worst of the muck off my gray suit as best I could. I contemplated going back out onto the street, tracking down the leopard-gator, and showing her just how much I appreciated her elbow to my ribs, but tempting as the thought was, I'd come to Ruination Row to do a job, and I didn't want to get distracted.

Several weeks back I'd had a run-in with an ancient Bloodborn named Orlock who, it turned out, fancied himself as a sort of Darkfolk version of Noah. He'd spent the last few centuries gathering one-of-a-kind objects, animals, and in some cases people, and adding them to his already vast collection. Orlock viewed himself as a preservationist working to protect the Darkfolk's culture and history. I viewed him as a senile old vampire with more than a few screws loose, and I was determined to free those beings he'd imprisoned in his collection. Orlock was too powerful to take on directly, so I made a deal with him: I'd retrieve artifacts that he wished to add to his collection, and he'd pay me by releasing some of the people he'd captured. The number of people he'd let go each time depended on the rarity of the object I brought him, and I often had to haggle with him over my "fee." Of course, I reserved the right to pick and choose which jobs I'd take. I wouldn't acquire an object for Orlock just because he coveted it. But more often than not, the artifact he desired was insanely dangerous and in the possession of some less-than-upstanding citizen who intended to use the device to commit appalling acts of mayhem.

Case in point: the Argentum Perditor.

Silver is a controlled substance in Nekropolis. It's highly poisonous to any number of Darkfolk, but especially to Bloodborn and Lykes, and the only ones who can use it legally are those Arcane who need the metal as a spell component. But you can buy anything on the streets of Nekropolis that your black little heart desires—if you have the darkgems to pay for it, of course. There are any number of silver suppliers in the city, but the most well-known is a man who calls himself the Silversmith. His true identity is a carefully guarded secret, and he only deals through intermediaries. Not even Orlock knew who he really was. But the ancient vampire knew one thing: the Silversmith was in possession of the Argentum Perditor, a mystic weapon that was like King Midas' touch, turning its targets into solid silver. And Orlock wanted it—bad.

As far as I was concerned, Nekropolis would be better off if a weapon that powerful was locked away in Orlock's collection, and I'd spent the last few hours making inquiries around Ruination Row to see if I could get a line on how to contact the Silversmith. I wasn't sure how I was going to get the Argentum Perditor away from him once I found him, but I figured I'd worry about that later. Improvisation has always been one of my strong suits.

So as much as I wanted to go after Leopard-Gator and put a few dents in her scaly hide, I was going to have to let her insult pass. Not only am I the city's only intelligent, self-willed zombie, I'm also its only private investigator—and once I accept a job, I keep at it until it's done.

I started toward the mouth of the alley when I heard a loud buzzing behind me. I still have emotions, but I don't feel the physical effect of them, so I didn't experience a sick surge of adrenaline upon hearing the sound, even though I was pretty sure what it was causing it and the thought terrified me. I turned to see a cloud of small creatures the size of gnats rising from the trash, and I realized I'd must have disturbed them when I'd landed in their midst. The mass of creatures was so thick it looked like black smoke, and my worst fear was confirmed: I was facing a carrion cloud. The cloud was the larval form of carrion imps, nasty little creatures that scour the alleys of Nekropolis on a never-ending quest for dead flesh to devour. The imps perform a useful function, I suppose, but considering that I *am* dead flesh, you can see why I prefer to avoid them whenever possible.

But as bad as carrion imps are, their larval form is far worse. Carrion clouds are absolutely ravenous and they move fast as lightning when they sense a food source is near. Once they begin to feed, they can strip away every bit of meat from the bone within seconds. Even if I was at my freshest, I wouldn't have been able to outrun the cloud, and given my current condition, I knew I wouldn't be able to take more than a single step toward the street before the larvae were on me. There was only one thing I could do, and without pausing to consider the ramifications of my actions, I reached into my pants pocket and gripped an ancient copper coin, its features worn smooth by the long passage of time. I willed the coin's magic to activate and closed my eyes as the buzzing swarm of larvae rushed forward to engulf me.

A jolt of what felt like electricity surged through my body's dead nervous system, startling me. Normally all I can feel is pressure, as when someone or something is pushing against my body, but this level of sensation was so intense that it momentarily stunned me. I collapsed to my hands and knees, the carrion cloud still swarming around me, and as the electric sensation gave way to a gentle tingling all across my body, I wondered if what I was experiencing was the feeling of being eaten alive by thousands of ravenous insects. But then the buzzing sound grew fainter, and I risked opening my eyes.

The carrion cloud had moved away and was slowly heading deeper into the alley. I stared at it for several moments because something seemed strange about the cloud, about the whole alley, really. Everything appeared sharper, colors richer, lines more distinct. It was like I'd been viewing the alley through a hazy sheen that had been lifted, and now I could see it clearly.

As a zombie I don't need to breathe unless I want to speak, but right then I inhaled through my nostrils, and instantly regretted it as stench so thick you could take a bite out of it burned my nasal passages like acid. I was wracked by a sudden coughing fit so violent that I ended up retching, and if there'd been anything in my stomach to bring up, I'd have spilled it onto the alley floor and added to the noxious muck coating the ground.

After a few moments, my coughing fit subsided, and I rose to my feet. My body moved with unaccustomed ease, and I felt so unbalanced that I nearly fell. I reached out to place a hand against the wall to steady myself, and I gasped as my flesh came in contact with brick. It felt cold and rough and solid, and the sensation was so intense that for a several seconds all I could do was gently rub my fingers against the brick and marvel at how it felt. It was then that I knew for sure that the coin's magic had done its job. I was alive again.

Magic isn't uncommon by any means in Nekropolis, but magic *this* powerful was rare indeed. The coin had once belonged to Charon, the ferryman who carried spirits to the afterlife in Greek mythology. It had been given to me by Lord Edrigu, master of the dead, as a reward for a service I'd performed for him. The coin could restore the dead to life for a period of twenty-four hours, but it was a one-time offer. Once the coin's magic was spent, the holder could never be granted life again, not from *any* source. So I was human again, and the clock was ticking.

Keeping one hand on the wall to maintain my balance, and trying to breathe shallowly so the stench of the alley wouldn't induce another round of coughing, I reached into my jacket pocket and removed my hand vox and dialed Devona. Like a lot of homegrown machines in Nekropolis, voxes are flesh-tech, devices fashioned from organic material, and now that the nerves in my hands functioned normally, I was repelled by the warm, soft feel of the vox. I could feel it throbbing gently, as if blood circulated through it, and I felt an impulse to drop the damned thing. But I held onto it and waited for Devona to pick up. But she didn't. Instead, I got her voicemail.

"This is Devona Kanti, owner and proprietor of the Midnight Watch. I'm sorry to miss your call. Please leave your number, and I'll call you back as soon as I'm able."

Once the vox's tiny mouth was finished recreating the sound of Devona's voice, it said, "Beep!" The vox's mouth exhaled gently as it spoke, and the feeling of its warm breath on my ear made me shudder.

"It's me. I had to use Charon's Coin. I'll explain later, but I'm human now, and I'm on my way home."

I disconnected and tucked the vox back into my suit jacket, glad to be rid of the thing. Devona was my partner, both personally and professionally. Normally she'd have come with me to Ruination Row to help search for the Silversmith, but she was a security expert, specializing in both the mundane and mystical aspects of the craft, and today she was helping to overhaul the wardspells for Diamonds are a Ghoul's Best Friend, one of the largest jewelers in the city. It was a huge account, and landing it had been quite a coup for her business. She was determined to do an excellent job for her new client, and I knew from experience that, like me, once she got her teeth into a job, she didn't let go until it was finished. So it was no surprise that she hadn't picked up when I called. She'd no doubt set her vox to silent mode, but she'd get my message eventually. And once she did, I knew she'd be thrilled.

Devona and I had been together for a while now, and she longed to start a family. But as a zombie, I'm not exactly fully functional in certain key anatomical areas, if you know what I mean. Hard to father a child when there's no lead in your undead pencil. Another problem is that Devona is half vampire, half human. Normally her kind is sterile, like mules back on Earth. But with twenty-four hours of human life granted to me—along with the aid of a fertility charm created by Papa Chatha, the houngan who provided my preservative spells—we had a chance to conceive a child. But though I'd had Charon's Coin in my possession for a while now, I'd been hesitant to use it, and I'd only done so now in order to avoid becoming a meal for several thousand hungry imp larvae. So even though I'd just called Devona and told her I was headed home, I had mixed feelings about it.

It wasn't that I didn't want to have children. I just wasn't sure that Nekropolis was the best environment to raise them in. Four hundred years ago, Earth's Darkfolk—vampires, shapeshifters, magic-users, demons, and the like—had decided they'd had enough of humanity and emigrated to another dimension where they built a vast city called Nekropolis. Here they could live openly, without the need to remain concealed from the humans who were increasingly outnumbering them. But as you might imagine for a city filled with monsters, Nekropolis can be an extremely dangerous place, and the idea of bringing innocent new life into this world made me uncomfortable, to say the least.

Devona and I weren't even sure *what* our child might be. She was half human, and I'd be all human when we conceived our baby. As best as Papa Chatha could figure, that meant there was an excellent chance our child would be completely human, or close enough to it. Some humans did live in Nekropolis. The Darkfolk maintained magical passageways that led back to Earth, mostly so they could continue to import goods and services, and a number of humans found their way here every year. That was how I'd originally come to the city, chasing a warlock who'd committed a series a murders in my hometown of Cleveland.

According to the laws of the Darkfolk, it's forbidden to prey upon humans, but so many of the Darkfolk are predators by nature, and they consider that law more of a guideline than a firm rule. Add to this the fact that Darkfolk outnumber humans by at least ten to one, and the reality is that humans, for all intents and purposes, live as second-class citizens in Nekropolis.

Zombies, intelligent or not, are considered to be the lowest form of life in the supernatural food chain, and I knew firsthand how the Darkfolk treated those they viewed as lesser beings. Given all this, I wasn't sure bringing a child—and a potentially *human* child at that—into this world was the most responsible thing to do. So I'd been conflicted about using the coin. But now circumstance had forced my hand, and I was human again, but only for a single day. I didn't have any more time to wonder if having a child was a good idea. If we were going to try to get pregnant, we had to get started as soon as possible. I didn't want to disappoint Devona, and besides, even with the fertility charm, Papa Chatha had warned us there was no guarantee we'd conceive. So maybe my worries would turn out to be for nothing in the end. But either way, I decided I needed to get home to my love.

That settled, I stepped back out onto the street.

The Sprawl is the most urban of Nekropolis' five Dominions. Even at its best, it normally looks like something out of a Hieronymus Bosch fever dream, but Ruination Row is in a nightmarish class by itself. The streets look like they're made from the craggy gray hide of some rhinoceros-like creature, and the distorted buildings look like they're constructed from a bizarre mix of insect chitin, bleached bone, and pulsating discolored organs. The traffic roars by at lethal speeds, the vehicles ranging from mundane cars imported from Earth to more outré machines like meatrunners, carapacers, and ectoplasmonics. The sidewalk was crowded with pedestrians, most of them Darkfolk, in search of the foul, debased pleasures that can only found in Ruination Row.

I'd originally come to Nekropolis as a living man, but I'd only been in the city a few days before I'd died and been resurrected as a zombie. That was several

years ago, and in that time I'd forgotten how overwhelming the city can be on a sensory level. Standing
there, my newly restored living senses were inundated
with an ocean of sensation—sights, smells, and
sounds—and the sheer amount of data was too much
for me to process. All I could do was stand in the middle of the sidewalk, frozen in place, eyes wide, mouth
hanging open. I don't know, but I wouldn't be surprised if I drooled a little. I swayed, dizzy, gray nib-
bling at the edges of my vision, my mind threatening
to shut down to protect itself from the overwhelming
sensory onslaught. I fought to hold onto consciousness. Passing out on the streets of Nekropolis is not an
effective long-term survival strategy.

A tall thin being—I couldn't tell if it was male or
female—wrapped from head to toe in strips of moldy
gray cloth came toward me. Perched on his or her
shoulders was a large bird with multicolored plumage
and a wickedly hooked beak. The mummy paid no attention to me as it walked past, but the pharaoh's eagle
riding on its shoulders glared at me with disconcert-
ingly intelligent eyes, let out an annoyed squawk, and
snapped at me. That hooked beak came within an inch
of slicing into the flesh of my cheek, but the eagle
missed. The bird glared at me one last time, but it
didn't leave its perch to attack, and eventually it turned
around to face forward again as its owner continued
walking down the street.

The eagle's near miss shocked me back to full awareness. As a zombie, I don't have to worry about getting
hurt. Minor cuts and bruises mean nothing to me, and
broken bones are merely annoyances to be tended to

later. Even losing a limb or two, or being decapitated, isn't a major concern. All I need to do is gather up my pieces and pay Papa Chatha a visit. He always sews me back together.

But I was alive again, and that meant not only could I be hurt, I could be killed. And though I wasn't 100 percent certain how the magic of Charon's Coin worked, I had to assume that if I died during the next twenty-four hours, I'd stay dead. This meant I needed to do something I hadn't done in years: be careful. If I got cut, I'd bleed. And if a pissed-off monster tore my arm out of its socket, it would be more than an inconvenience. It would likely be the end of me. So the best thing I could do was head home, keep my mouth shut, and avoid making eye contact with anyone along the way.

I put my hands in my pants pockets, lowered my gaze to the sidewalk, and started heading east, in the direction of the apartment I shared with Devona, but I only got a few yards before someone walked up to me and said, "Matthew Richter?"

The voice was a smooth, warm baritone, and I felt a strange pull when I heard it. Even though I wanted to ignore whoever it was and keep going, I stopped and raised my head to look the man in the eye.

He was a demon. His kind can vary widely in physical appearance and ability, but they all have several things in common. Their eyes contain multicolored flecks which rotate slowly around the pupils. All Demonkin, regardless of type, have those flecks, and they remain no matter what form a demon assumes. Another aspect they share is the almost hypnotic quality of their voices. As a zombie, demon voices have no effect on me, but as a human, I felt the power in this one's words. It was like I was compelled to listen to him, whether I wanted to or not. Demon voices can be resisted, but it takes effort, and I'd been out of practice for the last few years.

This demon was humanoid for the most part, bald, with dusky red skin, pointed ears, serpent scales beneath his eyes, a thick black soul patch on his chin, and slightly pointed teeth that were so white they almost gleamed. Despite all this, he was handsome enough, though he probably didn't get too many gigs as a male model. He wore a black turtleneck, black slacks, black shoes, and—naturally enough—black socks. Normally, I would have made a smart-ass remark about his lack of sartorial imagination. I mean, wearing black in a city full of monsters where the sun never shines? How much more clichéd can you possibly get? But I was still struggling to adjust to my newly restored senses. Everything was too bright, too loud, too *much*, and I felt almost as if I was drunk. I felt sick, too. My throat was dry and sore, there was an uncomfortable gnawing sensation in the pit of my stomach, and I kept hearing a strange thrumming in my ears. After a moment, I realized that I was thirsty and hungry, and the thrumming I heard was nothing more than the beating of my now living heart.

The demon spoke again, and this time he sounded annoyed. "Mr. Richter?"

I did my best to ignore the powerful sensations I was experiencing. "That's me," I said. My voice sounded strange. The tone lighter, the words more clearly enunciated.

The demon smiled, displaying his sharp white teeth. "I hear you've been looking for me."

I was having trouble concentrating, and at first the demon's words didn't sink in. But then it hit me.

"You're the Silversmith."

"My real name is Gilmore, and as long as we're in public, I'd prefer you use it. And before you get any ideas . . ." He reached into his pocket and pulled out a silver metal rod about six inches in length. On the end of it was a clawed hand, and Gilmore raised the rod and pointed the claw at me. "It might not look like much, but believe me when I say it packs a hell of a wallop."

It might've looked like nothing more than a back-scratcher, but I had no doubt that the weapon Gilmore wielded was the Argentum Perditor. But I pretended not to recognize it. I'd made no mention that I was searching for the artifact during my inquiries around Ruination Row, so Gilmore had no reason to think I knew what his little toy could do. And I'd learned long ago that the more cards you keep concealed from an opponent, the better.

But I wasn't in the mood to get into a pissing contest with a demon right then. As the saying goes, at that moment I had bigger and more important fish to fry.

"I *was* looking for you, it's true. But something's come up, and I'm needed elsewhere. Tell you what, why don't you give me your card and maybe we can do business later?"

He arced one of his thick black eyebrows. "I suppose next you'll say, 'Have your people call my people and we'll do lunch?' I'm not an easy man to find, Mr. Richter, and once found, I'm ever harder to dismiss. So . . ." His lips drew away from his mouth in a predatory smile. "Why don't you tell me what you want with me?"

What I most wanted was for him to get the hell out of my way so I could continue heading home. Instead, I said, "I use a lot of specialized equipment in my job. Holy water, silver bullets . . . I'm always on the lookout for new suppliers. Word on the street is that you're the go-to guy when it comes to silver, so I figured it was time I made your acquaintance."

I carry a 9mm pistol in a shoulder holster, and my bullets are coated with silver, dipped in a mixture of holy water and garlic juice, and both blessed and cursed by powerful magic-users. You never know who or what is going to try and kill you in Nekropolis, so it pays to be prepared.

At that moment, I considered going for my gun. Normally, my zombie reflexes are so slow that I can't out-draw anyone, but since it doesn't matter if an opponent gets the first shot in, my lack of speed is never an issue. If an opponent manages to hit me, all that it means is that I'll eventually need to get Papa Chatha to repair the damage. Shooting second is more than good enough when bullets can't kill you. But now my reflexes were once more those of a living man, and that meant I might be able to draw my gun before Gilmore could activate the Argentum Perditor. Then again, I'd had trouble simply standing back in the alley, and I still didn't feel all that steady on my feet. I hadn't adjusted to my newly restored body yet, and that meant there was a good chance I'd fumble when I tried to draw my 9mm, giving Gilmore more than ample opportunity to turn me into a silver statue. And if I got silverfied before I could get home and was able to, uh, make my delivery to Devona, she'd kill me.

So no gunplay for now.

Gilmore leaned toward me and inhaled deeply then, and I felt suddenly paranoid. Demonkin senses aren't always as keen as those of Bloodborn or Lykes, but they're sharp enough, and I feared Gilmore might smell that I'd turned human. One of the things you want to avoid at all costs in Nekropolis is having someone consider you prey—especially *easy* prey. I had a couple things going in my favor, though. For one thing, Gilmore had no reason to suspect I'd been restored to a living state. For another, my transformation had only affected my body. My clothes were still the same, and not only did a pungent eau de zombie still cling to them, they were stained from the gunk I'd landed in when I fell in the alley. With any lucky, my rancid-smelling clothes would help disguise my now human scent.

Turns out I had nothing to worry about. He leaned back and his smile became more relaxed.

"I can smell the silver on you, so perhaps your story is true. But I've heard rumors on the street as well, Mr. Richter. It seems that a number of powerful magical artifacts have been stolen from their owners over the last few weeks. The thefts have two important things in common. The owners are all, shall we say, *unconven-*

tional business people like myself, and *you* were spotted in the vicinity around the time of each theft, Mr. Richter."

I shrugged. "What can I say? I get around. Doesn't mean I had anything to do with the thefts." Inwardly, I cursed my luck. Gilmore might not be a genius, but it seemed that he was more than smart enough to put two and two together.

"So this leads me to two possible conclusions. Either you were looking for me for the reason you claimed, in order to secure a new supplier of silver bullets, or you were looking for *this*." He wiggled the Argentum Perditor for emphasis. "The problem is, how do I determine the truth?"

If he knew I was currently human, he'd try to force me to confess using the persuasive power of his demon voice. If he did, I might be able to resist. Then again, I might not. Hopefully, he'd continue thinking I was still a zombie.

I tried to speak more slowly and less distinctly as I replied to further the impression that I was still dead. "You could always take my word for it."

He laughed. "Demons aren't known for being the trusting type." He thought for a moment. "I think I'll invite you to accompany me to my home. The public face of my operation is a small business called One Man's Trash. Perhaps you saw it during your inquiries? It's not far from here. I specialize in selling 'reclaimed treasures' imported from Earth. You'd be surprised what some Darkfolk are willing to pay for the junk I carry in my shop. My real business lies in the chambers underneath the shop, of course. I have a number of devices there that will allow me to extract the truth even from a zombie." A gleam came into his demon eyes, and he bared his teeth once more. "This is going to be a lot of fun."

He jabbed the Argentum Perditor into my side, and the metal claw hurt like a bitch. I had to grit my teeth to keep from reacting.

"Let's go. That way." He nodded eastward, in the direction I'd just come from. Seeing no other recourse for the time being, I nodded, turned around, and started walking down the sidewalk, Gilmore at my side, the Argentum Perditor aimed at me.

We walked for several minutes in silence after that. I kept a close eye on the pedestrians we passed, hoping to spot a familiar face. I have a lot of friends in the city, and even more enemies, and any one of them might provide a way to distract Gilmore. But I didn't see anyone I knew, friend or foe. And I couldn't rely on Devona to come to my rescue. The voicemail I'd left for her said only that I was on my way home, and once she heard it, she'd have no reason to suspect I was in trouble and come racing to Ruination Row to help me. It looked like I was on my own.

We'd just passed High Stakes, an extreme piercing parlor run by a descendent of Vlad Tepes, and were approaching a Sawney B's, a fast-food joint for cannibals on the go, offering such delectable treats as lady fingers, marrow shakes, and homunculus nuggets. A trio of Bloodborn stood on the sidewalk in front of Sawney B's, sipping plasma shakes. Given that Bloodborn are for all intents and purposes immortal, it's difficult to tell their ages by looking at them, but I knew these there were young as vampires went. Older Bloodborn feel uncomfortable around technology, if they don't disdain it completely. But younger ones tend to embrace it, often to the point of getting themselves cybernetically augmented. Genetic and technological alteration wasn't uncommon for the Darkfolk, considering that their supernaturally strong constitutions allowed them to withstand medical procedures that would kill a human being.

These three vampires—two male, one female—were almost completely clad in metal, making them seem as if they were wearing suits of armor. Wires, cables, and gears were visible at their joints, and their eyes had been replaced by small holoprojectors that glowed with internal green light. Their heads had been shaved, the woman's too, and their left incisors had been painted a bright ruby red. The latter was the calling card of the Red Tide, a vampire street gang that was one of the most deadly in Nekropolis. Even for their kind, they were considered vicious killers, and they had one other important quality: they were notoriously sensitive about their cyber implants.

As we drew closer, I called out, "What are you guys drinking? Motor oil?"

Gilmore jabbed the Argentum Perditor into my side, and I couldn't keep from wincing. I hoped he hadn't noticed.

One of the males, this one of Asian descent, turned to look at me, his green eyes shading red.

"Shut up, smart-ass, or we'll stick our straws in your carotid and see how you taste," he snarled.

The woman, who was black, let out a high-pitched

laugh that had an electronic edge to it, as if she had a synthesizer unit attached to her vocal cords.

"I'm not afraid of you junk-heaps," I said. "Looks to me like your warranties are about up."

Gilmore leaned over to whisper in my ear. "I know what you're trying to do, and it won't work. Keep walking."

But we weren't able to do that. The three cyber-vampires dropped their shakes and, traveling so swiftly they were little more than blurs, they moved into the street to block our way. All of their eyes glowed red now.

The second male, who was white, looked me up and down, then wrinkled his nose in disgust.

"Where the hell have you been, man? Smells like you just swam a few laps in a sewer."

His companions laughed.

"I'm surprised your nose still works," I said. "I figured you'd have an air filter or something stuck in there."

The cybervamp snarled, grabbed a handful of my shirt, and pulled me close to him. Around us, pedestrians had either stopped to watch the incipient mayhem or they were giving us plenty of room as they moved quickly to get out of our way. The attention was just what I wanted. I hoped Gilmore would be reluctant to use the Argentum Perditor in front of an audience in order to avoid anyone suspecting he was the Silversmith.

Of course, now that I'd pissed off a trio of vampires, I had to find a way to keep them from killing me.

"You need to show more respect for the Red Tide,"

the cybervamp said in a low and deadly voice. His breath smelled foul, like rotten meat, and I had to fight to keep from gagging.

"Maybe a brainwipe would teach him some manners," the girl said, grinning.

The Asian vamp nodded eagerly. "Do it!"

The Bloodborn who had hold of me smiled, and his holo-eyes glowed a darker red. "This is going to hurt. A lot. On the plus side, once I'm finished, you won't remember it. But that's only because you won't remember *anything*."

He opened his mouth and extended his tongue. The end split bloodlessly in two to reveal a thin black wire with a silver needle on the tip. I understood what he planned to do with me. The wire was going to shoot forward like a striking serpent and the needle would imbed itself in my skull. The cybervamp would then send a jolt of energy into my brain, scrambling it and erasing my memories. When he was finished, not only wouldn't I know my name, I wouldn't even remember that there were such things *as* names.

I had only a split second to do something, but I had no idea what. I'd grown so used to relying on my zombie state to get me out of trouble that I couldn't think of any way to avoid getting mindwiped. It looked like my attempt to get away from Gilmore had backfired, and while I'd still be alive when it was over, I'd no longer be *me*.

"Enough of this foolishness," Gilmore said. He pointed the Argentum Perditor at the three Red Tide vampires and the claw on the end glowed with a bright silvery light. All three of the gang members turned to look at the claw, transfixed by its glow, and as I watched, the metal of the cyber-implants transformed into silver—and silver is highly poisonous to Bloodborn.

The flesh connected to their implants instantly began to smolder and blacken, and the cybervamps shrieked in agony. The one that had been just about to mindwipe me released me, and all three of them began to tear at their implants, as if desperate to remove the silver that was poisoning them. They fell to the ground, shrieking and clawing at their bodies, and Gilmore looked down at them, smiling with satisfaction.

"I do *so* enjoy my work," he said. Then he looked at me and jabbed the Argentum Perditor into my side once more. "No more tricks. Understand?"

I nodded, and we stepped around the screaming vampires and continued heading eastward.

Evidently, I'd been wrong about Gilmore. He wasn't worried about revealing his true identity. Then again, it wasn't as if the existence of the Argentum Perditor was common knowledge. Maybe he was counting on no one being able to associate the three silverfied Red Tide vamps with the Silversmith. Or maybe he just didn't give a damn. Demons can be like that.

We'd gone less than half a block before coming to a bar I'd passed earlier called Born of Man and Woman. It was a humans-only place, one of the few in the city, and a number of its patrons were standing on the sidewalk, watching us as we approached.

"I'm warning you," Gilmore said as we drew closer. "Don't say a word."

The half dozen men and women weren't exactly the

shy, retiring type. They were well muscled, heavily tattooed and pierced, and clad in denim, leather, and steel-toed boots. Humans need to be tough to survive in Nekropolis, and only the toughest can hope to hold their own in Ruination Row. It looked to me like these men and women were right at home here.

The tallest of them was a middle-aged man with long brown hair and a full beard. He had a wicked-looking scar on his right cheek, and wore an Apocalyptica T-shirt beneath a leather vest, and in his right hand he gripped the rubber-coated handle of an aluminum bat. He stepped forward to meet us as we approached.

"We heard there was trouble on the street with some Redfangs," he said in voice roughened by too much booze and too many cigarettes. "We came outside to see what was up. That was some mighty powerful magic you used to deal with them, demon."

"Just a little spell to overload their circuits," Gilmore lied smoothly. "Nothing special about it. Now if you'll excuse us . . ."

Gilmore made to step around the man, but he raised his bat to block the demon's way.

"My name's R.J. I own the joint." He nodded to the bar. "It's a kind of oasis, you know? A place where humans can go to be around their own kind and relax."

Gilmore struggled to keep the irritation out of his voice as he spoke. "That's all very interesting, but I don't see—"

R.J. interrupted. "We humans look after each other here in Ruination Row." His gaze flicked to me, then returned to Gilmore. "Looks to me like you're forcing this man to accompany you. That doesn't sit well with me, demon, and it doesn't sit well with my friends."

The other men and women gathered on the sidewalk shot Gilmore dark looks as they murmured their agreement.

Gilmore looked at R.J. for a moment before throwing back his head and laughing.

"You think this man is *human*? That's hysterical! This is Matthew Richter. The zombie detective?"

R.J. looked at me again, more closely this time. "Heard of him. Can't say I know him." He inspected me a moment longer before adding, "Skin looks like that of a living man." He reached out, gently pinched a bit of my cheek between his thumb and forefinger and rolled it around a bit. "Feels real," he said and he pulled his hand away.

Gilmore frowned. "Take a look at his clothes," he said.

"So the man's a mess," R.J. said. "That doesn't make him a zombie."

I was beginning to worry. The last distraction I'd tried to arrange hadn't worked out so well, and the last thing I wanted was for R.J. and his friends to be transformed into silver statues. I needed to find a way to end this—fast. If only I'd still been a zombie, none of this would have . . .

Then I realized I'd been going about this all wrong. I'd been thinking of being human as a weakness. Instead, I should have viewed it as a strength.

I carry all sorts of weapons on my person, and some of them have sharp edges. While Gilmore's attention was on R.J., I reached into one of my pockets and found a switchblade. I clicked it open and ran my index finger along the edge of the blade. Then I removed my hand and held it up for everyone to see.

Gilmore goggled as he looked at the line of blood trickling from the wound on my finger.

I smiled at him. "Like you told me, I didn't say a word."

Gilmore spun toward R.J. and raised the Argentum Perditor, but he was too late to avoid getting a face full of aluminum. Demons are tougher than humans, but not tougher than half a dozen. R.J.'s friends moved in and started working on Gilmore, punching and kicking, and it didn't take long before the demon was lying on the ground, moaning in pain, his arms and legs bent at awkward angles, his face swollen, bruised, and bloody.

When my fellow humans stepped back, I bent down and pried the Argentum Perditor out of Gilmore's hand and tucked it into my pocket. I wiped the blood from my finger on Gilmore's shirt before straightening. Then I turned to R.J.

"Thanks for the help," I said. I offered my hand to shake, and R.J. grinned as he took it. The man's grip was strong and warm, and it felt good to shake another man's hand—another *living* man's—and really feel it.

"No problem," he said. "All the Darkfolk can be a pain in the ass sometimes, but demons really annoy me." He gave Gilmore a last half-hearted kick the ribs, and the demon moaned loudly. R.J. turned back to me. "You want to come on in and have a drink? It's on the house."

I was tempted. It had been several years since I'd tasted anything, and a drink sounded damn good right then. But I had somewhere very important to be.

"I'll have to take a raincheck," I said. "But I want to thank you all one last time. Lately, I've been worrying that Nekropolis isn't the best place for a human to live, but now . . ." I smiled. "Now I think it's not so bad."

R.J. smiled. "Not so long as we watch out for each other."

We shook hands one last time, and I headed west once more, while R.J. and his friends returned to their bar. We left Gilmore lying on the sidewalk, moaning and trying to find the strength to get to his feet. I knew the demon would recover, and eventually he'd come looking for me, determined to make me pay for what I'd done to him, but right then, I didn't care. All that mattered to me was getting home, putting my arms around the woman I love, and for the first time since I'd met her, knowing what it felt like to touch her.

BENEATH THE SILENT BELL, THE AUTUMN SKY TURNS TO SPRING

Eugie Foster

The bell at Dojoji temple pealed at noon to mark the day's peak. Its voice was silver and light, water kissed by the sun. It matched the tolling in Alan's head, the same tone, the same cadence, even the same tempo—each reverberating note sounding in tandem with the phantom bell haunting him. For the first time in almost a year, ever since he'd started hearing the incessant ringing, he felt hope.

Ryoseki looked up from his meditations to find Soryo Kuro and Soryo Yusai standing before him, their heads bowed.

"Forgive the intrusion, Sensei," Kuro said. "There has been some commotion in the *shōro*. One of our visitors is demanding to purchase the temple bell, and even though we have explained to him that this is impossible, he refuses to desist."

The old priest did not seem surprised by this, although no one had ever made such an outrageous request before.

"I will take care of it," he said.

Alan jittered from one foot to the other, pacing around the belfry's stone perimeter, wishing he could light up. He didn't care what his doctor said, the patch did nothing for his nicotine cravings. He checked his watch again. Where had those priests gone to anyway?

At the end of his circuit around the *shōro*, Alan startled. The old man in the saffron robes seemed to materialize out of nowhere, standing placidly and gazing up at the huge bronze bell as though he were as solid a fixture as the stone Buddha statue in the courtyard.

The man bowed, un-stonelike. "I did not mean to startle you. I am Ryoseki, Dojoji's *jūshoku*."

"*Jūshoku*. That's head priest, right? Finally, someone in charge." Alan reached for the pack of Dunhills in his suit jacket only to stop mid-motion with a scowl. "I want to buy this bell. I don't care how much it costs. And don't give me some crap about not needing material goods. Your temple does charity work. Think of what you could do with an extra million or two for homeless orphans or blind puppies or whatever cause you like. And I'm talking U.S. dollars, not yen."

"That is a very generous offer. May I inquire what you will do with our bell once you are in possession of it?"

"I don't know yet."

"I see." Ryoseki contemplated the bell's ornate rim where a pattern of curlicues was stamped into the metal. "You are American, yes? Will you be wanting to relocate it overseas? It is quite heavy. Many tons."

Alan frowned. He hadn't thought that far ahead, which was unlike him. He never made an acquisition bid without thorough research and a prospectus plan and strategy. But this bell was different, more important than abstract numbers and profit margins, essential to have no matter the cost.

"And the *shōro* will need to be disassembled," the priest continued. "Or did you wish to purchase that as well?"

"You think I'm joking?" Alan yanked the sterling silver case from his pocket and extracted an embossed business card. "My name is Alan Brandt. Maybe you've heard of me? I have the means to buy what I want, and I want this bell."

Ryoseki accepted the card and its inked pedigree—CEO, EMBA, CFA—with a polite nod. "Did I do something to indicate that I was not treating your request with the utmost sincerity? That was not my intention. I merely wished to know if you had already considered the practical aspects of this transaction or if I could offer any suggestions."

"Don't you want to know why I want it?"

"I would be glad to hear your motivations."

Alan studied the other man's face. Was he mocking him? He was an astute reader of expressions. He had to be in his line of work. But the priest's cordial facade gave away nothing.

"For the last year, I've had a bell ringing in my head at noon and midnight," Alan said, "every single day, without fail. You'd think twice a day wouldn't be that bad, but I can't concentrate, can't sleep, can't do anything but count down the minutes until the next time it rings. I've seen neurologists, otologists, neurotologists, and psychiatrists, been scanned, probed, and psycho-analyzed. They can't find anything. My board is on the verge of ousting me with a 'no confidence' vote, and I can't blame them. I'm utterly distracted. And it's getting louder."

"Yet though you are tormented by the tolling of a bell," Ryoseki said, "you wish to possess ours."

"That's right. Because when it rang at noon, it sounded exactly like the one in my head. I don't know what it means, but it's important."

"So it is." The priest turned on his heel.

"Hey, where are you going?"

"If you are to purchase Dojoji's bell, you will require documentation and an official receipt, will you not?"

"Uh, yeah—"

"Well, come along then."

Bemused, Alan followed the priest down a little path to a cottage on the temple grounds. The front door opened to a tidy room with western furniture: a wooden desk and a pair of chairs. A display case filled with books and a modest Buddha figure seated in lotus position, more bookend than icon, took up the remainder of the space.

"Please have a seat," Ryoseki said. "Would you like some tea?"

Alan nodded, stifling another urge to reach for his cigarettes. This was territory he knew, the Japanese custom of small talk and socializing before getting down to business. Annoying but unavoidable.

The priest set a small kettle on an electric plate and spooned fragrant leaves into the water. "You know, if you wish to smoke, I don't mind."

Alan immediately pulled out a cigarette and lit it. He took a long drag, sucking the smoke deep into his lungs. Exhaling, he felt tension dissipate in the plume of blue smoke.

"God, I needed that."

The lines around Ryoseki's eyes crinkled. "I thought so."

"Hey, I noticed your English is really good," Alan said.

"Thank you. I spent several years studying overseas when I was a boy." The priest took a sip of tea, his expression lost in a whorl of steam. "This isn't your first time to Japan, either."

"My company partners with many Japanese holdings, but I've never been outside Tokyo before."

"Yet you have come all the way to Wakayama Prefecture to our humble temple. Are you familiar with the tale of Kiyohime? It is Dojoji's most famous legend."

Alan blinked, his stock banter thrown off by the abrupt subject change. "Er, no."

The priest set his cup down. "Kiyohime was the only daughter of a powerful *daimyo*, a military lord high in the shogun's regard. The *daimyo* was also a religious man. So when a traveling soryo named Tomozo and his young novice, Anchin, were caught in a torrential storm, it was to the *daimyo's* house they went to shelter for the night.

"The *daimyo* commanded that a large feast be laid,

and afterwards asked the priests to give a sermon from
the Lotus Sutra. Soryo Tomozo was an old man with a
fondness for beer, and he was a bit lazy to boot. Sur-
feited on fine food and drink, he found the lord's request burdensome and commanded his novice to
conduct it in his stead.

"Now Anchin was an earnest young man, elated to
be entrusted with this duty. His sermon was fervent
and full of passion, so much so that it roused a match-
ing fervor in the lady Kiyohime. The two young people
discussed scripture until the fire burned low and everyone else had gone to sleep. And in the manner of
such things, they fell in love.

"Imprudent things were done. Impetuous things
were said. And when morning came, they parted with
a promise. Anchin pledged that he would return for
Kiyohime. And Kiyohime vowed that she would love
no other."

Alan took a last pull from his cigarette and absently
lit another. He'd been prepared to have to feign interest in the old man's natterings, but found himself un-
characteristically drawn in.

"Tomozo and Anchin resumed their travels," Ryoseki continued, "and Anchin confided in his mentor
confessing what had transpired between himself and
Kiyohime. As etiquette forbade Anchin to visit alone,
he begged Tomozo to accompany him again to the
daimyo's residence.

"With reservations, Tomozo agreed, but he also reminded Anchin of the other promises he had made, the
ones to the temple and to Buddha. Did he intend to
recant those in the name of love? Anchin was an hon-

orable man, and he did not want to come before Kiyohime in disgrace, so he promised Tomozo that he would fulfill his spiritual obligations as well.

"Weeks passed as Anchin readied himself to take his temple vows, but on the eve of his ordination, he received tragic news. Believing herself scorned and in despair, Kiyohime took her father's *kaiken* and slit her own throat. She left behind a poem:

> *Is it true that a man's heart changes swiftly as the*
> *   autumn sky? Surely yours cannot be so cruel.*
> *I cannot stop thinking of you. But it seems your*
> *   feelings changed.*
> *Broken promises are the winter snow.*

"Anchin was overcome by guilt and grief. He would not eat, would not sleep. He would only pray and meditate. Tomozo worried about his young charge and convinced him to participate in a ritual to renew and cleanse the spirit.

"That evening, Anchin struck the temple bell eleven times. But before he could strike the twelfth peal to accomplish the ritual, Kiyohime came. She had become an angry ghost, a *yurei*. Her body transformed into the shape of a huge serpent with only her face unchanged by her rage.

"Anchin hid beneath the sacred bell, but when Kiyohime could not drag him forth, she engulfed the bell in her coils. And so baleful was her fury that the bell turned white-hot and molten, incinerating Anchin within it."

Alan stubbed out his cigarette in his empty tea cup and fumbled for another, surprised to discover he was down to his last one. Another surprise, the afternoon had faded to nighttime during the priest's narration, and they sat in shadowy near-darkness. The only illumination came from the main temple's lighting, bleeding in through the window.

Again anticipating him, Ryoseki flicked on a desk lamp. The wan light of its single bulb only made the shadows seem longer and the night darker.

"Dojoji was without a bell for a long while," the priest said, "until a new one was cast and blessed in a purification ceremony of many weeks. But I have long believed that Anchin and Kiyohime's story is not yet done. Your presence here, Alan Brandt, confirms it."

Alan frowned. "*My* presence?"

"The temple bell is part of your karma and compels your destiny. You are bound to it by the wheel of death and rebirth, beholden to debts incurred by a former existence."

Alan leaned back and crossed his arms. "I don't believe in destiny or reincarnation."

"Nevertheless, the voice of the temple bell sounds in your head."

"And you think it's because I have to repay my karma." Alan shrugged. "Believe whatever you like so long as I can have that bell."

Ryoseki drained the dregs of his tea and stood. "Then it is time."

Alan rose. "Time for what?"

The priest lit a candle lantern from behind his desk and tucked a linen-wrapped bundle into his sleeve. "Time for you to restore the balance of your karma. Or, if you prefer, time to inspect your prospective purchase before finalizing our transaction." He beckoned for Alan to follow him into the night.

There were no electric lights in the *shōro*, and its thick timbers and winged roof admitted little of the main temple's illumination. The great bell within was a towering blackness. Ryoseki's lantern bobbed as he climbed the steps, awakening flickering shadows over the bronze patina.

"Are flashlights prohibited? It's a little hard to 'inspect' anything by candlelight," Alan grumbled.

"They are not prohibited," Ryoseki said. "But modern lights and electricity deter spirits, and tonight we wish to invite them."

Alan rolled his eyes. "Okay, fine. Consider it inspected."

"You have only examined the outside."

"After that story, you don't seriously expect me to get inside it, do you?"

The *jūshoku* shrugged. "You are not here merely to buy a bell, Alan Brandt. You are seeking answers. I have shown you the text, but only you can read it." He extended the lantern.

Alan took it, swearing under his breath, and ducked beneath the bell's rim. "Well, I don't see anything, answers or otherwise." His voice echoed in the metal confines.

"Exactly."

"What do you mean 'exactly'? Is that one of those riddles that has no—?" Alan trailed off. "Hey, there's no clapper."

"Temple bells are rung by means of a large wooden

striker from without." The priest's voice drifted to him, slightly muffled. "But this one has never had a striker. And as you can see, it has no internal clapper either. Last year marked the 1000th anniversary since Anchin suffered Kiyohime's wrath and still every effort to install a striker has failed—beams became rot-eaten, supports that give way, chains that always break. The bell is mute and always has been."

"But I heard it."

"You did. Two bells in your head instead of one." Ryoseki shuffled closer. "And now all the players are assembled."

The bell boomed, a single, crashing note.

Alan dropped the lantern and clamped his hands over his ears. "What the hell are you doing?" he shouted. He could still hear it, feel it, thrumming deep in his bones.

"I am finishing the ritual begun by Anchin a thousand years ago. Here, take this." Ryoseki set a slender shape down—the linen-wrapped something now unwrapped—and toed it beneath the bell's edge. It rasped along the *shōro's* floor, steel on stone.

Alan stared at the knife by his foot. Curved and long as his forearm, it was an ancient samurai's weapon. The hilt was stained and faded from time and use, but the edge was still bright.

Still bright? Alan's breath caught. The lantern had gone out when he dropped it, but he could see. Light glimmered behind him, steadier than any flame. And it was moving closer, swelling his shadow against the bell's curved darkness.

Alan lunged for the knife. Grabbing it, he spun around.

*   *   *

"Father would disown me if he knew. But I don't care. I don't even care if he kills me for loving you, Anchin. The only thing I fear is you forgetting me and leaving me bereft and alone."

"Kiyo, I will love you always and forever. I promise I will come back to you. We will marry and live together like happy mice, quietly and simply."

Her words of love and his cruel lies. Broken promises and shame. Worse, despite his duplicity, she still pined for him, still loved him.

Keen rage and bitter desire, an impossible, torturesome duality. Her heart was a bleeding conflagration, burning without surcease. The *kaiken* opened her, releasing the fire, spilling it out in a boiling fountain.

But it wasn't enough. She still burned.

Alan reeled, catching himself on the curved bronze at his back. Suspended between juxtaposed images of American businessman and Japanese princess, memories of a distant past overlaid more recent recollections. The *kaiken* in his hand, the edge of it slicing his flesh, the crimson spray shockingly red in his mind's eye. He touched his throat, expecting to find ravaged tissue and a drench of heat, was surprised not to.

"Beloved, at last."

Alan raised his head. Reflected in the unshined bronze, an apparition of a young man regarded him, faintly translucent and cloaked in a nimbus of gold. Anchin.

"I waited for you." Kiyohime's words billowed black and hot from Alan's mouth, smoky dragon's breath in lieu of tobacco. "You never came." It was too much for Alan to accept, kinesthetic impressions of a monstrous serpent spitting fire that was also a woman. Senses engulfed and overwhelmed, the tousled strands of Alan submerged, and Kiyohime darted forward.

Anchin's ghostly form reached out. "Forgive me. Fate was unkind. I meant to come."

Kiyohime ignored the proffered hand. "Easy to say now, when our time is past and all that remains is a mournful tale."

Anchin's hand fell away. "Is this truly what you want? To be locked together in this cycle of suffering?"

An ember kindled in her chest. She knew this fire, knew how it must end. Again. "Why not?" she demanded. "If this is all of you I will ever have, if this is all you will give me, why should I let you go?"

Anchin's eyes fixed on her, still pools of sorrow. "Your rage is a demon that consumes us both. I would free you from it, even if you don't wish the same for me. What if I give myself to this demon willingly, will that appease you? Will that sate it?"

"What do you mean?"

"I will gladly surrender myself to be devoured and razed to nothingness if it will end your spirit's torment."

Kiyohime sneered. "Nothingness? Isn't oblivion what all good little *soryos* yearn for?"

"You misunderstand. I am offering you my eternal spirit to consume. Destroy it and I will never know nirvana or enlightenment. I will be nothing, negated."

Fury churned in her, leaping with greed. She bared his teeth—part grin, part grimace. "In that case, I accept."

Anchin bowed his head. The apparition shrank, falling into itself—translucent features and ghostly limbs lost in a contracting orb. It continued to diminish, flattening into a disc, then a slender needle. But although it decreased in size, its brilliance remained undimmed.

The bell tolled, familiar and unrelenting, rising to a deafening crescendo as the needle flared zinc-white.

Light receded, the white brand becoming the pale, rose-fawn rays of dawn.

Kiyohime observed the morning with detachment, an impartial observer. Without needing to see the stark walls of a novice's cubicle or feel the rough wool of priestly robes, she knew the eyes belonged to Anchin, her consciousness now riding in his body.

The bell's clamor had paled too, sounding as though from a distance. And in similarly muted tones, Anchin's voice jangled in her head: "This is the day of my immolation. When night falls, your *yurei* will find me. All you must do is join it, two flames into one, and when you sunder me to ashes, my spirit as well as my body will be consumed."

"That is all good and well," Kiyohime said. "But it is only sunrise. Why must I wait for a whole day's passage before I may feast?"

"Did you not want to savor my suffering? Won't it be over too quickly otherwise, this opportunity to relish my anguish?"

"There is savoring and there is tedious delay. I am not interested in the latter."

"Then only bid 'quicker,' and time will dash forward."

"Fine. Qui—" Kiyohime's impatience was interrupted by the entrance of an old priest. Those lined features, that portly figure. She remembered him.

"Anchin, you must eat something." Soryo Tomozo frowned at the untouched bowl of rice. "And by the haggard look of you, you haven't slept either."

Anchin acknowledged the other man's presence with a listless glance before resuming his silent litany of prayer.

Tomozo padded in and kneeled beside Anchin. "My son, there is such a thing as too much austerity."

"Sensei, I am grateful for your concern," Anchin mumbled, "but I wish to be alone." His voice was rough and thick, absent even a suggestion of bell tones.

"I have left you alone, and look at you, one foot already in the yellow waters of the afterlife." Tomozo exhaled, shoulders sagging. "Even fools may realize truth upon reflection and meditation, and this old fool has had a lifetime of reflection in which to recognize his many faults: a proclivity for drink and indolence, and a cowardly disposition. But I am not so much a coward as to allow you to destroy yourself with guilt and self-recrimination when by rights, the fault and responsibility is mine. I am to blame for Kiyohime's death."

Anchin looked up at that. "What do you mean?"

Tomozo wrung his hands. "I connived to keep you apart, always finding some excuse to put you off when you suggested going to her."

"Why?"

"I told myself that it was in your best interests. After all, you were due to take your vows and she was a highborn young lady. Such creatures are known to be frivolous and fickle. But really, I was afraid. The *daimyo* is a powerful man with a reputation for lopping off the heads of those who displease him, and I feared he would hold me responsible for entangling his daughter with a penniless priest."

Anchin was silent for a long while. "Thank you for your honesty, but it changes nothing," he said at last. "It was my neglect that caused her to despair. The worth of a man lies in his actions, and all I gave her were words."

Tomozo reached into his sleeve and pulled out two bundles of paper secured with string. "My inventory of sins is not done. These are the missives you entrusted me to convey to the lady, undelivered. And these are the ones she sent that I withheld from you."

Anchin accepted the two packets. "She didn't even have my words to reassure her?"

"My life is not long enough for me to atone for my misdeeds. I am truly, profoundly sorry."

Anchin said nothing, only gazed at the sealed, unread pages in his hands.

"Tonight I will sound the temple bell in order to entreat Kiyohime's spirit for forgiveness," Tomozo said. "Please, it would mean much if you came and prayed with me."

Anchin gave the barest nod, and the old priest rose to go.

After Tomozo departed, Anchin unbound the cache of Kiyohime's letters and selected one. It was tied with a red ribbon, and a single cherry blossom fell out when he opened it. The petals were withered and dry, but they retained a wisp of fragrance, delicate and sweet.

With a pang, Kiyohime recalled the day she had

written it. Seated beneath the sakura trees, each brush-
stroke crafted with devotion, each character imbued
with longing.

Anchin began to read:

My Dearest Anchin,
*   You are doubtless occupied with your devotions, and*
I fear I am bothering you with my trivial ramblings.
How fine it must be to have such purity of dedication,
such clarity of purpose. Alas, no matter how I pray or
meditate, I remain fanciful and scatterbrained. I have
begun to wonder if that night we had was a dream, a
sweet vision crafted by a fox spirit. Please, if I am a
nuisance to you, do not spare me this candor. I think it
is better to know the truth than to linger in delusion.

The ember in Kiyohime's chest flared, hurtful and
sharp. "Quicker," she whispered.

A claxon of bells and a burst of light scoured away
sight and sound. When she could see and hear again,
morning had yielded to afternoon. Anchin kneeled
before their letters, opened and neatly arrayed—his
and hers in tidy piles. A band of sunlight picked out
fragments of text from his stack:

*   . . . only a short while until we may be together . . .*
will you mind very much, the life of a priest's wife? I
cannot give you riches, but I lay my heart at your . . .

"Quicker!" she cried.

Between glaring brilliance and strident bronze notes,
afternoon turned to dusk.

Anchin gave a hoarse yell and flung himself down, his hands scrabbling at violently torn paper strewn like fallen leaves across the floor.

"Quicker," Kiyohime gasped. "Quicker, quicker!"

The crashing light could not blind nor the booming bell deafen her fast enough to blot out the raw anguish. It didn't matter. When the serpent consumed Anchin's spirit, this pain would end too.

In the storm-thrashed darkness, Anchin staggered, his arms aching with the effort of plunging the heavy striker against the temple bell. His breath came in ragged gulps, laboring in his too-tight chest. He was glad for it, glad he had insisted on ringing the bell. It was a token of penance, this final effort.

Bronze notes thundered to the skies, summoning the gods and spirits to come and bear witness. But it was something else that heard and came, not a god or spirit, a smoldering mote of rage. It coalesced, drawing shape and dimension from each stroke of wood on metal.

Kiyohime recognized it, this mote. It was herself reflected in a mirror shaped like a serpent. She called out a welcome and felt the rushing reply: *Soon, soon. I am coming.*

Anchin fell to his knees, panting. A nacre vial slipped unnoticed from his sleeve and rolled beneath the bell's rim. He dragged himself up, clinging to the striker, and hauled it back once more.

But Kiyohime had seen the pearly glint out of the corner of Anchin's eye. "What is that?"

A scroll of memories unfurled, mislaid before in a run of "quicker"s:

Descending a cramped stairway into Dojoji's neglected cellar. Fashioning a brittle posy from dusty jars and pots, desiccated flowers that had once been the deep red-purple of twilight; a spray of shriveled berries, green as envy; a gray root bulb shaped like a baby's hand curled into a fist. And steeping these into a milk-white elixir drained into an iridescent vial—the same vial that rolled, empty, beneath the temple bell.

"What did you do?" she cried. A princess's knowledge of herb lore could not match a learned priest's, but it was enough to recognize the nightshade and the moonseed, enough to know death when she saw it.

"I was already coming to you." Silvery notes chimed in her head. "You only hastened me along."

Her chest ignited to blazing agony. She writhed, burning but unburned, brimful of fire. The fire demanded release, like she knew it must, the same as before. It breached the cage of her body, another verse reprised. But when it crested and broke, there the script changed. It didn't singe off her limbs and flay her skin, didn't remake her into armored scales and sinuous coils. It streamed from her eyes in a scald of tears.

Kiyohime wept. For herself, for Anchin, for their squandered lives. And most of all, for every lost moment of their love.

The bell pealed, a sonorous crash of sound.

A fragment of memory stirred, echoes of a duplicate bell. Buried and somnolent, Alan awakened, resurfaced. The tolling in his head, the bell only he could hear, it rang out in a trio of unisons—the bell of the future, this one from their past, and the inescapable din in his head. He recognized it now. It was Anchin, his voice, his spirit, finding Kiyohime's spirit, returning as he had promised to do.

A thought away, the serpent sundered apart the temple's gate, rushing toward the *shōro*.

"Stop! Go back," Kiyohime-Alan, both of them as one, implored it.

But it was mindless, heedless of all but its terrible purpose.

"Why can't I stop it? Why is it still coming?"

A trill of chiming notes sounded as Anchin crumpled beneath the bell's rim. "We are spectators of a tragedy already played through," his spirit-voice replied. "The events are set; only the repercussions may be rewritten."

The serpent arrived in an inferno gale, pouring over the *shōro's* topmost stair.

"How can I bear to watch myself kill you?"

"What transpires here has been and must be, but you are not obliged to stay. Say 'quicker' and this moment will end."

Alan felt their malice wind around the bell, saw through Anchin's eyes the glow of its fury redden the bronze. One word and he could escape the coming horror. It was ready on his tongue.

But that was the reckless impulse of a bygone life. Must he squander another thousand years reprising the same lesson? He listened to the memory of sound still trembling in the air and found the conviction he had lacked before.

"These moments are the dregs of a precious cup wretchedly spilled," he said. "Even if they are bitter, I won't waste them again. I won't leave you."

Within the blistering cage of metal, Anchin lifted his head. "Kiyo?"

She stretched her hand to him, a reflected echo of a moment yet to be. "Forgive me. I should have trusted you."

Without hesitation, Anchin took her hand. "There is nothing to forgive." They came together as the bronze bell flashed white-hot around them.

Reunited at last, they did not notice when the end came in a molten cascade of metal, when Anchin's body blackened and turned to ash. Their union was perfect, one heart, one spirit joined. But though it was perfect, it was not endless.

The wheel turned, inexorable, and its next pass sundered them apart. But even in parting they were joyous. Though it might take a thousand years, they knew they would touch again. And this time, it would be forever.

Ryoseki sat in the darkened *shōro* and pressed the illuminate button on his watch. He knew without having to consult the glowing display that it was almost midnight, but he found it soothing to watch the timepiece's measured movements. The twelve hour cycle was etched into him, noon and midnight, in the rhythm of his pulse, his breath, each blink of his eyes. The bell had tolled for him, a steady, predictable cadence to mark the days of his life.

As a child it had troubled him, the incessant ringing that no one else could hear. But then he had come to Dojoji and the bell had spoken to him. It told him of the karmic debt he owed to remedy the course of three wayward fates: his, Anchin's, and Kiyohime's.

The second hand swept to the apex of its circuit. Midnight. It seemed to linger for an extra beat, a prolonged second, before starting its next circuit. And for the first time in his life, there was no ringing, no peal of bells to mark it.

Ryoseki closed his eyes and listened to the silence.

THE VERY NEXT DAY

Jody Lynn Nye

The first thing people noticed on the busy New York street was the broadsheet newspaper clutched in the small man's hand. That was odd, because his costume would surely have set him apart anywhere outside of Lapland, or wherever winter ruled. It ought to have stood out on a fine day in September like a sore thumb. His coat, which reached over his round belly nearly to his knees, was made of fur, russet red like a deer's hide, and lined with longer white fur. A hood with a long peak lay on his shoulders, revealing wavy white hair worn very long and a shining white moustache and beard that seemed as if they had been growing for centuries, if not decades. His boots of black leather shone like mirrors, as did the silver buckle of his black belt. Normally, they would not expect to see a man dressed as Santa Claus sooner than December, but today everyone in Manhattan felt a bit indulgent and nostalgic.

"Nice outfit," the man in the newspaper kiosk said, glancing up. "Giving the suit an airing today?"

"Why, no," "Santa Claus" said. "This is what I wear all of the time."

The newspaper vendor shrugged. A harmless nut, but he looked like the real thing, and that made him feel good. He pushed the flat wool cap back on his head and scratched his scalp. Like a boy again.

"Just in town for the day?"

Santa slapped his chest with his hand and looked up at the tall buildings—the tallest in the world. He felt a thrill to see them. "Why, yes! It's a fine city. I never do get to see them in daylight. Always by moonlight or starlight." He glanced down at the paper in his hand.

The vendor nodded toward the newspaper. "Nice piece of writin' there, ain't it?"

Santa nodded. "Truly. I would be convinced, if I were a child."

Something in the way the old man said the last word sounded disappointed. The newsman gave him an encouraging grin. "Everyone was, if you ask me. Wanna copy of today's paper?"

"No, thank you," the old man said. "I haven't finished with this one yet." He folded it up and put it in his pocket. Then he eyed the newsman, counted the gaps in his smile. "You should take better care of your teeth, you know."

The newspaper vendor felt his face go red. "Don't you make personal comments to me, geezer!"

"But you promised me," "Santa" said. "In your letter. If I brought you that stuffed leather horse, you'd clean your teeth every day, just as your mother asked you."

The newsman's mouth dropped open. "But that was forty years ago!"

"A promise is a promise."

"Yeah." He ran his tongue over the remaining teeth in his mouth. "I will, Santa. I really will. Thanks. And thanks for the horse. I really loved it. I gave it to my first daughter when she was born."

"You were a good boy, Louis," Santa said, offering his free hand for a shake. Louis clutched the leather glove.

How absolutely marvelous that he knew everything there was about a child just by looking at him, Santa thought as he turned away from the wondering eyes. Then he paused, confused. *How did I know all that?*

What was going on inside his head was not nearly so amazing as what was outside it. New York was a place of wonders! Santa gazed around him in wonder, taking it all in. Men and women wore clothing made of the most exquisite fabrics, soft and evenly woven and dyed in colors that had heretofore existed only in rainbows and spring meadows. Gentlemen in brilliant white linen jackets tipped their flat straw hats to ladies whose long, shining hair was piled up in a pumpkin shape on their heads. The streets themselves were surprisingly clean. Men pushing barrels on wheels stopped to sweep and scoop up refuse deposited by horses.

He had expected to be overwhelmed by the odor of sewage and rotten vegetation on top of the smell of coal fires that filled the air. Instead, there was a new scent, a sharp burning scent. Horses drew carriages through the streets as well as on narrow metal rails, but over his head and in the windows of the many, many shops, tiny lights encased in glass shone. They were not candles, they were light bulbs. The smell was that of *electricity*. Such things did not exist in many places yet, that he knew, but this was a city that had to have everything new as soon as possible. He walked between tall, stone buildings with shining bronze doors. Fantastic, swooping designs were pressed into them. Art Nouveau, they called it. Beautiful. New World, new art. New music poured from the doors of clubs.

From a point at the very tip of the island, he saw in the harbor a magnificent statue, a woman facing away from him, with a torch in her hand raised in welcome. He did not have to see her face to know that she was Liberty herself. She had been a gift. Santa had not given her, but he knew when something had been tendered with love or respect. He felt as if *he* had been given a present, to see something that represented such an ideal.

Children who had been looking out into the harbor noticed the small man in their midst. They broke away from their parents and came tearing toward him.

"Santa!" "Santa Claus!" "Sinterklaas!"

They danced around him, laughing, and he shared their delight. Little girls in bows tied on top of their heads, boys in knee pants, urchins without shoes. They hugged him, tugged on his coat, tried to clamber into his arms, though he was scarcely taller than they were.

They felt in his pockets and came up with handfuls of hard candies wrapped in bright cellophane. Their eyes were alight with happiness.

"What are you doing here?"

"Where are your reindeer? Can I say hello to Dancer?"

"Mama said you would bring me a train for Christmas if I am good. Will you?"

"Well, well, well, we will see!" Santa said, chucking a chin here and offering a hug there. "Are you helping your mother with the chores? She needs help now that your new brother has arrived."

"Aw," said Steven, the boy who wanted the train. "I *guess*."

"Good for you! Then you will be on my good list for this Christmas!"

Steven glowed with pride.

With every child's question, Santa felt himself growing stronger and more alive. How marvelous it was to interact with the little ones whom he usually glimpsed asleep in their beds, if at all. He knew of the dreams they had and wishes they made. They were a joy awake. He loved to be with them all.

They all knew everything about him, and because they did, he knew everything about them. Glynnis had a lisp that made her friends tease her. Fridur had recently come to the United States with his parents from the Netherlands. They were poor, but making their way. His mother took in washing, and his father worked on the docks. Evelyn was from a wealthy family, but her brother had just died of typhoid. All of them had been good except Mick. He was cruel to ani-

mals. Santa regarded him with stern pity. He did not
have to say anything. The boy shrank away from his
bright gaze. He knew too much about Santa to imagine
that his sins were hidden from him.

What did Santa know about himself? More memories
came to him as he spoke with the children. He lived far
away, where it was cold. They were unclear as to where,
as each of them had a different idea. He drove a sleigh
with reindeer. He made toys. Not all by himself. Little
men helped him. They loaded the sleigh on Christmas
Eve, and he drove all over the world. He brought toys
for good children, and punished bad ones—no, he
brought rocks and coal for bad ones. His assistants did
not beat children any more. He was glad of that.

"How do you go all the way around the world in
just one night?" a boy with big brown eyes asked. His
name was Julian. He was ten, and his grandfather had
been a war hero.

"My reindeer are very swift," Santa said. "I have
worked out the very best route possible. I am always
home by dawn." He knew in his soul that it was absolutely true. The other children nodded eagerly.

"But it's impossible to go to every house with children! There are millions of them!"

"It takes magic," Santa explained. "You do believe
in magic, don't you?"

Julian crossed his arms. "My daddy said that magic
doesn't exist. Just science."

"Isn't there room for both in your heart?"

"But you think with your head, not your heart!"

Santa tapped his own temple. "A smart person
knows that he should listen to all the parts of his body."

"Who brings you presents, Santa?"

What a good child, that little girl with long yellow braids tied with blue ribbons. Her name was Caroline. She was just eight.

He stroked her hair, marveling at the silky strands. "Why, you do, children. Every smile, every laugh, every thank you is a gift to me."

"That's funny," she said.

"Why do you believe in me?" he asked. "Is it because of this newspaper article?" He showed them the paper from his pocket. Caroline shook her head.

"Oh, no, I always believed in you. Daddy and Mama and Granddad and Gamma say you are real. But I know I heard you in my parlor last Christmas."

Santa remembered; the memory as vivid in his mind as in hers. "When I left you the doll with golden braids, just like yours."

"Yes!"

"So you was just pretendin' to be asleep!" Mick said.

"No, she was really asleep," Santa explained. "She was dreaming. You can hear me in your dreams. Sometimes you can see me, too." He knew that Mick had. The boy had also dreamt of those helpers that punished bad children. Mick believed, even if he didn't behave.

"Come away, sweetheart," said a slender woman in a white shirtwaist, a tiny blue jacket trimmed with maroon braids and a graceful, long blue skirt that swept the pavement. A tiny hat made of feathers was perched upon her hair. "We must get you to school."

Caroline didn't want to let go of his hand. "But, Mommy, it's Santa Claus!"

Mary, that was her name, detached Caroline's hand. "No, sweetheart, just someone dressed up as him." She looked Santa up and down. Her expression was disapproving. "Good day, sir."

"Good day," Santa said. He watched them go, feeling his heart grow heavy.

Mary thought he wasn't real. Her mind embraced something hard that was pushing her away from the belief that she had had as a child herself. Though she stopped short of telling Caroline Santa Claus wasn't real, she . . . doubted. He felt his flesh thinning on his bones. Skepticism ate away at his very body. It hurt. He put a hand to his aching ribs. He had never felt pain before. It was unpleasant.

"Don't worry," Evelyn said, slipping her hand into his. She looked up trustingly into his eyes. "I believe in you."

"Thank you, my dear," Santa said, touched.

So did her father, who tipped his hat as he came to retrieve his daughter. Peter's eyes were filled with wonder.

That abated the ache a bit more, but it didn't rebuild his flesh completely. The children drifted away, some to school, others to hang around the waterfront. They were happy he was there. They felt comfort in his presence. They did him good as well.

He lit his pipe and took a deep breath of the fragrant tobacco smoke. Life felt good. He must see more of the city, and speak to more children.

As he was turning away, an urchin on the docks who had hung back from the group ran up and kicked him in the shin.

"I hate you!" he said, fury in his filthy face. "All I wanted was a pocketknife! You didn' leave me nothin' but a dirty piece of coal. Said I been a bad boy!"

"But you had been bad last year, Donald," Santa said. His leg hurt, but it meant that the boy believed in him. "I was disappointed in you. I hope not to be, this year."

Donald was too angry to see the connection. He spat on the ground and ran away, but he glanced back to see if Santa was watching him. The adults went about their business, carrying loads and checking off lists. They were too busy on a work day to pay attention to what children cared about. But, truly, what could be more important?

Children looked at him and knew what they saw. They knew he existed. It was only when they peeked around the newel post and saw their parents placing gifts under the tree that they began to understand that he had not come to their house, that the presents had a much more prosaic origin. But he was here now. They could see him. All the things that they knew about him were true. He had reindeer and a sleigh and a workshop. He would get back to work as soon as he could, if only they didn't stop believing in him.

But a child had doubted his existence, because other children had told her he *wasn't* real. He read the newspaper column again. His heart squeezed with regret.

No. He was real! Life was joy. Life was precious. All those rooftops, his trips around the world every year high in the sky on his reindeer-drawn sleigh never engendered fear in him. He did not fear the tight confines of chimneys, though his handsome fur suit often was the worse for all the soot. But it must be true. He had never existed before. And something was trying to push him out again now that he had been made real. Science. Science denied him.

And it was all around him. Twinkling lights that were not made of fire, encased in light bubbles of glass. Everywhere he walked, he saw fascinating new inventions, wonders in themselves. Human beings defied the darkness, pushed back ignorance, spread knowledge in new ways. They had chained the lightning. Small wonder that it had pushed from them that little comfort of someone giving them simple gifts out of love. Was he no longer relevant?

Santa did not want to go away again. He could not imagine anything more wonderful than being here among people, seeing how they lived, how they felt. Cold fear made a knot in his belly. He did not recall what it was like before he had appeared on that street corner. The thought of not existing again worried him.

It was the nature of life to want to remain alive. What did he have to do to stay that way?

As he walked through the bustling city, he saw no place where he belonged. He touched upon the lives of people only once a year. Here and now he was misplaced in time.

I'm not satisfied to exist only one day, he thought.

Peddlers pulling carts glanced up and saw him. Women doing their day's shopping noticed him. Men in waistcoats, collars and ties peered his way. Most smiled, and then looked away hastily. A few stared openly. He greeted them with a cheerful wave. They saw, they hoped to believe, and they doubted.

The next time a man caught his eye and turned away with a sheepish expression, Santa hurried after him. He was panting by the time he caught up with the man at a busy corner. He took his arm. The man, in his late thirties, prosperous, with a lush mustache waxed at the ends to curl upward, clad in a fine wool coat reaching to his knees, a silk waistcoat adorned with a heavy gold chain and a top hat made of silk, shied like a horse at the sight of the little man in fur.

"Do you know who I am?" Santa asked. "You do, I can see it in you."

The words came to Alfred's lips unwillingly. "You are Santa Claus," he said.

"But you only think I look like Santa, don't you. What would it take for you to believe that I *am* Santa Claus?"

Alfred shook his arm loose. "You are nothing but a strange old man in a fur suit. You are mad. You need a doctor to help you. Good day!" He rushed off, skirting under the nose of the policeman directing traffic and a goods van loaded with clanking cans of milk.

Santa was, briefly, all of those things that the man said, but the rest of the millions of children who did believe in him dispelled the bad and left the good. Alfred did not totally disbelieve, that Santa could see in his heart, but he doubted so much that he had to deny belief completely. How very sad. The pain returned, eating the muscles in his legs. His cheeks began to feel sunken. He felt himself slipping away. He looked around for help. Few people would meet his eyes.

Doubt was his enemy. He must banish doubt, and continue to live.

One didn't have to prove an article of faith to children; one only had to let them believe. Adults needed proof. No, adults needed to believe the child within, who still knows there is a Santa Claus.

The only proof, if proof it was, that he was worthwhile lay in the palm of his hand. He read the words again, and they filled his heart with joy and hope. That reply to a simple child's query was a complex construction. It had brought him into existence for the first time.

But who had written it? His greatest ally and savior in this city of modern wonders was the man who had penned these moving words.

He returned to the kiosk on 34th Street and held out the sheet of newsprint. "Louis, how do I find the man who wrote this?"

"At the *New York Sun*," Louis said. He pointed down the long street that intersected with 34th. "That's Broadway. Take it to Chambers and look for the clock."

"Thank you, my friend."

Louis grinned. His teeth looked cleaner already. "My pleasure, Santa. He's gonna be really surprised to see you."

"I would like to meet the man who wrote this," Santa told the stout, uniformed porter at the bronze and glass door of the newspaper office.

The big man sneered down at him from his great height. "I bet you do. A lot of crazies came out of the woodwork after yesterday's editorial." He eyed Santa skeptically. "Your outfit's a lot better than most of 'em.

You can go ahead, if you want. It'll give everyone a good laugh."

He passed Santa along to a copyboy, who brought him to the city desk editor, who laughed hard enough to attract everyone within a three-desk radius. They all chuckled at Santa, but they agreed with the door porter, that it would be great fun to send him in to Mr. Church.

The doubters in the Sun office greatly outnumbered the believers. Santa could hardly push his way through the agony that ate away at him. It was only the uniformed black porter who took his arm who made it possible for him to get up the stairs to the third floor. His strength was in rags by the time he reached the female receptionist at the desk outside the editor's office in the busy newsroom. She regarded him with sympathy but no understanding. Margaret had always been that way, Santa knew. It would do him no good to tell her so.

"Mr. Church is in a meeting. You may wait." She gestured to a hard backed chair against the wall.

If he had thought the streets of New York were noisy, they were silent as a winter's night compared with the newsroom. Typewriters clattered under the fingers of men and women alike. Copyboys, many no older than ten, ran up and back with their arms laden with sheets of paper. Men shouted over the din at one another. Under his feet Santa felt the thrum of the presses, the heartbeat of the *Sun*.

At last, the door swung open. Two men in short plaid jackets emerged, shoving notebooks into their pockets. They eyed Santa speculatively as they went by. Matthew felt a wave of nostalgia, but Henry saw only an old man in a red fur coat. Santa understood. Henry covered the new scientific advances. He was on his way to meet Mr. Westinghouse. Matthew wrote about baseball, so he maintained faith and hope in a way that was almost childlike. Though, he would have died on the rack before he would admit it to a living soul. He was off to see a Giants game that day at the Polo Grounds.

"Go in," Margaret told Santa.

"Well, Mr. Claus," Frank Church said, putting out a hand to Santa. He was a tall, spare man with bushy eyebrows. "My colleagues told me you were here." He smiled, lifting the corners of his luxurious mustache a trifle. "Please, have a seat. I can give you a few moments. What may I do for you?"

"It is about your editorial," Santa said, producing the newspaper.

Mr. Church looked amused. "Yes, I assumed that was so. What about it?"

"Well, to be straightforward, it seems to have brought me into existence. Your words moved me deeply. I assume that they moved thousands of your fellow New Yorkers to belief, and for that I thank you. So many people feeling the truth of your eloquent plea has caused me to appear in their midst. I rather like it, and want to continue to *be*. I have come to ask for your help."

Frank nodded. "So you want me to believe that you are the true Santa Claus. Who sent you? Haley at the *Times*? It'd be just like him."

Santa found his skepticism to be perfectly natural. Frank was a grown man who had seen tragedy and horror in his life, yet he felt Frank's desperate hope to believe in the fairy tale that he had written about just the other day. He had grown to be an adult, yet a spark of faith and wonder remained.

"Mr. Haley did not send me. I am Santa Claus," Santa said, reassuringly. "You should know what to look for. You expressed it most beautifully in your column."

"I . . ." Frank did not know what to say. "It was for the sake of that child, you know. She ought to be allowed to remain a child as long as possible."

"I do understand that," Santa said. "But I should not have to explain to you how important it is for science and simplicity to coexist. One must not fear to be a little child again, when times of wonder are at hand."

"You are not a simple thing, Mr. Claus," Frank said. "You seem to be well-educated and a philosopher to boot, but I think I have to decline. I'm not equal to the task." Frank's defenses were growing. Santa felt logic and science teaming up to push him out of the world.

"I can prove my reality to you, but that would defeat the purpose, would it not?" He searched Frank's face. "I think that I have my answer."

The pains spread across his whole body now. His back and sides ached. His nerves were exposed, and his soul was starting to spread out again across the universe. How sad that he should not be able to enjoy this world a little longer. He fetched a breath, but it caught on the pain.

"Shall I call for the nurse?" Frank asked. He was not

a heartless man, merely mortal and conflicted, as any human being was.

"No, it will pass, as I will. I thought you could help me to live longer." Santa smiled. "I should be grateful for the day—and I am. It's a gift I never knew. When one is an ideal, one's feet never really touch the pavement, you see. I have seen electric lights, and liberty, and the joy in little children's faces. It is enough."

"There isn't a touch of irony in you, is there?" Frank said, his brow drawn into a furrow. "How I wish I could be that way."

"You have been, at times. As you were when you wrote that lovely piece. It is oblique suggestion, not proof, but I could sense your whole heart in it. You have always been that idealist. I admire that in you. That is why you chose journalism as your career. You believe in truth. You'd rather be honest than liked."

"You were briefed very thoroughly about me," Frank said. "Was it my wife told you my story? My brother?"

Santa smiled. "One of the things that I discovered today that people know about me is that I can see into their hearts. It is true. I . . . I was not going to do this, because it will spoil your natural faith, but it will quell your skepticism." He reached into his pocket and took from it a carved wooden lamb. He set it on Frank Church's desk. It was painted white and had a blue ribbon around its neck.

"You wanted this when you were very small, when you saw it in the Christ Child's crèche. Your mother told you that it was not right for you to take it. I couldn't give it to you then, but you shall have it now."

Frank's face went through a rainbow's worth of expressions, from outrage to astonishment to grief to outright wonder. He took the lamb and ran a finger on its knobbly head. "No one knew that. No one could have remembered that." He stood up. "I shall do whatever you wish, Santa. But come with me now! I shall take you to visit little Virginia. She's the one who precipitated me into writing my piece. She will be delighted beyond reason to see that she was not wrong to believe."

Santa held up a hand. "Oh, no, Frank. She's the one person that does not need to meet me. You convinced her very thoroughly indeed with your poetry. Her friends are a trifle embarrassed that they doubted, as are their parents. It's you who needed to be reassured. And me."

Church's eyes widened. "Why you? You are Santa Claus."

"I am what all of you have made me. If you cease to believe, and you just proved how easy a thing that is to do, then I do not exist. I celebrate the birth of the Christ Child. How I do that and what people expect of me differs from person to person. Some resent me. Some hate me. What you wrote will help me be in this world for a little longer. I want to exist."

"You shall," Church said, his thin face passionate. "You live forever."

"So you said in your lovely letter, sir. But these are New Yorkers. I feel as if I am fading already. No matter what we do here today, I cannot last. The shared belief that you caused is passing away. By tomorrow, I shall be a memory again, though a cherished one, I hope."

Frank looked aghast. "No! I believe in you."

Santa shook his head. It hurt a little to move. "But you doubt what you see. You cannot help it. It's a natural thing. We cast aside that which does not allow us to walk freely, to explore, to make our own decisions, right or wrong. It is . . . human. They have to be free to say there is no Santa Claus. But wonder, magic and love must always be allowed in children's lives. If you help to give them that, and you have, I will always live a little. That will satisfy me. I did not think it would, but it does, because it is what children need. It is better for me to be a dream, to live in that unseen world you spoke of."

"I will always assert the truth of your existence," Frank Church assured him. "The veil to the unseen world is torn asunder, and I see the glory I wished was there."

Santa felt the twinge of doubt that lessened the force of the statement. "Ah, no. You are already wondering if I am making a fool of you. You know the Santa you believed in would not do so. Your Santa keeps your letters, dreams and wishes to himself. But you needn't believe me completely. Keep being a cynic, so you can prevent others being fooled. The moment you don't doubt, then you stop being of use as a newsman, and I would not ruin a distinguished career such as the one you have built for yourself."

Church laughed. "I feel sad, you know. You have given me the best Christmas gift of my life, and I do not mean the lamb. I wish I could give you what you want."

Santa laid his finger beside his round little nose.

"Ah, but you have. You gave me this day. To be manifested and see what I mean to people makes me wiser than I was. But let us smoke a pipe together and talk. Tell me about this wonderful city. Then, when the time is right, I shall depart, without regrets."

Frank Church smiled. "Up the chimney?" he asked, with a nod toward the fireplace in the corner.

Santa laughed, his belly jiggling up and down with merriment. "Since that is what you wish for, it would be my pleasure."

THE DESTROYER

Kristine Kathryn Rusch

I discovered the house during one of my last crazy full moons. Nestled in the trees at the very edge of my twenty-acre territory, the house was small, white, with big windows and a large porch. In the back, a barn no longer used by cows, but still smelling of them, and to the side, a garage for a single car that seemed to be the only vehicle which used the dirt road.

I collapsed in old straw in that barn, beneath rotting eaves, and slept off wounds from my inadvertent partying. I was terrified by my own lack of control; I knew if I didn't stop fighting over females, I would end up like the old black tom that I repeatedly chased off the hill. He had only one ear, no fur on that side of his head, and a white orb in place of his eye that occasionally oozed. He could still fight—and did, every full moon—but afterwards, he never seemed to recover.

He was in that barn too. Normally, just coming off

the full-moon crazies, I would have killed him, but I was too tired. Besides, when I was myself, I rather liked him. That night, we actually talked like equals—alphas who worried about their prides. He confessed he had only seen two more summers than I had, that once he'd been as strong and powerful and terrifying as I was.

And then he said the thing which changed it all. He said, had he to do it again, he would take the Bargain.

The Bargain—offered, they say, only to what the humans call "feral" cats, not to the pampered indoor variety. Once a year, cats of a certain age—no less than two, no more than four—got to try being another creature for twenty-four hours. The easiest to become were the ones we knew: dogs, horses, cattle.

Human.

Only no feral cat chose human. Except the old black tom.

It scared him so badly, he said, that he hid in that very barn for twenty of his twenty-four hours. He felt big, and stupid, and different. Then at the moment when the gods let him choose between remaining human or reverting to feline, he reverted. And had the best six months of his life.

Until the following summer, when he lost his first fight. Then his second. And finally his third—to me—becoming instantly old, and a half-breath away from dying.

He was the one who told me about the Bargain, and he was the one who showed me the Others. He said if he had real choice, he would have become them.

Just before dawn, we snuck out of the barn and sat

by those huge glass windows, watching the gray-haired human woman inside, her slim hands preparing dishes which she then gave to the Others.

They looked so wonderful then: the silver and gold female, tail high, the epitome of female beauty; the long-haired white male, so dainty that he seemed unreal; the black-and-orange female with the asymmetric eyes, and the stunning gold male with the square leonine face, the one that the black tom said looked just like me.

I had a flashback at that moment to my kittenhood. I had seen that woman before. She had found my mother, my siblings, and me underneath an abandoned house. She had actually caught me, just before I could run to my family, and held me.

She called me a little ball of fluff. She called me cute. She called me precious. My heart pounded so hard I thought it would come out of my chest. My mother watched from behind a board, her eyes glittering, tail switching. The woman said I was too young to come with her without my mother, so she set me down and I ran for my life, my mother catching me with one strong paw and holding me down.

The woman said she would come back with help to "rescue" us.

But when she came back—if she came back—we were gone. Mother had moved us to an old-growth stump half an acre away. It was warmer and drier than that abandoned house, but much more cramped.

Mother warned us that we should never ever let the humans take us because we would disappear forever.

She said the woman had taken her other kittens in the past and she never saw them again.

One early fall evening, Mother died horribly outside that stump, when she led a pack of coyotes away from us all. We were old enough then to survive on our own—barely—and we managed. All except my sister, who died in kittenbirth not six months later.

I'd like to say the old black tom taught me that my mother was wrong about humans, but the nice man on the hilltop was already changing my mind. He put out food every morning, and the neighborhood ferals ate there. Most of us avoided the humans entirely—I don't think they ever knew they were feeding up to ten cats a day.

But I began to watch the nice man. He felt safe. Safe in a way I hadn't felt since I came to consciousness under that house. I started to understand cats who lived with humans. I heard tell of domestic cats that lived for twenty summers, that spent their final years sleeping in the warm sun instead of hiding from coyotes or bear.

That morning, with the old black tom I should have hated, watching the woman and the other cats—the pampered ones, the tom called them—I felt something I had never felt before. Envy. They had daily food, a warm bed, no predators, and no full moon wars. The Others got along, and the woman took care of them.

I went back almost every day and watched, wishing I could go inside. Then I'd go up my hilltop and see the kind man. I ate his food and slowly—ever so slowly—I let him touch me.

The windows in the kind man's house weren't as big as the woman's, but when I climbed on his car, I could see inside. He too had pampered cats who received the same kind of treatment the Others got.

The man told me I could join his family. He ran his hand along my back and spoke soothingly to me. But I had so many bruises from the fights that he would inevitably brush one and then I couldn't help myself: I'd scratch him and run away. He had to trap me to take me to that frightening place, the one that stopped the full moon fights somehow. Only I didn't know that would happen. I figured it out later.

I figured a lot out later.

After everything changed.

The changes started in the house in the woods. Another car came up the dirt road, swerving and nearly hitting the old black tom. Then I thought it the old black tom's fault. Now I think it was intentional. The old black tom and I, we hid while a big man, soft like a pampered indoor cat, walked to the door and let himself in. He brought the woman bags of rich-smelling bags of food and other things.

Lately, she hadn't been going out. And instead of walking around her kitchen to feed the Others, she grabbed onto things—the chairs, the counters, the door frame. She moved like a cat who had been in a bad fight and nearly lost.

Five days later, I found the silver-and-gold beauty cringing near the old barn. I tried to calm her, but she fled. It took me two more days and the promise of food to get her to come near me.

I tried to take her back to the house, but she wouldn't go.

He hates us, she said. He wants us all dead.

I did not believe the woman would let that happen, but the silver-and-gold beauty said the woman was dying. The beauty could smell it—the sickness, the loss. The beauty wasn't going to stay with that man.

So she stayed with me. Roaming the hillside, jumping at every noise, eating the nice man's food.

And a few more days after that, the handsome gold cat joined us, and then the white one. They had escaped through a broken basement window along with the black-and-orange cat, who was not with them. The white one led us to her, collapsed beside the road. He said we had to help her, and I said she was going to die. Her leg was crushed, the bone sticking out, and her eyes were glassy.

Again, the gold cat said we must help her, and I said the only thing we could do was make her die faster, which I didn't relish, and the gold cat said, in his superior way, that humans would know what to do.

So I said we need to take her back to the woman, and the gold cat told me—sadly—that the woman was gone. She had died quicker than the gold cat had expected. The white cat said he would not have left the house had the woman still lived, no matter how awful that man was to them.

They all had wounds, mostly healing, but the black-and-orange cat's were the worst.

The gold cat again said we had to get her help and I knew only one way to get the kind of help he wanted.

So I lifted the black-and-orange cat gently in my teeth and carried her up the hill. She passed out from the pain. The Others trailed after me, and we brought her to the nice man at the very time he was bringing out dinner.

I put her down near the food, and he took her away. He came back without her, and I thought I had made a mistake, but the gold cat told me that I had not, that humans worked together to solve problems, something I did not realize.

Humans had prides as well.

They just weren't obvious.

At first, the Others tried to live with me. But they made so many mistakes—not fleeing the predators, not understanding the full moon crazies, not sleeping in a protected place. One by one, they let the nice man catch them, and one by one, they vanished from my hilltop.

I saw them again, inside the nice man's house, but it wasn't the same. The tension, the fear, remained in their eyes. They jumped at loud noises and did not sleep soundly.

They were forever changed.

Especially the black-and-orange, who could no longer walk without a limp. I had been right; had she stayed another night, she would have died. But she had a life indoors again, pampered and protected and safe.

I wished I could live that life. But whenever the nice man tried to pick me up, I scratched him. Whenever someone else stood with him at feeding time, I fled.

I was, he said, too feral to ever be tamed. He had

waited too long, he said. I could not adapt to the pampered indoor life.

I believed him. I saw what my life had done to the Others. Just a short few weeks in the wild, and they were not the same. They didn't even sit in windows any longer, gazing out at the world with longing. Now they sat on the nice man's floor and stared upwards, protected by walls, afraid to leave.

I wished they would go to the open windows so I could tell them what I saw.

I saw that man, that horrible man, the one who had brought food, stomp the old black tom with his boots. The old black tom had died there, beneath those feet, and I could do nothing.

I had thought the old black tom would die in a full moon fight or running from coyotes. But he had died in a place he loved, for no reason at all.

Then I realized what happened to the silver-and-gold beauty, why she would not go back. How the white cat had lost some of his lovely fur, and why the gold cat wouldn't even go back to that yard. I knew how the black-and-orange cat had lost her leg.

Then the man invaded my barn. I thought, perhaps, he was looking for us, looking to injure us. But he dug a hole instead. A large one, long and rectangular.

On a breezy full-moon night before the Others were adopted by the nice man, but after the nice man had saved the black-and-orange, I tucked them into the hollow of that old-growth stump my mother had found, then came down the hillside to watch the fights and remind myself why I was happy to be free of those urges.

Instead of seeing fights, I saw the man with the woman in his arms. I was downwind, and I could smell her. She had been dead at least a day.

He put her in that hole and covered her with dirt. I could still smell her, just not as strong. If I could, coyotes and dogs could as well. She would be uncovered soon. Then he covered the dirt with rocks and I figured only the desperate would dig around them.

I stayed hidden as he walked by. I watched those boots, remembered how he had stomped the old black tom, and wondered if he would stomp me, too. I did not get close.

The horrible man stayed in the house. It was his now. He had conquered the territory, first taking out the weaker animals, and then the woman.

It was wrong. He did not take an unclaimed territory. He took it for his own, but not in a constructive way. When a young tom takes over territory, he takes responsibility for all inside it.

This man did not. He was a destroyer. He emptied the territory of all inside, like coyotes would. But unlike coyotes, he did not travel through.

He looked like he planned to stay.

And I had no choice but to let him, even though his house was in my twenty acres. He was bigger, stronger, and more violent. The kind of violent that did not care who—or what—it stomped, even if it got nothing in return.

The next night, the moon still seemed full. I sat on my hilltop and watched the animals caught in their fever, fighting and copulating and running mindlessly across my acreage. I did not miss it, but I felt strangely left out.

Midway through the night, the party moved elsewhere and I did not move with it. Instead I enjoyed the pale silver light—and the silence.

Until someone said, *Traditionally, fairy tales give you three wishes. And technically, that's what you'll have. But we only claim two wishes, because the third is the one you must reserve for that last hour.*

I started: I did not see or hear anyone approach. For a moment, I thought I was getting old like that black tom, but I was not. Because no one could have anticipated the silvery see-through creatures sitting on either side of me.

They looked like they were made of moonlight. They were not quite cats—a bit too big, a bit too sleek— but they felt like cats. Cats crossed with something else, something older, something wiser.

Are you talking to me? I asked.

No one else is around, they said. They both spoke at the same time, and somehow that did not surprise me, not until later, when I actually thought about the whole experience.

I asked, What are you talking about when you say wishes?

And then I knew: they were talking about the Bargain.

My heart started to race, but I did not move. I had learned in all of my fighting not to let the opponent know exactly how you feel.

You have twenty-four hours to try a new form, they said. *You may choose that form—lion, dog, human, whatever you want. And you may have one other wish to ease that transition, whatever that wish may be.*

That's two wishes, I said. You mentioned three.

The third will either turn you back into yourself, or it will guarantee you remain in the new form. We will not let you waste that wish. We reserve it until the last minute of the twenty-fourth hour. We will appear to you then. Will you make the Bargain?

Why is it a Bargain? I asked. What do you get from it?

For the first time—the only time that night—they looked at each other. Then the one on my left said, *We get entertainment*, as the one on my right said, *We get enjoyment*.

I did not want to know more. But I knew what I wanted. I wanted to control the hilltop. I didn't want anyone to take even a corner of it from me.

I want to be human, I said.

That is the hardest wish, they said. *Make sure your second wish helps you.*

I did not know exactly what they meant, but I remembered what the old black tom said. He said he had become human, he had felt weak and stupid. Others would ask for strength. I did not.

I want human smarts, I said. I do not want them to know I'm a stranger to their culture. I want to understand it all the moment I arrive.

The cat creatures twitched their tails and tilted their heads. Then they nodded like humans.

You have twenty-four hours. In the last minute of the last hour, we will find you.

And they vanished, taking the pretty silver light with them.

As well as all of the smells and most of the sounds. The hilltop grew dimmer and I was cold.

I looked at myself. I was naked, with pale skin, long legs and long arms. Ginger hair feathered my body, not heavy enough to protect me. Next to me, a shirt, pants, undergarments, and shoes. Those, I knew, were a product of my second wish, just like my ability to put them on.

I did not like the shoes. I needed to feel the ground beneath my feet.

I sat for at least an hour to get my bearings. I had two perceptions: My feline thoughts, which felt more comfortable, and the human understandings overlaying them. I knew then that my vague plan to conquer the hilltop would take more effort than I thought.

To conquer the hilltop as a human would take more than one night. I would need to build an identity, find a way to earn money, find a way to buy a home— here—on the hill. It would take time, years perhaps, and even though I knew humans lived longer, I was not sure I would.

I almost wished I had not asked for understanding. Then I remembered the old black tom and how he had hid during his human time because of the ways the change made him feel. I remembered how I liked him, and the crunch of his bones beneath that man's boot.

I could not conquer the hillside as a human, but I could remove the destroyer from it.

I stood, stretched, and felt bigger than I ever had in my life. The old black tom had been right; there was a vulnerability to this body despite its size. Its fingers had thin nails, not claws. Its teeth were even, strong, but not sharp. I flexed the fingers, watched the muscles, realized I had only a few advantages, and the greatest of these was size.

Down the hill I went, to the trees and the house. It was harder to walk my usual route—there were tree branches and bushes blocking my way. I couldn't go under them. I had to go around.

Finally, I went to that dirt road, and trudged to the house.

With my new knowledge, I could find a phone and call the police. I could tell them about the body in the barn. Even if they accepted my testimony, even if they arrested that man, they would have to prove he had killed her, and that might be difficult. Then they would lock him up in a room and feed him three times per day, turning him into a pampered cat, although—I suspected—he would be more like the Others, never quite able to accept his good fortune.

I did not want him to have good fortune. Human solutions did not seem like solutions to me. I knew the customs. I knew how to use them. But deep down, I did not understand them.

Perhaps I should have asked for understanding, not smarts. But I had asked for what I had asked for, and unlike the old black tom, I would not waste this opportunity.

I would use it to secure my hill.

The house was dark. The destroyer slept later than the woman ever had. I knew he was there, though. His hated car sat in the driveway, its engine still warm.

I did not try the front door. Doors were for humans. I found the broken window in the basement, the one the Others had escaped through. I slid inside, the glass cutting at my clothing. I had to ease my shoulders through one at a time and twist my torso. Humans were not very flexible.

I could not jump to the floor. I had to slide toward it, breaking my fall with my hands. I tumbled, winced at the pain, and stopped flat on the concrete floor.

Dust rose around me and made me want to sneeze. I couldn't see well, as if I was already old and going blind. Humans couldn't smell things, couldn't see things, couldn't hear things. It was a wonder they survived at all.

A real human in this basement would grab a tool or bring one. He would climb the steps and use that tool to attack the destroyer.

But I did not know how to use tools. And I had the benefit of surprise.

I crept up the wooden stairs on all fours, not because I had to, but because it felt more comfortable. I stopped and listened a lot, worried that my weakened powers would make me vulnerable.

But all I heard as I reached the top was a faint snoring not too far away. I stood, walked quietly, although not as quietly as I wanted. Bare human feet slapped against a surface. They didn't pad the way a cat could. Everything about this body was big and loud and uncomfortable.

I thought I would like the size. I thought it would give me a feeling of power. It did not.

The kitchen stank of rotted food. The place was

filthy, papers scattered everywhere. I looked at them, realized I had acquired another skill. I could read. I saw a woman's name on an account ledger, money deposited after she had died, automatic payments coming out, keeping the lights on and food in the refrigerator.

No one would come here. No one would know.

This place was too remote for other humans. Apparently she had liked that, with her animals and the silence. He, somehow, had taken advantage of it.

Then a voice: Who the hell are you?

I turned, and saw him, my heart pounding. I had lost my advantage—he knew I was there. By rights, he should have sprung, attacked me before I attacked him.

But he had not.

He did not look the same. He wore a robe over boxer shorts, and he was barefoot. The boots were nowhere to be seen.

Oddly—or not so oddly—he was smaller than I was. Shorter, not nearly as powerful as he had seemed from the ground. He gave off a faint stench I recognized.

He was afraid.

My advantage had come back. I had learned in those full moon fights how to use someone else's fear. You did not give them time to overcome it.

I gave him no time at all.

I launched myself at him. I did not fight him like a human. I fought him like a cat, with clawed hands and sharp teeth, going for the vulnerable spots, the soft underbelly, the throat.

He tried to push me away. He could not. He had no defense against frenzy, and I did not give him one.

I destroyed him, the way he destroyed the old black tom, the way he had tried to destroy the black-and-orange, the way he had destroyed the woman who had lived in this house.

I destroyed him, and when I was done, I studied him for a moment.

I could, I suppose, have called humans to help me with him or what remained of him. They would come, clean the house, take him away, find the woman, and know some of what had happened.

But this house was remote, isolated. It had checks coming in and bills being paid. And he had an identity, one he was leaving behind.

I could clean this place. I could stay here. And I could bring in Others. I knew where they lived, how to tame the feral ones, how to make the lost pampered cats safe. I would leave the broken window alone for those who did not like being confined, and I could find food. Eventually, I could learn enough to survive, only not as a destroyer.

Cats buried excrement all the time. They buried excrement to hide traces of where they were, what they had been. He was excrement. I could put him deep in the ground, so no one would scent him.

No one would look. I would make certain of that.

I continued to study him—or what was left of him. I could carry him, and dig a hole for him. I could clean the walls, and figure out how to live here.

Or I could claim it as part of my territory after the humans had cleaned it out. It would take them a long

time to settle the accounts, to figure out what had happened to the woman, to find out who he was.

Besides, I did not like to be confined.

I picked up the phone and dialed 911, but said nothing, leaving the phone off the hook. I knew that would
work, because I knew human details, although I did
not understand them.

Someone would arrive, take the body away, and remove the smell of death. They might board up the window, but they wouldn't close all of the crawl spaces. I
would find a way in, or my pride would as I continued
to form it. We would eat the food of the nice man and
we would sleep out of the rain and we would be safe,
or as safe as we could be, here at the edge of my territory, in my world.

At the last minute of the twenty-fourth hour, when
the catlike creatures came for me, I exercised my last
wish. I returned to my old life.

And I did not regret it.

I am old now, older than the old black tom had ever
dreamed of being. I am careful about how I make my
way to the top of the hill. I know some young tom will
try to take my turf from me, and I don't care as much
as I thought I would. I would cede most of it to him, if
he asked, so long as he left me the house.

The humans call it the death house. The nice man
who still feeds me cautions me to stay away from it,
saying no one knows what happened there. I do not
tell him I live there now, with other ferals and the occasional refugee for whom I must find a home.

My original Others look healthy and younger every
year. They have now moved to the windows, and their

eyes have less fear. I have not told them what I did. I do not know how.

But on late summer afternoons, I imagine doing so as I doze in my safe place. I imagine telling the old black tom about my choices during my Bargain.

I like to think he knows what I did.

But he probably does not.

His life ended on that overgrown driveway. Mine will end in the woods nearby. When the time comes, I will leave my house, my territory, and die the way my kind does. Alone, so that no one follows the stench of death.

I like our ways. I understand them.

And while I remember all that I have learned about the humans, I still do not know what it all means.

I'm not sure I want to.

I am simply glad there are the nice ones to balance out the destroyers.

I no longer wish I could be different. I like my life. I like the choices I have made. And I like sleeping here, on my porch, in the hot, hot sun.

INTO THE *N*TH DIMENSION

David D. Levine

The fence around Dr. Diabolus's lair is twenty feet tall, electrified and topped with razor wire. I'd expected no less. From one of the many pouches at my belt I pull a pair of acorns and toss them at the base of the fence.

I exert my special power. Each acorn immediately sprouts, roots digging through asphalt as the leafy stem reaches skyward. Wood fibers *KRACKLE* as the stems extend, lengthen, thicken, green skin changing to grayish bark in a moment. Leaves *SSHHH* into existence; branches reach out to the neighbor tree, twining themselves into rungs.

Before the twin oaks have reached their full height I spring into action, clambering up the living ladder as it grows, creeping along a limb even as it extends over the razor wire. It's a dramatic, foolhardy move, but I can't delay—Sprout is in peril! The branch sags under my weight, lowering me to within 10 feet of the ground, and I leap down with practiced ease.

Again I concentrate, and the two trees wither away behind me, a gnawed patch of asphalt and a few stray leaves the only sign they'd ever existed. I feel their pain as they wilt and die, but I don't want my intrusion discovered sooner than necessary. The loss of their green and growing lives is just the latest of the many sacrifices I've made. I press onward.

Slippery elm makes short work of the side door lock; mushrooms blind security cameras and heat sensors. These bright corridors, humming with electricity and weirder energies, are cold places of steel and concrete, offering me no plants or plant matter to leverage my powers. I've faced worse. I prowl quickly, silently, keeping my head down, all senses alert to any trace of the kidnapped Sprout.

Voices! I duck into an alcove as two of Dr. Diabolus's goons round the corner. As soon as they've passed I spring out behind them, tossing seeds at their feet. Fast-twining English ivy ensnares one before he can cry out, but the other evades its tendrils. "Phyto-Man!" he gasps.

POW! my fist responds. He drops cold beside his still-struggling comrade, whose eyes glare with hatred above his smothered mouth. I direct the ivy to bind the unconscious goon as well, so he'll raise no alarm when he awakes.

Even their underwear is synthetic fiber. Dr. Diabolus is thorough, I'll grant him that.

Deeper and deeper into the cavernous lair I probe, keeping an eye on the pipes and conduits that line the ceiling, smaller leading to larger, following the branch to find the trunk. I know Dr. Diabolus; wherever he's holding my sidekick it will be near his latest contrivance, and all his inventions require massive amounts of power.

If only he'd gone solar instead of stealing plutonium, we might have been allies.

At last I come to a massive, vault-like door, all steel and chrome, set in a concrete wall into which many thick conduits vanish. But nothing is more persistent than a plant. I tuck dozens of tiny dandelion seeds into the crack between door and jamb. Their indomitable roots reach deep, swelling and prying, until with a *WHANGG* of tearing metal the door bursts from its frame.

With my own muscles I wrench the shattered door aside and burst into the chamber. Dr. Diabolus turns to me, cape swirling. "You disappoint me, Phyto-Man," he sneers, his artificial eye glowing red. "I expected you here half an hour ago."

"Traffic was terrible," I quip. The chamber is dominated by a complex machine, seething with arcane energies that make my head swim, but there's no sign of Sprout. "What have you done with my sidekick, you fiend?"

"I sent him to . . . the *N*th Dimension!" He pulls a lever on the control panel before him. A ten-foot iris of blue steel in the center of the machine *SNICK*s open, revealing. . . .

Looking into the opening makes my eyes feel like they're being pulled out of my head. It's as though all the colors of the palette have somehow been smeared together with . . . others . . . forming impossible combinations of hue and tone that swirl sickeningly. But worse than that, the weird amalgam of color seems to *bend* . . . around a corner that isn't there. It's painful to see, even harder to look away.

CHANGG! Something hard and cold fastens onto my bicep, breaking the spell. "What?" I cry. Before I can move, a second steel claw *CHANGGs* onto my other arm. *CHANGG! CHANGG! CHANGG!* I'm caught like a fly, steel bracelets ringing my arms, legs, and neck. Jointed metal arms haul me off the floor, suspend me in the air before the gloating Dr. Diabolus.

"*HAHAHAHAHA!*" he laughs as I struggle in vain. "You've foiled my plans for the last time, Phyto-Man!"

"If you've harmed Sprout—!" I growl through clenched teeth, straining against the imprisoning metal.

"My dear Phyto-Man, I must confess . . . *I don't know!*" He works the controls and the arms propel me, none too gently, toward the yawning portal. The uncanny colors swirl crazily, filling my vision, seeming to tug at every fiber of my being. "But whatever has become of your Sprout, you will shortly be joining him there. *Bon voyage*, Emerald Avenger!"

The arms thrust me forward. With a *SPRANK!* the five claws open simultaneously, flinging me into the swirling abyss.

A hard, gritty surface presses against my side. I'm cold, my head is spinning, and everything hurts. There's a thin, rushing sound off in the distance. Traffic?

I sit up and open my eyes. And immediately I wish I hadn't.

There's nothing to see but a cracked and filthy concrete floor and my own hands, but they're all wrong . . .
seriously wrong. The floor curves *away* from me in
every direction—the same impossible curvature I'd
seen in Dr. Diabolus's portal—despite the fact that it
looks and feels flat. And the surface looks like . . . like
concrete multiplied by itself. Cracks are crackier. Grit
is grittier. It's all realer than real; it pounds on my eyes
as though I were staring into the sun, though there's
barely any light. And the color is not just gray, but a
weird amalgam of thousands of different grays
blended smoothly together. A whole shining rainbow
of grays.

My heart is pounding. I've faced death many times,
fought monsters, escaped from traps, but I've never experienced anything this disturbing. Always before the
threat came from outside, but now it's me—my own
perceptions—that have changed.

My hands, too, are a disconcerting, amplified version of themselves. I turn them before my eyes, and as
they rotate I seem to see both sides at the same time as
the front. In color they are . . . kind of an ultra-pink, not
the plain pink I've seen every day of my life but an eye-
hurting blend of unnatural shades. Pinks that don't
exist, have never existed. And as I look more closely I
see disturbing swirls of texture in my skin, spiraling
like microscopic galaxies, like nothing I've ever seen
before.

I swallow and rip my attention away from my own
fingers. Have I been drugged? I shake my head hard,
but that just makes the headache and dizziness worse.
I pound my fists on the ground, but though I feel the

impact and the pain there's no comforting *THUD*, just a muffled thump so faint and distant I might as well be imagining it.

"Hello?" I call. No, nothing wrong with my hearing; my voice bounces back to me from the darkness, echoing off the distant, unseen walls.

To my surprise there's an immediate reply. "Michael?" The voice is heartbreakingly familiar. I feel a twinge of hope.

"Sprout?" I peer into the darkness, hoping for a glimpse of green tights and pointed shoes. It's a ridiculous outfit. Why have we never changed it?

And why have I never wondered that before?

"It's me, Michael. Richard."

A familiar figure appears in the dim distance, but with everything so strange here I can't afford to relax. "Is this a secure area? We should stick to code names . . ."

"No need. There's no Sprout here, and no Phyto-Man either."

Worries spring up in my mind—impostors, hypnosis, possession, brainwashing—but I decide to bluff it out in case there are unseen observers. "Well, I'm here now, Sprout."

"This all seems very strange, I know, but don't worry. Everything will be all right."

Despite his reassurances, there's a strangeness about Sprout as he approaches. He's wearing street clothes, in colors and textures as hallucinogenic as everything else here, and his face combines familiarity with an alien super-reality exactly as my own hands do, but the really disturbing thing is the way he moves. Each step flows into the next with a weird gliding motion that propels him forward seamlessly, without transitions. It's like he's rolling toward me on a treadmill, constantly cresting a hill that isn't there. I push down feelings of nausea and . . . and fear. Never in all my adventures have I faced anything as disquieting as this place. "Where am I?"

"Dr. Diabolus called it the Nth Dimension, but the people here just call it the world." He's reached me now, and the mingled concern and relief in his face match the conflicting emotions in my own heart. "I'm so glad you're finally here."

He bends down and helps me to my feet, a disturbing reversal, and I find that I move with the same unnatural glide that he does. Even more disturbing, I find I'm naked. "My costume!" I cover myself with my hands as best I can, but the loss of my belt pouches, my carefully nurtured collection of seeds, leaves me feeling not just nude but defenseless.

I reach out with my powers. Perhaps a seed from a discarded Fig Newton lies in a crack on the floor, a seed I can grow into leaves to cover my nakedness. But there's nothing; my powers are dulled almost to nonexistence. I can feel wood beams supporting the ceiling high above, but I can't warp them to my will.

I'm helpless. For the first time in . . . I can't remember when.

"Don't worry," Sprout says, "no one here wears costumes. I brought you some clothes." He turns, the motion revealing sides and back, width and depth and thickness, all at once. I groan and nearly lose my balance. "Oh!" he says. "I'm sorry. Try closing one eye. It helps."

I do, and it does—the colors are still wrong but the disorienting sense of everything being too far away and too close at the same time is greatly reduced. Sprout—Richard—reaches into a rustling paper bag and hands me a folded bundle.

Putting the clothes on is a challenge. Each trouser leg recedes like a portal to another world; buttons and zippers feel much larger, more detailed than they should. I close my eyes completely and let my instincts take over. It makes a big difference. How many times in my life have I dressed myself? But this still feels like the first time.

I sit on the filthy floor to tie the unfamiliar shoes. "That's better," I say. "Now let's get to work." Maybe action will still the trembling dread in my heart. "There's no time to lose—we need to get back to our own dimension and defeat Dr. Diabolus before it's too late!"

Richard smiles and shakes his head. I'm starting to get used to the weird multi-dimensional effect. "Don't worry, there's plenty of time." He puts out a hand. "Come on. I'll explain over coffee."

Sprout's lack of concern raises anew the questions I'd had about drugs, hypnosis, imposters. But lost in a strange, incomprehensible world, I have no better alternative to offer. I take his hand.

His hand is warm and soft in mine. When was the last time I'd grasped it without gloves, without haste, without danger all around?

He leads me across the floor—now that my eyes have adapted a bit to the darkness and strangeness I see that the space is a cavernous, disused warehouse—to a corroded metal door. It opens with a muted squeak of rusty hinges, not the *SKREEK* I would have expected, but once we pass through it to the street I'm assaulted by a cacophony of sounds, visions, and smells more intense than New Year's Eve in Metro City. Cars in an astonishing variety of designs and colors careen by, with the same seamless motion as Sprout's walk but a hundred times faster. Each one seems to zoom in from the horizon and vanish away to infinity all in a moment, but even as they speed by I can't help but notice their scratches and dents and chips in the paint and a hundred other details. It's a dizzying kaleidoscope of color and detail.

"Whoa!" I cry out as Sprout hauls me back from the curb.

"Careful, big guy." He pats my shoulder. "You're not invulnerable here."

"Well, I've never been in Dynamic Man's league . . ."

"No, I mean you can *really* get hurt easily. It doesn't take much, and it takes a *long* time to heal. Look at this." He pulls up his sleeve, revealing a hideous scab on his elbow. "I scraped this on a brick wall when I first got here. Just a little scrape, nothing I'd even have noticed if I were in a fistfight with the Demolisher, but it hurt like a son of a bitch—"

I've never heard such language. "Sprout!"

"—and a month later it's still not all the way better."

A *month*? Immediately I'm on high alert again. Has the imposter slipped up? Sprout only disappeared the day before yesterday.

But he notices the change in my expression—faces

here seem more subtle, more expressive—and puts up a hand. "Sorry. We're on a monthly schedule. One or two of our days, more or less, is a month here. I should have told you right away." His eyes dip to the sidewalk. "There's a lot I should have told you, before."

My suspicions are only slightly allayed, but I still have little alternative but to stick with this person, whether or not he's the Sprout I know. Whoever he is, he just saved my life.

We walk to a coffee shop. Safe from the chaos of the street, I can begin to appreciate the wonder of this world—the colors and textures, the tears in the vinyl seat's upholstery, the individual grains of spilled sugar on the laminate tabletop. My spoon makes a tiny *tink-tink* noise as I stir my coffee. The flavor is astonishing—rich and sweet and dark. "So you've been here a whole month?"

He nods. "I showed up in the same place you did. It's the closest analog in this world to Dr. Diabolus's lair. It took me quite a while to figure this place out, but I finally did."

"You always were the brains of this partnership." Before Sprout, there had been no Phyto-Computer, no chemical lab, and no advanced cross-breeding program in the Hidden Greenhouse. I'd really been little more than a thug with a green thumb.

"This world . . . it's like a layer above our world. Everything here is . . . bigger. More complex. More detailed. Even the color spectrum . . . there's an *infinity* of different colors here, Michael."

I think back on the time I fell into the Hollow Earth,

and how I had to help the downtrodden people there throw off the tyrannical overlord Karg before I could return to the surface. "Then they must have even bigger problems than we do. More villainous villains! More despotic despots! More disastrous natural disasters!" I find myself grinning with anticipation. "This could be our greatest adventure!"

"You might think so, but I haven't seen any sign of it. There *aren't* any villains here."

"It's some kind of Utopia, then?"

"Not really." His face squinches up the way it does when he's thinking hard. "There are people who do bad things. But every time someone does something that seems entirely villainous to me, a whole bunch of other people come along and say it was really the right thing to do. I'm kind of confused, really." He shakes his head. "Even bank robbers have their defenders here. And there are tornadoes and hurricanes and earthquakes, but they're . . . diffuse. I mean, yeah, people get hurt, but you never see the President's daughter trapped under a collapsed building or someone racing to get the secret plans to the hidden base before the whole Eastern seaboard becomes uninhabitable."

"Sounds . . . boring."

"Oh, it's not!" His eyes brighten and he grabs my hands across the table. "It's the most wonderful place, Michael. There's art and culture and nature like nothing you've ever seen. Not just stuffy charity balls where the only exciting thing is when The Rutabaga tries to steal the debutante's diamond necklace. I can't wait to show you *Turandot*."

I pull my hands from his. "Whoa, whoa, *whoa*, kiddo. We're not here to be tourists. We're here for a reason. And once our job is done here, we'll go back where we came from. That's the way the world works."

"Not this world. In this world you can do whatever you want, make the best of what you've got, succeed or fail or just muddle along. You're not limited to playing the role you were born into, fighting the same villains and foiling the same plots over and over again. Not like our world." He reaches into his hoodie's front pocket, pulls out a slim colorful magazine. "To the people here, we're *fictional*."

The title of the magazine is *The Amazing Phyto-Man*, issue 157. On the cover, a hulking over-muscled brute with a ridiculous green outfit and a caricature of my own face smacks a tentacled monstrosity in the beak. The pages inside are divided into squares and rectangles, each bearing a picture and some text.

It shows the whole story of how I got here. Over the fence, down the corridors, the confrontation with Dr. Diabolus, the metal arms flinging me into the portal.

I feel as though the world has been jerked out from under my feet. "This is impossible. Absurd. Some kind of hoax."

"It's no hoax. There were ten copies of this one on the rack I bought it from. All our friends have their own publications too." He taps the final panel, showing me screaming as I fall into the swirling colors . . . but the colors on the page are the flat, limited palette of the world I came from. "This is how I knew you'd be arriving here."

I stare at the page. It's wood pulp with vegetable inks. My powers are weak here, almost nonexistent, but I can feel the minuscule thread of green life in it. In some ways this stupid little magazine is the only thing in the whole chromium-and-vinyl coffee shop that's *real*.

The only thing that's real. . . .

I turn back a page. It's one large panel, with Dr. Diabolus laughing *"HAHAHAHAHA!"* as I struggle in the grip of the metal arms. I stare at his flat, cartoonish face.

I exert my power.

It's not easy. What I'm trying to do is unlike anything I've ever done before. My teeth grind together; my pulse pounds in my temples.

This is as hard and as strange as the very first time I ever made a seed sprout.

It had been an apple seed, a discarded pip from my lunch, that happened to be lying on the floor the day that eerie green-glowing meteorite had crashed into the experimental greenhouse with its stocks of Growth Serum X. That tiny seed, and the potential apple tree within, had been all that stood between me and certain death as the heavy beam had come crashing down toward me. As though in a dream I'd sensed its potential, I'd reached out, I'd *pulled* harder than I'd ever pulled on anything before . . . and the tree burst into being, root and branch and leaf cushioning the beam's fall and saving my life.

That had been the first time I'd felt that green power flowing through me. Now I feel it again, a thin green thread of life pulsing in the dead, flattened wood pulp before me. But this time it's different somehow, pulling at me even as I pull at it.

Sweat stings my eyes and runs down my nose. I keep straining . . .

And then Dr. Diabolus blinks.

The caricature face turns fractionally toward me, its look of triumph beginning to change into one of astonishment . . .

It's more than I can sustain. I collapse, my breath rushing out in a whoosh as I fall back into the padded seat. The page before me reverts to its previous form, but I feel a sense of triumph.

Sprout snatches the magazine away. "What did you *do*?"

"I used my powers. I touched our world. I made a *change*."

"So what?"

"We can *use* this!" I pound the table. "I don't know how, but somehow we can use this magazine to get back to our own world!"

"Hush!" Sprout pats the air with his hands; I notice that the server and the other patrons are staring. I sit down, noticing as I do that I'd surged to my feet. "Michael . . . I don't *want* to go back to the world we came from."

"We *have* to!"

He looks at me for a long moment, his expression unreadable.

And then he bolts from the table.

I stare stupidly at the door as the little bell over it tinkles, then take off after him.

Sprout's fast, but ever since that day in the experimental greenhouse I've been stronger and tougher and faster than most people, and at least some of that seems to have come through the portal with me. I manage to make it through the door before his heels vanish around the corner.

Running in this world is a kaleidoscopic, hallucinogenic experience. Walls seem to rush at me, a riot of color and texture; cars veer and swerve, horns blaring. But I keep my eyes fixed on Sprout's blue hoodie as he dashes across streets, pushes through crowds of protesting civilians, runs down alleys.

Block after block, I'm gaining. Sprout was always the smart one in our partnership, but I'm the one who battled The Piledriver to a standstill. Soon, I'm only a few feet behind.

We're racing down an alley, dodging around dumpsters and piles of newspaper, when I get almost close enough to touch him. He looks over his shoulder . . . and trips on a bundle of magazines. He tumbles on the concrete with an "oomph" that sounds almost like something from our original world.

I catch up to him just as he's sitting up. Bright red blood runs from his nose; there's a rusty smell. "Guh?" he says.

I bend down, put an arm around his shoulder. "Are you all right, old buddy?"

He stares into my eyes for a moment, blood painting his nose and mouth.

And then he kisses me.

I taste blood. I feel his warm lips soft under mine.

I kiss him back.

Then, horrified, I push him away. "What are we *doing*, Sprout?"

"Kissing. And you liked it as much as I did." His bloody lips twist into an ironic smile. "If you couldn't figure that much out, I guess I really am the brains of this partnership."

"But . . . but you're just a kid!"

He glares at me. "I'm twenty-two, Michael."

Twenty-two? It's strange to realize that he's right. He was fifteen when I adopted him after Maniac killed his parents, but that was . . . seven years ago. Where did the time go? How had I failed to notice he'd grown into a lithe, attractive young man? "Even so . . . it's . . . it's *wrong*."

"Maybe where we came from. Not here." He pulls a bandana from his pocket, wipes his mouth. Blood still trickles from his nose but it's slowing. "This world is better than ours, Michael. It's complex and it's mundane and it's sometimes tedious, but it's not just the same round of villains and fights and secret identities over and over again. It's *real*, Michael. And here I can be what I've always wanted to be, instead of just playing a role." He holds out the bandana. "And so can you."

Sprout keeps holding out the bandana.

After a while I take it, and wipe my own mouth.

Then I stand up.

"I'm a hero, Richard. It may be a role, but it's the only role I know."

Sprout just looks at me. The expression on his blood-spattered face is a sick compound of longing, sadness, and disappointment. Perhaps I'm learning how to understand what I see in this world.

I wonder what the expression on my own face tells him.

"Give me the magazine, Sprout. We'll take it to the warehouse where we came in. I figure that's the best place to try going back to our world."

"No."

Sprout lies at my feet, looking so small and weak, the front of his blue hoodie stained black with his blood. I could take the magazine from him easily. "I'll find another copy."

"You don't have any money to buy one."

"I'll steal it."

He gives a weak little laugh. "Liar."

I have to smile myself. "Okay, maybe not." I sit back down. "Come back with me, Sprout. You know it's where we belong."

He sits up, leans against me. His shoulder is warm, the only warm thing in this cold, garbage-strewn alley, and I let it rest on my chest. "Give this world a chance, Michael. You've only just arrived. I've already found a job at a nursery. You could work there, too." He looks up at me. His nose has stopped bleeding. "We could share the apartment."

I consider the idea. I put my arm around my sidekick, lean back against the filthy brick wall, and think very hard about it. This world is amazing, with its details and colors and motions and flavors. And to share it with Sprout would be . . . something I hadn't even realized I desired.

But in the end, it's duty that wins out. "I'm sorry,

Sprout. Even if I wanted to—and there's a part of me that does, believe me—it's more than just you and me. There are people depending on us back home. If we don't go back there, who'll keep the Scimitar Sisters in check?" I give him one last squeeze, disentangle myself, and stand up. "Coming?"

"You're sure I can't change your mind?"

I'm so, so tempted. "I'm sure."

"Then I'm coming too." He stands, brushes himself off. "I'd rather be a cartoon hero with you than alone here."

We walk hand-in-hand back to the warehouse. As we pass the coffee shop, I pause. Sprout looks up at me, expectant. "I, uh . . . I still have some of my powers here." I clear my throat. "I wonder if there's. . . .if there's any way we can bring . . . some of this world, back to ours?"

"I don't think so." He points to a small shield printed in the corner of the magazine's cover. "There are rules against it."

Finally, we find ourselves again in the dark, echoey space where we entered this world. I think about how strange it looked to me when I first arrived, and I realize I've grown used to these new perceptions. My old world will seem so flat and colorless by comparison.

Sprout stands beside me as I spread the magazine out in a patch of sunlight. There is no joy in me as I contemplate the garish images full of POW and KRUNCH, only a dull sense of obligation. "It's not too late to change your mind," Sprout says. "We can make a life together here."

"I'm sorry, Sprout. Our world needs saving." But

even as I say it, I know I'm trying to convince myself as well as him. I hold out my hand.

Without a word, he takes it.

I bend down and stare hard at the last page, showing my cartoon avatar falling into the vortex between worlds. I exert my will, block out all other sensations, focus my powers on the ink-saturated wood pulp. Somehow, I know, I can use this image of the portal to return myself and Sprout to the world where we were born.

It's the hardest thing I've ever done.

I concentrate. I work my power. I push and pull and strain . . . this is as hard as the time I used pea vines to temporarily close up the Grand Canyon. Harder.

I strain still more intensely. The printed vortex begins to whirl.

I feel again, just as I did on that first day in the experimental greenhouse, the deep connection between my soul and the green life underlying the page . . .

I feel the warmth of Sprout's hand in mine.

And I realize that the connection runs both ways.

With an unprecedented effort of will, I reverse my power.

Where before the meteor's green energy had flowed into me at my moment of greatest need, now I send the energy flowing from myself into the printed page.

I scream in pain as the power drains from me like my life's blood.

The image before me springs to life. Just as the metal claws release, the cartoon me on the page reaches down and tears open his belt. Seeds of all descriptions

pour out in their thousands, most falling into the vortex, but many others sprouting and twining and filling
the portal with leaves and stems and branches. I
bounce off the web of vegetable matter, springing right
back toward Dr. Diabolus. WHAM! My fist connects
with the villain's chin.

Then all is blackness.

Later. I open my eyes, and the first thing I see is Dr.
Diabolus's lab. Everything is flat, static, in eight garish
colors. But then I blink, and realize I've fallen face-first
into the magazine spread on the floor before me.

I sit up. I'm no longer looking at the last page of The
Amazing Phyto-Man issue 157. It's now the first page
of issue 158, a single large panel. In it Dr. Diabolus,
threatened by an enormous Venus flytrap, cowers at
the controls of his dimensional portal, through which a
grinning Sprout steps to take the hand of Phyto-Man.
All's well in Metro City.

"Michael?" Richard is just awakening beside me.
"Wha . . . what just happened?"

It takes me a long, reflective moment to find an answer to his question. "I . . . I sent the power back where
it came from, I think." I look within myself. It certainly
isn't in there anymore. "It's with him now." I tap the
page.

Richard's eyes dart from the page to my face. "But
that's you."

"Not any more. I'm just Michael now." I stroke the
flat, cartoon version of myself with my fingertips.
"Phyto-Man is back where he belongs. I don't know

how much of me went with him, but I hope . . . I hope he enjoyed his day in this world. Maybe he can use what I learned here to make Metro City a better place."

"But what about us? What happens next?"

I close the magazine. "I don't know. Isn't it amazing?"

EPILOGUE

Jim C. Hincs

According to Claire's phone, it had been three days and forty-seven minutes since the cave-in.

In the first few hours, as the ringing in her ears began to die and the dust settled, she had explored every inch of the thirty-foot stretch of tunnel, from the useless elevator shaft to the impassible wall of fallen rock.

Her head pounded, every beat a pickaxe against the inside of her skull. Her mouth was dusty and dry like old rags, and her lips were cracked. For three days, she had drunk nothing but her own urine, her only food an old apple-cinnamon granola bar she had brought down with her.

Dust in the air scattered the light from her helmet lamp, painting a static-like blur over the rubble where the ceiling had collapsed behind her. Broken, flat-surfaced slabs of stone that must weigh at least a ton apiece protruded from the debris, along with splintered timbers and a twisted electrical conduit.

Rock crunched under her boots as she moved closer, searching the dust for eddies that might indicate airflow. She knew it was pointless. She would be wiser to sit and rest, to conserve her energy. But she could only sit for so long before the despair crushed her as inexorably as another cave-in.

"Anthony! Tim!" Her shouts sounded faint to her ears, still half-deaf. After three days, her team had long since escaped . . . assuming they had been far enough back when the mine shaft collapsed. "Nicole, Ann? Anyone?"

She prayed they had escaped. That they were even now on the surface, telling the officials of White Lion Energy that Claire Howell might still be alive, and planning her rescue . . . a rescue which would still be days in coming, at best.

It had taken a day and a half to send Claire's team in after the first methane explosion trapped sixteen people in the coal mine. With a second cave-in so soon after the first, they would be even more cautious.

She moved to the far end of the tunnel. A yellow sign on the metal gate proclaimed this elevator shaft six. The gate had crinkled like cardboard during the cave-in.

Her lamp might as well have been a nightlight for all the good it did. According to the readings she had taken at least a dozen times, there was no hope of escape here. The shaft went down only 318 feet before hitting an obstruction. It should have gone far deeper, meaning either the elevator car was jammed or else the shaft itself had collapsed.

"Hello?" Her words bounced back from the shaft, weak and distant. "This is Claire Howell. Can anyone hear me?"

Nothing. Just like the last hundred times she had tried. She backed away from the elevator and sat against the wall. She tried her radio again, to no avail. She checked her phone next, knowing there would be no reception. "Too bad." she muttered. That would have made a great commercial. "More bars, even a half mile underground."

She tapped the phone's screen, smearing dust over the glass as she pulled up her e-mail. The battery was at 68 percent. Plenty of power to write her goodbyes. If she was ever found, and if the phone was plugged back in, it should automatically send her messages.

Her hands shook, and she closed the app with a violent swipe of her finger. They would find her. She just had to wait. Had to stay sane long enough for them to dig her out.

If they could even reach her.

If they were willing to risk another team for the sake of one surveyor.

The fear grew stronger with every breath of stale air. Her throat tightened. She would have wept, but her body was too dehydrated for tears.

She opened up the e-book app on her phone. When she was a child, when she had bad dreams, her father would come into her room and tell her stories until she calmed enough to sleep.

She scrolled to a collection of short fiction by H. C. Howell. Her throat tightened at the dedication: *For Claire.*

For years, she had told herself she'd get around to reading her father's work, but life always got in the way. She choked on a laugh. That wouldn't be a problem much longer, would it?

Pushing back the fear, she switched off her helmet lamp and scrolled to the first story.

"The one good thing about the zombie apocalypse is that it's a short-lived apocalypse."

Clara Hamilton took the non-sequitur in stride. She didn't recognize the British man with the cane, but it wouldn't be the first time a student hadn't bothered to show up until midway through the semester. "Thank you, but we were discussing the respiratory system."

"Oh yes, they've got lungs." The man leaned back in the molded plastic chair, crossing his feet beneath the desk. He ignored the muffled laughter of the other students. His voice was light, but his eyes burned. "Otherwise they wouldn't be able to groan. But think about it. The flies and maggots would devour them. Have you ever seen zombies picking the bugs off of one another like chimps? And they can't heal, so any injury will go gangrenous just like that." He snapped his fingers. "The trouble is, while they'll die off within weeks or even days, that doesn't help you tonight."

Glass shattered somewhere in the building, making Clara and several of her students jump.

"We don't have much time, darling." The man

jumped to his feet, graceful and fluid as a dancer. "Henry Cornwell the Third, at your service."

Clara set her notes onto the desk and moved to open the doorway. She saw students and one teacher hurrying through the hall, but nothing to indicate mass panic or—she flushed to think she had even considered it—zombies.

And then she saw the blood. One of the students clutched his arm to his side. Blood dripped through his fingers, leaving a speckled trail on the tile floor.

Another window broke, this one closer. Screams reverberated through the hallway.

Clara spun back to her class. "Nobody panic." Ten years of teaching everything from elementary school through community college had honed her voice, allowing her to slice through the fear and confusion.

A sharp popping sound came from the east wing of the building. A gunshot? Protocol for a school shooting was to go into lockdown and wait for the police, but that was the first shot she had heard, and wouldn't explain the wounded student in the hall. She turned to the stranger. "Not that I believe you, but how many zombies are we talking about?"

Henry pursed his lips. "Pretty much the entire research department from the lower level. Some will make their way up the stairs while others circle around outside and smash their way in through the windows. Your best hope is to make for the roof."

Clara didn't move. "Who are you?" She was positive she had never seen the man on campus, and she knew she would have remembered that accent.

"A friend."

*   *   *

A time traveler. Claire remembered her father talking about this story now. One man, sent from the future to save his great-grandmother's life and prevent the zombie plague.

"Everyone to the stairs," Clara shouted, waving her students down the hall. The fire alarm began to ring. Raising her voice, she asked, "How did it happen?"

"There was an accident. Do the details really matter?"

"I want to know."

"Experimental treatment for end-stage medullablastoma."

Clara stared blankly.

"Brain cancer. It usually hits children." He gave Clara a gentle push into the hall. "On the bright side, it does cure cancer. Or at least renders it moot . . ."

"Oh, God." Clara slowed, staring at the woman staggering down the hall behind them. Professor Cassidy's suit jacket was dark with blood. Her face was torn, and she held her right arm at a strange angle.

"She's gone," said Henry, pulling Clara away. "You can't help her."

Another zombie was smashing through the doors near the stairwell. The students screamed, pushing and trampling one another in their rush to escape this new threat. Clara grabbed a metal trash can, the only thing she could find to use as a weapon, but Henry was faster. His cane whooshed through the air like a sword.

The first blow dislocated the zombie's wrist. The second smashed the elbow of the opposite hand.

*   *   *

"A time traveling ninja?" Mom had shaken her head as she looked up from the manuscript. *"Really?"*

Dad laughed. *"A little over the top?"*

"Just a little."

"Oh, come on. Ninjas vs. pirates is clichéd, but ninjas vs. zombies? This is going to be awesome!"

"Hello?" Claire's heart pounded with fear and hope. She set down her phone and checked her radio: nothing but static.

The imagination expected silence, but the earth was rarely still, even this far down. Air moved through the tunnels. Occasionally the rocks shifted ever so slightly, sprinkling dust from the roof and causing the beams to groan like a haunted house. But this had been something different. Almost like laughter.

Or maybe it was another hallucination. Dreams and reality had blurred together for the past day or so as dehydration set in. She glanced back down, forcing her eyes to focus as she skimmed to the end of the story where Henry and Clara fought zombies in a carnival of gore and violence.

"*This* is why you locked yourself away every night while I was growing up?" Her tongue was swollen, slurring her words. "So a British ninja could beat a zombie to death with its own arm?"

The laughter came again. She could *feel* the sound in her bones. There was nothing cruel in the laugh. It was almost rueful. "Who's there?"

Nothing. She was alone. Alone and trapped, death closing in from all sides. And no time-hopping ninja was going to pop in and save her ass.

She stood, wincing as aches and bruises made themselves known. She had battered every inch of her body during the cave-in, and she was pretty sure she had sprained her left elbow. At first, she had counted herself lucky to have survived at all. Now, she wasn't sure.

Claire had gone ahead to check the elevator shaft while the others took air quality readings. She remembered deafening thunder. The ground had shifted. A feeling of *pressure*, and then cold panic, as her body reacted even before her mind realized what was happening.

The roof had split behind her. She flung herself forward. Dust blinded her, but she kept crawling along until she reached the gate to the elevator shaft. Terror had nearly driven her to yank open the gate and keep going, just to escape the crushing death behind her.

The shaft was still an option. Maybe the quick death was the merciful one.

She returned to the elevator shaft, studying the flat concrete walls. There was no cable, just a set of dirty metal tracks on either side, and several steel conduits bolted into the concrete.

Three hundred feet until an obstruction. But there were other tunnels. If she remembered right, there should be another level around two hundred feet down. She couldn't remember if shaft six stopped there or not.

If so, those tunnels might not be blocked off. Or they could have collapsed even worse than this one.

Not that it mattered. Even at her best, she never could have made the climb in one piece. But at least the fall would be quick. She stretched out one foot, hesitated . . .

The phone buzzed. She jumped, nearly tumbling forward. Her body shook uncontrollably as she backed away and pulled out phone from her pocket.

The screen was dark. It had been another delusion, a cruel prank of the imagination.

She collapsed, clutching the phone in both hands. There was no point in conserving the battery anymore. She stared at the e-mail icon, but couldn't bring herself to open it. Instead, she opened the reader, picked another story at random, and began to read.

The man sprawled on Jackson's living room couch had a dreamlike quality, both unreal and *too* real. He wore a black suit with a thin red tie, like he had just stepped out of a bad 80s sitcom. A black patch covered his right eye. He held the TV remote in one hand. "Did you know KITT was a chick?"

Jackson stared. "Huh?"

"The car from Knight Rider? They gave her a man's voice, but that Trans Am was all woman. What I wouldn't give for a night in her garage." He glanced up. "Then you've got Optimus Prime. The new one, I mean. From the movies. Queer as Liberace. The flames are a dead giveaway." He let out a sharp, coughing laugh.

"How did you get into my apartment?"

"Don't you recognize me, Jackson?" The man tapped his eye patch. "I haven't seen you since you did this to me."

"You've got the wrong guy." Jackson backed away, one hand reaching for his cellphone.

"Six years ago, the corner of Maple and Second."

"Six years—" He *had* gotten into an accident on that corner, taking out a neighbor's mailbox and smashing the car's right headlight and fender. He stared at the man's eye patch.

"There we go." The man chuckled. "There's that slack-jawed look of disbelief."

"You're . . . you're my car."

"Your father's car, actually."

Jackson and his father had spent two years restoring the car, a 1973 Triumph TR-6 convertible. The curves of the body were almost sensual. Black with red pinstriping and redwall tires, the car had sat untouched in the garage for four years until Jackson was old enough to help rebuild it.

He knew that car as well as he knew his own body: the feel of the bucket seats, the faint smell of oil and dust and old cigarette smoke, the cracked wood-grain paneling and the solidity of the walnut gear shift knob. He had only driven it twice before the accident, but in his dreams, he had taken that car all over the country.

Claire flushed, remembering how sweaty her palms had been as she dialed the phone to tell her parents about the accident. The car had still been drivable, but her father had never returned the keys.

Jackson shook his head. "That's—"

"If you say 'impossible,' I'm going to chuck this remote at you. The whole 'That's impossible!' scene is so overdone and clichéd. Either I'm real, in which case you need to get over it, or else you're having a mental breakdown." He tossed the remote onto the couch and jumped to his feet, moving to the entertainment center to examine a row of dusty trophies. "So you're still swimming, eh?"

"I've been on the university swim team for two years now."

"Good for you." He picked a medal off of one of the trophies. "Still doing the 100 meter freestyle?"

"And the 50." Whatever was happening, the man— the car?—didn't appear threatening. "How—no, why are you here?"

"That's a better question." He replaced the medal. "How long's it been since you and your dad talked?"

"We talk," Jackson said, too quickly.

"I don't mean saying hi when you go home to do your laundry. I mean really talked."

"He's busy. We both are." Jackson pointed to the stack of books on the coffee table. "I've got finals in three weeks—"

"I'm here because I want to go for a drive."

Jackson blinked. "Well, you're a car, right?"

"Smartass. Yeah, I'm a car. And tomorrow I get scrapped. But I get one day's freedom first, and I want what anyone would want in his last day."

"To take a drive?"

"To go home. To be with my family."

Claire scrolled back to the first few pages of the collection, checking copyright dates. This was one of her father's final stories, finished when he was in hospice, waiting for complications from a failed kidney transplant to kill him. "You never told us you wanted to come home," she whispered.

Guilt surged through her. She pushed it back, con-

centrating on the story and the memories it evoked.
Long afternoons in the garage with her father. The
pride the first time they turned the ignition and the engine coughed to life.

"I loved that car, Dad." She had been a bit of a nerd
in school, but showing up at school in a gleaming convertible when most of her friends were driving five
hundred-dollar rustbuckets, seeing the looks on the
other kids' faces . . . it was one of the best moments of
her high school life.

She remembered his voice, full of frustration. "If
you loved it so much, you should have been more careful."

"It was only a headlight." It had been October, and
the leaves had begun to fall. The roads were slick after
a recent rainfall. "You were more worried about that
stupid headlight than you were—"

"That's bullshit and you know it."

"Sure, I know it *now*." Claire scrolled back through
the story, skimming the ending. Jackson and the car returned home, and Jackson found a way to save it from
the scrap yard. "Is that why you wrote these things? So
you could invent happy endings for everything?
There's always a solution. Always a reason for what
happens. And closure for everyone who needs it."

Real life didn't work that way. In real life, stories
ended in divorce, or in slow, ugly death as your organs
failed one by one, or alone in the darkness hundreds of
feet below ground.

"You were right about one thing, Dad. I want to go
home." Not back to her apartment. Not to her boyfriend, or to any of her friends from school. She wanted

to be back in that messy house, with her father's typewriter clacking away from his attic office while her
mother graded papers in her recliner.

She closed her eyes, remembering the occasional
ding of the typewriter. She used to love that bell when
she was a little kid, back before Dad switched over to a
word processor. It was a magical sound, the ring of an-
gels and fairies and other wondrous things.

Darkness brought imagination to life. She could
hear him typing, the sound coming from behind the
cave-in. The bell stopped, and the tapping took on a
lighter, plastic sound. Once the family went digital in
the nineties, they had needed two computers: one for
Dad and one for the rest of them. Floorboards creaked
as he stood and paced, working through a plot point.

She clung to those sounds, listening with every cell
of her body, until they were more real than the rock
and the dust and the despair; until she recaptured, just
for a moment, that feeling of security, of being a child
and listening to her father's voice as he pushed the
nightmares away.

"Dad?"

The rocks digging into her body reminded her
where she was, and what had happened. She flipped
on her phone. 5:49 p.m. The battery had run down to
30 percent. She closed her eyes, trying to recall that
feeling of peace and safety that had lulled her to sleep,
but the typing had stopped, and she was alone.

She blinked, trying to clear her vision. Did she have
time to read the entire collection? She scrolled to the
last story, a sword and sorcery tale called "Spellbound."

* * *

Jokra the orc hurried through the tunnels, clutching her father's stolen spellbook to her chest. The only light came from the book itself, a faint glow to illuminate the obsidian walls around her. The shouts and screams of combat faded behind her.

The attack had come without warning. ~~Goblins~~ Dwarves poured into the orc lair, pushing their oversized, wheel-mounted crossbows. One dwarf would steer and aim while another turned the crank, automatically reloading and firing faster than the orcs could respond. Jokra could still hear the clank of the chains as they spat steel-tipped death at her friends and family.

She passed the garbage pits, barely noticing the stench of mold and rotting meat. She veered left, toward the underground lake. Only when she reached the edge of the lake did she stop.

She mopped her face with her sleeve and fought for breath. The cavern was quiet, save for the rhythmic dripping from the stalactites far overhead. [tk: check w/Andy re: cave formations; would an obsidian cave have stalactites?]

Claire tapped back to the copyright page, searching for the date of this story, but "Spellbound" wasn't listed. How had one of Dad's drafts made it into this book? He had started using those "tk" notes after switching to a computer. He could search for those two letters to find places where he needed to come back and fix something. The editor deserved to be shot for leaving his edits and notes in the published copy.

*   *   *

Jokra sat, folding her legs and opening the spellbook in her lap. There was power here, magic enough to save her, if she could only find it. Her father had fallen before he could protect her, but if Jokra could decipher his secrets, she might yet save some of her friends. Or at least herself.

A distant splash made her ears shoot up. She held her breath and searched for the source of the sound. There it was again, a quiet paddling, as if someone was swimming toward her. [tk: Sounds like a ripoff of Gollum and Bilbo from *The Hobbit*.]

There it was again, a quiet, padding footstep at the edge of the lake, as if someone was circling toward her. The spellbook was a beacon to anyone in the cavern. It was too late to hide, so she tried to pretend she hadn't heard anything. One hand crept slowly toward the knife tucked through her belt.

Whoever it was, it was no orc. The movements were too tentative, almost frightened.

She jumped to her feet, yanking the knife free.

A goblin stood before her, a crude spear ready to throw. The tip was sharpened bone, lashed in place by some sort of seaweed fibers. His blue skin was pale, wrapped tight around his bony limbs.

"I thought there were no goblins left in this mountain," Jokra said, stepping sideways. That spear might not even penetrate her clothes, but a lucky shot could still kill her.

"You mean you thought you'd killed us all?" The goblin's voice was rusty, but firm.

Jokra ~~nodded~~ grimaced. "The dwarves drove us underground. We had to—"

"No, you didn't." He stepped closer, shifting his grip on the spear so he could keep the point aimed at her neck. "They attacked you again, didn't they? I can hear the screams."

Jokra tilted her head. She couldn't hear the battle, but goblin ears were larger, their senses sharper. "They'll kill you too," she said. "Unless there are others?" If so, maybe they could rally and catch the dwarves by surprise.

"I'm alone." His words were flat. Empty. Hopeless.

"And the orc and the goblin learn to work together and defeat the dwarves, right? Jesus, Dad. It's no wonder you could never quit your day job." Talking cars, ninjas and zombies, orcs and goblins . . . this was her father's legacy, the product of endless nights locked in his office, away from his family.

A bemused chuckle from the darkness. Or maybe that was her mind continuing to torment her. She couldn't tell anymore. Her hands and feet tingled, and she felt nauseous. Her heart was beating too fast, and she was breathing like she had just done twenty minutes on the exercise bike, despite the lack of any real exertion.

"The least you could have done was write a story telling me how to escape from a mine cave-in," she said.

Another chuckle, this one tinged with sadness. Someone else *was* here, sitting across the tunnel, almost close enough to touch. She could make out his shape from the light of the phone. She reached for her helmet lamp.

"Don't."

The familiar voice made her throat knot. She clasped her hands in her lap, afraid to do anything that might shatter the moment.

"Jokra doesn't defeat the dwarves."

"She—what?"

"She's outnumbered a thousand to one. The story isn't about some *deus ex machina* that lets her live happily ever after. Magic doesn't work that way."

"Sounds like a fucking depressing story."

"Watch your language." A snort. "But yes. I can't imagine most editors taking this one."

"Are you . . . is this another hallucination?"

He sighed. "The 'Was it real or all a dream?' conundrum is almost as clichéd as 'But that's impossible!' Does it really matter, kiddo?"

"So how *does* it work?" The word "Dad" stuck in her throat. "Magic, I mean."

"You used to know. When you were younger. You'd climb out of bed and run around like a little tornado of destruction, bringing those stories to life. That's why the bedtime stories had to stop, because you'd never settle back down and go to sleep."

"I brought you back?" In her thirst-induced fog, it almost made sense. She could smell him now. The faint scent of Old Spice, the spearmint gum he chewed to try to hide the cigarettes on his breath. "The ninja would have been more helpful."

Another sad chuckle. "I'm sorry, Claire. It doesn't work that way."

"That story, 'Spellbound.' Mom and I went through your work after you . . . that's not one of your stories."

"It is now." He continued before she could ask him to explain further. "He knew he wasn't writing great literature. Nobody's going to be writing papers about his work a hundred years from now. But he loved that ninja zombie-slayer, the homesick car, even Jokra the orc."

"He?" She squeezed her head in her hands, trying to ease the pounding. "You're not him?"

"No writer is that good." Another laugh. "But your father poured himself into those stories. That's what you brought to life. Not the surface elements, but the heart of his writing. The core of his stories. Even the ridiculous ones."

She started to shake. "It's been three and a half days. They think I'm dead." She would be dead, soon enough. She doubted she could survive another day without food or water. "How does this end? Do I die alone in the darkness? Do they ever learn *why*, or is it just a stupid, senseless accident?"

"I don't know." A strong hand took hers, and she felt him scooting over to sit beside her. "But whatever happens, you won't be alone."

She rested her head on his shoulder, feeling the soft warmth of his favorite flannel shirt. He was right; he wasn't her father. He was more like a blend of all of her best memories of her father. "What about you? I've got one more day at most, and you'll be trapped—"

"Don't worry about that. You brought me here, kiddo. Once you're gone, so am I."

"I'm sorry." She shuddered with unshed tears. "I didn't know."

"Hush." There was no fear in his voice as he wrapped his arms around her. "This is what he wanted.

What I want. Why do you think he wrote all of those stories?"

The phone in her lap gave a warning buzz. The battery would die soon.

"I should write my good-byes, but I don't know what to say."

"Write the truth. Share yourself with whoever gets that letter." He squeezed her hand. "I'll even promise not to criticize your spelling."

"That'll be a first." Her cracked lips tugged into a brief, faint smile. "Thank you."

She tapped open a new e-mail message and began to write.

ABOUT THE AUTHORS

Dylan Birtolo is a writer, a gamer, and a professional sword-swinger. He currently resides in the great Pacific Northwest where his evenings are filled with shape shifters, mythological demons, and epic battles. He has published a couple of fantasy novels and several short stories in multiple anthologies. He has also written pieces for game companies set in their worlds and co-authored a game manual.

He trains with the Seattle Knights, an acting troupe that focuses on stage combat, and has performed in live shows and for video shoots. In addition, he teaches at the academy for upcoming acting combatants. Endeavoring to be a true jack of all trades, he has worked as a software engineer, a veterinary technician in an emergency hospital, a martial arts instructor, a rock climbing guide, and a lab tech. He has had the honor of jousting, and yes, the armor is real—it weighs over 120 pounds.

Erik Scott de Bie is the author of numerous tales of speculative fiction, including the Forgotten Realms novels *Ghostwalker*, *Depths of Madness*, *Downshadow*, and *Shadowbane*. His short works have featured in anthologies such as *Close Encounters of the Urban Kind*, *Beauty Has Her Way*, *Cobalt City Timeslip*, and *When the*

Hero Comes Home. A fencing enthusiast, he can never pass up a good fight scene accompanied by the sound of ringing steel.

His piece "Ten Thousand Cold Nights" draws upon the Japanese myth of the competition between the legendary masters Muramasa and Masamune. Each challenged to make a better blade, the two smiths tested their respective masterworks in a stream. Mercilessly, Muramasa's bloodthirsty sword cut the leaves, fish, water, and the very air that struck its blade: it destroyed anything that came into its path. By contrast, Masamune's sword did not cut a single leaf or a single fish, and neither the water nor air was harmed by its edge. Muramasa boasted of his sword's deadly efficacy, all the while mocking Masamune for crafting a blade that could not cut anything. In the end, Masamune was declared the victor, as his discerning blade did not needlessly cut that which was innocent and worthy of preservation.

Married with cats, de Bie lives in Seattle. Catch up with him on erikscottdebie.com.

Eugie Foster calls home a mildly haunted, fey-infested house in metro Atlanta that she shares with her husband Matthew. After receiving her master's degree in psychology, she retired from academia to pen flights of fancy. She also edits legislation for the Georgia General Assembly, which from time to time she suspects is another venture into flights of fancy. Eugie received the 2009 Nebula Award for Best Novelette and was named the Author of the Year by Bards and Sages. Her fiction has also received the 2002 Phobos Award, been translated into seven languages, and been a finalist for the Hugo, Black Quill, Bram Stoker, and BSFA awards. Her publication credits number over one hundred and include stories in *Realms of Fantasy*, *Interzone*, *Cricket*, *Orson Scott Card's InterGalactic Medicine Show*, and *Fantasy Magazine*; podcasts *Escape Pod*, *Pseudopod*, and *Podcastle*; and anthologies *Best New Fantasy* and *Best New Romantic Fantasy 2*. Her short story collection *Returning My Sister's Face and Other Far Eastern Tales of Whimsy and Malice* is available from Norilana Books. Visit her online at www.eugiefoster.com.

Jim C. Hines' latest book is *The Snow Queen's Shadow*, the final book in his series about butt-kicking fairy tale heroines (because Sleeping Beauty was always meant to be a ninja, and Snow White makes a bad-ass witch). He's also the author of the humorous *Goblin Quest* trilogy, as well as more than forty published short stories in markets such as *Realms of Fantasy*, *Sword & Sorceress*, and *Turn the Other Chick*. He has never actually written a story about time-traveling, zombie-slaying British ninjas, but now thinks it could be fun. He lives in Michigan with his wife, two children, and half an ark's worth of pets. You can find his web site and blog at www.jimchines.com.

Jay Lake lives in Portland, Oregon, where he works on numerous writing and editing projects. His 2011 books are *Endurance* and *Love in the Time of Metal and Flesh*, along with paperback releases of two of his other titles. His short fiction appears regularly in literary and genre markets worldwide. Jay is a past winner of the John W. Campbell Award for Best New Writer, and a multiple nominee for the Hugo and World Fantasy Awards.

Tanith Lee was born in North London (UK) in 1947. Because her parents were professional dancers (ballroom, Latin American) and had to live where the work was, she attended a number of truly terrible schools, and didn't learn to read—she is also dyslexic—until almost age eight, and then only because her father taught her. This opened the world of books to Lee, and by nine she was writing. After much better education at a grammar school, Lee went on to work in a library. This was followed by various other jobs—shop assistant, waitress, clerk—plus a year at art college when she was twenty-five. In 1974 this mosaic ended when DAW Books, under the leadership of Donald A. Wollheim, bought and published Lee's *The Birthgrave*, and thereafter twenty-six of her novels and collections.

Since then Lee has written around ninety books and approaching three hundred short stories. Four of her radio plays have been broadcast by the BBC; she also wrote two episodes ("Sarcophagus" and "Sand") for the TV series *Blake's 7*. Some of her stories regularly get read on Radio 7.

Lee writes in many styles in and across many genres, including horror, SF, fantasy, historical, detective, contemporary-psychological, children and young adult. Her preoccupation, though, is always people. In 1992 she married the writer-artist-photographer John Kaiine, her companion since 1987. They live on the Sussex Weald, near the sea, in a house full of books and plants, with two black and white overlords called cats.

David D. Levine is a lifelong SF reader whose midlife crisis was to take a sabbatical from his high-tech job to attend Clarion West in 2000. It seems to have worked. He made his first professional sale in 2001, won the Writers of the Future Contest in 2002, was nominated for the John W. Campbell award in 2003, was nominated for the Hugo Award and the Campbell again in 2004, and won a Hugo in 2006 (Best Short Story, for "Tk'Tk'Tk"). A collection of his short stories, *Space Magic*, won the Endeavour Award in 2009. In January of 2010 he spent two weeks at a simulated Mars base in the Utah desert, and you can read about that at http://www.bentopress.com/mars/. He lives in Portland, Oregon with his wife, Kate Yule, with whom he edits the fanzine *Bento*; their website is at www.bentopress.com.

Seanan McGuire was born and raised in the San Francisco Bay Area, which probably explains her affection for the region, rattlesnakes and all. Her short stories have appeared in various magazines and anthologies, including *The Mad Scientist's Guide to World Domination* and *Westward Weird*. Mina Norton, the bartending alchemist, first showed up in *After Hours: Tales from the Ur-Bar*, and has shown no immediate signs of leaving.

Seanan was the winner of the 2010 John W. Campbell Award, and is currently the author of two urban fantasy series: the October Daye books, which follow the adventures a half-fae knight errant, and InCryptid, which focus on a family of cryptozoologists. She also writes as Mira Grant, author of the Newsflesh trilogy. To relax, she occasionally records albums of filk music. Unsurprisingly, Seanan doesn't sleep very much.

Seanan currently lives in a crumbling farmhouse with far too many books, several large blue cats, and an extensive collection of strange and unusual toys. When not writing, she attends more conventions than is strictly probable, resulting in her bringing home more books and more toys (although usually not more cats).

Jody Lynn Nye lists her main career activity as "spoiling cats." When not engaged upon this worthy occupation, she writes fantasy and science fiction.

Before breaking away from gainful employment to write full time, Jody worked as a file clerk, bookkeeper at a small publishing house, freelance journalist and photographer, accounting assistant, and costume maker. For four years, she was a technical operator and technical operations manager at WFBN-TV Chicago.

Since 1987 she has published forty books and more than one hundred short stories. Among her novels are her epic fantasy series The Dreamland, beginning with *Waking in Dreamland*; five contemporary humorous fantasies, beginning with *Mythology 101*; three medical SF novels; the Taylor's Ark series; and *Strong Arm Tactics*, a humorous military SF novel. Jody wrote *Th- Dragonlover's Guide to Pern*, a companion to red the Caffrey's popular world. She c---- on four novels, including ---- its solo sequel, *The Sh*----

Visual Guide to Xanth with Piers Anthony, and edited an anthology of humorous stories about mothers entitled *Don't Forget Your Spacesuit, Dear!* She wrote eight books with the late Robert Lynn Asprin, *License Invoked*, a contemporary fantasy set in New Orleans, and seven of Asprin's *Myth Adventures*, including the latest, *Myth-Fortunes*.

Her newest books are *Dragons Deal*, third in the Dragons series begun by Robert Asprin, and *View from the Imperium*, a humorous military SF novel.

Over the last two decades, Jody has taught in numerous writing workshops and participated on hundreds of panels about writing and being published. In 2007 she taught fantasy writing at Columbia College Chicago.

Jody lives in the northwest suburbs of Chicago, with her husband Bill Fawcett, a writer, game designer, and book packager, and one cat, Jeremy.

Fiona Patton was born in Calgary, Alberta, and grew up in the United States. She now lives in rural Ontario with her partner, Tanya Huff, a huge pile of cats, and two sweet Sheltie/Papillons. She has written seven heroic fantasy novels for DAW books. The latest, *The Shining City*, is due out in April of 2011. "The Sentry" is the thirty-third short story she has written for Tekno Books and DAW.

Jean Rabe tugs on old socks with her two dogs when she isn't writing. She's the author of more than two ˙˙ fantasy and adventure novels and more than 60 ˙˙˙She's edited twenty anthologies and ˙he cares to count. She lives in

Wisconsin, where she hibernates in the winter and roots for the Green Bay Packers, Chicago Bears, and occasionally the Pittsburgh Steelers.

Laura Resnick is the author of the popular Esther Diamond series, whose releases include *Unsympathetic Magic*, *Doppelgangster*, *Disappearing Nightly*, and *Vamparazzi*. She has also written traditional fantasy novels such as *In Legend Born*, *The Destroyer Goddess*, and *The White Dragon*, which made the "Year's Best" lists of *Publishers Weekly* and *VOYA*. An opinion columnist, frequent public speaker, award-winning former romance writer, and the Campbell Award-winning author of many short stories, she is on the Web at www.lauraresnick.com.

Kristine Kathryn Rusch is an award-winning, bestselling writer. In the science fiction field, she has won two Hugos and a World Fantasy Award, as well as several other awards. Her bestselling Retrieval Artist series has been called one of the top 10 best science fiction detective series ever by *I09*. She is about to publish her Diving into the Wreck novels, with *City of Ruins* and *Boneyards* upcoming. And her entire backlist—including short stories—is coming into print, starting with electronic books and moving slowly to print books. She also writes under a half a dozen pen names in a variety of genres. Find out more about her at www.kristinekathrynrusch.com.

Anton Strout is the author of the Simon Canderous urban fantasy series, as well as the author of half a dozen tales for DAW anthologies. Anton was born in the Berkshire Hills mere miles from writing heavy-weights Nathaniel Hawthorne and Herman Melville and currently lives in the haunted corn maze that is New Jersey (where nothing paranormal ever really happens, he assures you). He has been a featured speaker and workshopper at San Diego Comic-Con, Gencon, New York Comic-Con, and the Brooklyn Book Festival. In his scant spare time, he is a writer, a some-times actor, sometimes musician, occasional RPGer, and the world's most casual-and-controller-smashing video-gamer. He can often be found lurking the dark-ened halls of www.antonstrout.com.

Ian Tregillis was born to a bearded mountebank and a discredited tarot card reader, who settled in the Min-nesota Territory after fleeing the wrath of a Flemish prince. (The full story involves a sunken barge, taco-nite ore, and a stolen horse.) He received a doctorate in physics from the University of Minnesota before es-caping to New Mexico, where he consorts with writers, scientists, and other disreputable types. His first novel, *Bitter Seeds*, debuted in 2010. The second volume of the Milkweed Triptych, *The Coldest War*, is scheduled for publication in 2012. He is a member of George R. R. Martin's Wild Cards writing collective. His website is www.iantregillis.com.

Tim Waggoner's novels include the Nekropolis series of urban fantasies and the Ghost Trackers series writ-ten in collaboration with Jason Hawes and Grant Wil-son of the *Ghost Hunters* television show. In total, he's published over twenty novels and two short story collections, and his articles on writing have appeared in *Writer's Digest* and *Writers' Journal*, among others. He teaches creative writing at Sinclair Community College and in Seton Hill University's Master of Fine Arts in Writing Popular Fiction program. Visit him on the web at www.timwaggoner.com.

ABOUT THE EDITORS

Jennifer Brozek is a fulltime freelance author and editor. Winner of the 2009 Australian Shadows Award for edited publication, Jennifer has edited a number of anthologies with more on the way. Author of In a Gilded Light and The Little Finance Book That Could, she has more than 25 published short stories, is the creator and editor of the webzine The Edge of Propinquity, and is an assistant editor for the Apex Book Company.

On the RPG side of things, Jennifer is a freelance author and editor for many RPG companies including Margaret Weis Productions, Savage Mojo, Rogue Games, and Catalyst Game Labs. Winner of the 2010 Origins Award for Best Roleplaying Game Supplement, her contributions to RPG sourcebooks include Dragonlance, Colonial Gothic, Shadowrun, Serenity, Savage Worlds, and White Wolf SAS. She also writes the monthly gaming column Dice & Deadlines.

When she is not writing her heart out, she is gallivanting around the Pacific Northwest in its wonderfully mercurial weather. Jennifer is a member of Broad Universe, SFWA, and HWA. Learn more about her and her projects at www.jenniferbrozek.com.

Martin H. Greenberg (1941–2011) was the CEP of Tekno Books and its predecessor companies, now the largest book developer of commercial fiction and non-fiction in the world, with over 2,250 published books that have been translated into thirty-three languages. He was the recipient of an unprecedented four lifetime achievement awards in the science fiction, mystery, and supernatural horror genres—the Milford Award in Science Fiction, the Solstice Award in science fiction, the Bram Stoker Award in Horror, and the Ellery Queen Award in Mystery—the only person in publishing history to have received all four awards.

RM Meluch
The Tour of the Merrimack

THE MYRIAD　　　0-7564-0320-1
WOLF STAR　　　0-7564-0383-6
THE SAGITTARIUS COMMAND
　　　978-0-7564-0490-1
STRENGTH AND HONOR
　　　978-0-7564-0578-6

To Order Call: 1-800-788-6262

www.dawbooks.com

DAW 48

Gini Koch
The Alien *Novels*

"This delightful romp has many interesting twists and turns as it glances at racism, politics, and religion en route. Darned amusing." —*Booklist* (starred review)

"Amusing and interesting...a hilarious romp in the vein of 'Men in Black' or 'Ghostbusters'." —*Voya*

TOUCHED BY AN ALIEN
978-0-7564-0600-4

ALIEN TANGO
978-0-7564-0632-5

ALIEN IN THE FAMILY
978-0-7564-0668-4

ALIEN PROLIFERATION
978-0-7564-0697-4

ALIEN DIPLOMACY
978-0-7564-0716-2
(Available April 2012)

To Order Call: 1-800-788-6262
www.dawbooks.com

Sherwood Smith

CORONETS AND STEEL

"A lively heroine, mysterious ghosts, and a complex and intricate plot always get the action going..."
—*Publishers Weekly*

"Highly recommended for all fantasy and general-fiction collections, from urban-fantasy readers looking for something lighter but still complex to young women who grew up reading the Princess Diaries series." —*Booklist*

"A rousing adventure of doubles, political intrigue, and doomed romance. It's a delightful romp, with just enough loose ends to leave some hope that the doomed romance might not be so doomed at all."   —*Locus*

Now in paperback!
978-0-7564-0685-1

And now available in hardcover, the sequel:

BLOOD SPIRITS
978-0-7564-0698-1

To Order Call: 1-800-788-6262
www.dawbooks.com

Katharine Kerr

The Nola O'Grady *Novels*

"Breakneck plotting, punning, and romance make for a
mostly fast, fun read." —*Publishers Weekly*

"This is an entertaining investigative urban fantasy that sub-
genre readers will enjoy...fans will enjoy the streets of San
Francisco as seen through an otherworldly lens."
—*Midwest Book Review*

LICENSE TO ENSORCELL
978-0-7564-0656-1

WATER TO BURN
978-0-7564-0691-2

To Order Call: 1-800-788-6262
www.dawbooks.com

Celia Jerome

The Willow Tate *Novels*

"Readers will love the first Willow Tate book. Willow is funny, brave and open to possibilities most people would not have even considered as she meets her perfect foil in Thaddeus Grant, a British agent assigned to look over the strange occurrences following Willow like a shadow. Together they make a wonderful pair and readers will love their unconventional courtship." —*RT Book Review*

TROLLS IN THE HAMPTONS
978-0-7564-0630-1

NIGHT MARES IN THE HAMPTONS
978-0-7564-0663-9

FIRE WORKS IN THE HAMPTONS
978-0-7564-0688-2

And don't miss:
LIFE GUARDS IN THE HAMPTONS
(Available May 2012)

To Order Call: 1-800-788-6262
www.dawbooks.com